DESTINY

An Adventure from the Myrmidon Files

On the Texas border, a brutal massacre threatens to ignite a firestorm of violence that will destabilize an already fragile Mexican government and trigger an international crisis that knows no boundaries. The only clue, a cryptic message: The time for Destiny has arrived! Tam Broderick, leader of an elite CIA task force, code-name: Myrmidon, knows that the Dominion—a quasi-religious extremist group—is behind the attacks; now it's up to her and her team to find out what the Dominion's true goals are, and stop them dead in their tracks.

Praise for DESTINY!

"An action-packed, globe-spanning treasure hunt of an adventure by David Wood and Sean Ellis. Destiny hits all the right beats—full of historical mysteries and intriguing what-ifs—to keep the pages turning fast, with a satisfying and thrilling payout that you won't soon forget." **David Sakmyster, author of *The Pharos Objective* and *Jurassic Dead***

"Smart, suspenseful and action-packed, Destiny is an unforgettable ride! A perfect mesh of two incredible authors, Wood and Ellis hijack you on an absolutely thrilling adventure! An excellent read." **Ashley Knight - author of *Five***

"With an adrenaline-fueled search for an ancient relic with mystical powers and the introduction of a new powerhouse team, the Myrmidons, to set matters right, get ready for a new pulse-pounding adventure series brimming with action and intrigue!" **Rick Jones, bestselling author of the *Vatican Knights* series**

Books by David Wood

The Dane Maddock Adventures
Dourado
Cibola
Quest
Icefall
Buccaneer
Atlantis
Ark (forthcoming)

Dane and Bones Origins
Freedom (with Sean Sweeney)
Hell Ship (with Sean Ellis)
Splashdown (with Rick Chesler)
Dead Ice (with Steven Savile)
Liberty (with Edward G. Talbot)
Electra (with Rick Chesler)
Amber (with Rick Chesler-forthcoming)
Justice (with Edward G. Talbot-forthcoming)

The Jade Ihara Adventures
Oracle (with Sean Ellis)
Changeling (with Sean Ellis-forthcoming)

The Myrmidon Files
Destiny (with Sean Ellis)

Stand-Alone Works
Arena of Souls- A Brock Stone Adventure
Into the Woods (with David S. Wood)
Callsign: Queen (with Jeremy Robinson)
Dark Rite (with Alan Baxter)
The Zombie-Driven Life
You Suck

David Wood writing as David Debord

The Absent Gods
The Silver Serpent
Keeper of the Mists
The Gates of Iron (forthcoming)

The Impostor Prince (with Ryan A. Span- forthcoming)

Books by Sean Ellis

Mira Raiden Adventures
Ascendant
Descendant

The Nick Kismet Thrillers
The Shroud of Heaven
Into the Black
Fortune Favors
The Devil You Know (novella)

The Adventures of Dodge Dalton
In the Shadow of Falcon's Wings
At the Outpost of Fate
On the High Road to Oblivion

Chess Team/Jack Sigler Thrillers
(with Jeremy Robinson)
Callsign: King
Underworld
Blackout
Prime
Savage
Cannibal

The Jade Ihara Adventures
Oracle (with David Wood)
Changeling (with David Wood-forthcoming)

Other Works
Magic Mirror
WarGod (with Steven Savile)
Hell Ship (with David Wood)
Flood Rising (with Jeremy Robinson)

DESTINY

AN ADVENTURE FROM THE MYRMIDON FILES

DAVID WOOD
SEAN ELLIS

Gryphonwood

Gryphonwood Press

DESTINY- AN ADVENTURE FROM THE MYRMIDON FILES

Published by Gryphonwood Press
www.gryphonwoodpress.com

ISBN-13: 978-1-940095-29-5
ISBN-10: 1940095298

Printed in the United States of America
First printing: March, 2015.

PROLOGUE—AMBITION

Chihuahua, Mexico—May 14, 1916

The Lieutenant was awake before dawn and ready for the day's activities, which came as no surprise to cavalry scout Emil Holmdahl. The officer was like a wild mustang, champing at the bit, eager for action and hungry for glory, and today was the day that he intended to find plenty of both.

The Lieutenant was an ambitious man, driven and competitive, despite the fact that the glory he so clearly craved always seemed just out of reach. A graduate of the U.S. Military Academy at West Point, where he had been an outstanding swordsman, he had struggled academically, finishing in the middle of his class. He had competed in the 1912 Olympic Games but failed to earn a medal. Now, two months into his first military expedition, he had yet to prove his mettle in combat, and that was an itch he was desperate to scratch. At any cost.

After a month of serving as General Pershing's aide de camp and courier, the young officer had gotten one step closer to his desire when the General had given him command of a cavalry troop tasked with rooting out Villistas in the area, but thus far the search had been fruitless.

"I'm tired of waiting for those greasers to show up," the Lieutenant had said just a few days earlier. "I want to take the fight to them."

Holmdahl, a veteran soldier who had first seen combat in the Spanish-American War at the age of fifteen, knew that brave talk was just that: talk. Pancho Villa and his army of bandits had learned their lesson at the battle of San Geronimo Ranch, where the Seventh Cavalry killed seventy-five Villistas and nearly captured Villa himself. Instead of fighting in the open, the revolutionaries contented themselves with guerilla warfare, conducting hit and run attacks well away from the American troops, and blending back into the local population where they were treated as heroes. 'Taking the fight to them' sounded impressive, but in practical terms, it meant very little.

But something unusual had happened which promised to end the stalemate.

Shortly after sunset the previous day, a local woman had come to the camp, asking the Lieutenant to meet her outside the perimeter. Wary of a trap, or perhaps hopeful that the encounter would lead to the battle he longed for, the Lieutenant had marched out, one hand on the butt of his ivory handled Colt revolver, which he favored over the standard issue M1911A semi-automatic pistol and which gave him the appearance of a dime-novel gunslinger. Holmdahl, an expert marksman and cavalry scout had followed him to the edge of the camp, taking a position twenty yards away, ready to lay down, covering fire if the anticipated ambush occurred.

The woman had spoken briefly with the Lieutenant, then called out to someone in the darkness behind her. Fearing that this was the beginning of an attack, Holmdahl trained his rifle on something moving in the shadows, but instead of a raiding party there was just one old man, shuffling forward with the aid of a walking stick.

As the man got closer, Holmdahl saw in the faint moonlight that he was a gringo but that by itself was no reason to relax his vigilance. There were plenty of foreigners fighting with the Villistas; Holmdahl himself had fought with Villa's forces a few years earlier. However, Holmdahl's instincts told him that the old fellow was probably more interested in trading information for a few pesos than he was in deceiving the American officer and leading him into a trap. While keeping one eye on the shadows, Holmdahl managed to catch a few snippets of the conversation.

The newcomer gave the woman an avuncular pat on the arm, dismissing her, then faced the Lieutenant. When he spoke, it was with an asthmatic wheeze. "I've been hearing a lot about you lately."

"Then I must be doing something right," replied the Lieutenant in a tone that somehow managed to be both cocksure and suspicious at the same time.

The old man laughed. "You don't recognize me, do you? Well, why should you? I had lunch with your father years ago, when you were just a pup." He leaned closer and whispered something too softly for Holmdahl to make out.

The effect on the Lieutenant was startling. He leaned closer, squinting at the old man's face. "You're dead."

"Very nearly," agreed the old gringo. "And I'm content to allow that misconception to persist until the situation remedies itself. I would, of course, appreciate your discretion in that regard."

The Lieutenant cocked his head sideways. "Then why are you here? Is there something I can do for you?"

"There may be something *I* can do for *you*. You're ambitious. That's plain as day. You've come down here expecting to wrap yourself in glory." He paused and made a sound that might have been a laugh or a cough. "Maybe you will, maybe you won't. Villa's men are animals. Outlaws pretending to be heroes. Killing them will bring you about as much glory as shooting a wild dog in the street."

"It may be that you don't understand me as well as you think you do."

The old man shrugged. "I'm told that I am a singular judge of character, but we shall see." He held something out in one frail-looking hand. Holmdahl thought it looked like a leather tobacco pouch.

"What's this?" asked the Lieutenant.

"Glory." As if aware that Holmdahl was nearby and eavesdropping, the old man leaned in close again and spoke in a soft murmur.

The Lieutenant's eyes widened as he listened, and when the old man was done, the Lieutenant regarded the pouch in his hand as if it were a lit stick of dynamite. "Why are you giving it to me? This could end the revolution in a day."

"I used to believe that." The old man laughed derisively. "Men will always find a reason to go to war. If you take one reason away, they'll just find another. You'll see." He began to turn away, but then stopped. "You should pay a visit to Las Cienegas, tomorrow. It may prove… instructive."

As the old man shuffled back into the night, the Lieutenant opened the pouch and shook its contents into his palm. Holmdahl caught the glint of gold before the Lieutenant shoved the object back into the pouch.

Holmdahl hurried to join the other man, his curiosity now stronger than his good sense. "Who was that?"

The Lieutenant gripped the pouch tightly in his hand and gazed after the departing figure. He gave a short, harsh laugh. "I do believe it was the Devil himself."

"What was that he gave you?"

"Pancho Villa's greatest secret." The answer was murmured so softly, Holmdahl wondered if it had been meant for his ears.

After a night tossing and turning in his bedroll, haunted by the promise in those words, Holmdahl discovered that the Lieutenant's eagerness was contagious, but unlike the officer, Holmdahl's thirst was for something other than glory. The more he thought about what he had seen and heard, the more convinced he was that the secret the Lieutenant now possessed could only be one thing, and Holmdahl wanted it.

They set out at first light, heading for a nearby town, ostensibly to buy feed for the troop's horses. Today, they would be riding mechanical mounts: a pair of 1915 Dodge Touring Cars, painted a dull green of a sun-bleached prickly pear. Holmdahl rode in the lead car with the Lieutenant at the wheel, along with their civilian interpreter and two of the seven enlisted soldiers that made up their foraging expedition. As they rumbled across the roadless landscape, trailing an enormous column of dust, the Lieutenant asked Holmdahl for his opinion on the use of motor cars in military operations.

"I like 'em just fine for gettin' around the countryside," Holmdahl replied, having to shout to be heard above the chug of the engine and the creaking of the suspension as the tires bounced over one rut after another. "I ain't so sure about using 'em in combat, though. They make quite a ruckus. You can see 'em and hear 'em from miles away."

The Lieutenant pondered this. "I'm an old horse soldier myself," he began. "It's in my blood."

Holmdahl resisted the urge to laugh. At just thirty years of age, with no combat experience whatsoever, the Lieutenant hardly struck the image of a grizzled veteran cavalryman. Holmdahl, only two years older than the other man, had been a soldier in one form or another for more than half his entire life. Yet, he had watched the Lieutenant ride and practice with his saber, and had a pretty good idea what the man actually meant.

"Mechanized warfare is the future," the Lieutenant went on. "Armored cars and infantry tanks will replace the horse, mark my words. Mobile artillery platforms that can go roll up on an enemy position and let 'em have it." He took his hands off the steering wheel and smacked them together emphatically. As he did, the front wheel hit a stone, and the car veered off course.

Holmdahl just nodded. He knew the Lieutenant was right about the future. That was the thing about war; it was great for innovation.

But Holmdahl had been right, too. When they arrived in Rubio near midday, the plaza was so crowded they were unable to enter. There were at least fifty men, and while none of them were armed, Holmdahl could feel their anger smoldering, like a buried coal in a fire pit, just waiting for a stiff breeze to come along and fan it into violence.

He sank low in his seat and tipped the brim of his campaign hat down to conceal his face, careful not to make eye contact with any of the men. He had been hoping for a more subdued arrival in the town and a chance to ask a few discreet questions. "I do see a number of old friends here."

"That's why I brought you along." The Lieutenant pulled the car around in a wide circle so that they were facing away from the crowd. "Who are they?"

"Villistas." Holmdahl said it like a curse. Although he had once fought on the same side as Villa, Holmdahl's true loyalty had always lain with Villa's fellow revolutionary, Venustiano Carranza, currently the president of Mexico. Villa and Carranza had never seen eye to eye, but when tensions between the men reached the breaking point, Holmdahl had chosen to support Carranza. "Cardenas' men. I didn't see Cardenas, but I'll bet my last nickel he's nearby."

Holmdahl knew that name would get the Lieutenant's blood pumping. General Julio Cardenas was Pancho Villa's most trusted commander and the chief of his bodyguard. Cardenas was also a vicious killer, and the mastermind of the raid on Columbus, New Mexico, in which eighteen American citizens had been murdered. Outcry over the infamous "Battle" of Columbus had been the catalyst for the American Army's Punitive Expedition to hunt down Villa.

Holmdahl also knew that Cardenas and the other men of Villa's elite bodyguard went by the nickname "Los Dorados"—the Golden Ones—because, it was said, Villa paid them in gold, while all his other fighters received only silver pesos. Holmdahl thought again about the glint of gold he had spied the night before and recalled the Lieutenant's words. *Pancho Villa's greatest secret.* That could mean only one thing:

Treasure!

They headed north on a wagon road and soon arrived at a hacienda known as Las Cienegas, the place the Lieutenant's mysterious visitor had recommended they visit. This time, there was no reception committee waiting for them, just an old man whom Holmdahl recognized immediately.

"That's his uncle," he told the Lieutenant. "Cardenas' uncle."

"Let's go rattle his cage and see what flies out."

They approached the old man nonchalantly as if merely interested in socializing. Through their interpreter, the Lieutenant inquired if the old man knew where they might purchase a large quantity of corn. The old man dissembled and spread his hands in a gesture of helplessness. Holmdahl understood every word the man said, but feigned ignorance, waiting for the translation before asking, "What about San Miguelito Ranch? That's close by, isn't it?"

He saw a flash of wariness in the man's eyes at the mention. Rancho San Miguelito was indeed close, just six miles away. Less than two weeks earlier, the Lieutenant had ridden near there with "H" troop and marked it as a possible location where Villistas might take refuge. If Cardenas was in the area, San

Miguelito was the sort of place where he might lay low.

Evidently aware that his omission had aroused the suspicions of his visitors, the old man just shrugged again. "Yes. You could ask there."

The Lieutenant turned to Holmdahl, a fierce grin on his face. "I believe we will."

The cars tore down the road to Rancho San Miguelito, once more trailing a telltale plume of dust. Holmdahl knew that the cars would easily outpace any informants that might have been dispatched to warn their quarry. As they rolled toward the open main gate on the east side of the walled compound, Holmdahl spotted a group of men skinning a cow in the front yard. One of them broke away and ran into the house.

The Lieutenant slowed the car to a crawl, watching the other men for any sign of trouble. After just a few seconds, the man who had gone into the house rejoined his compatriots and went back to work as if nothing had happened.

"He's here," the Lieutenant said. "I can feel it."

He steered off the road and drove along the outer perimeter of the compound to the northwest corner, and then waved the second car forward. "Pull around to the south wall," he told the driver. "We're going to smoke that son of a bitch out and drive him toward you."

As the other car pulled away, the Lieutenant grabbed a rifle and jumped out. He sent two of the soldiers south, along the western wall, and then motioned for Holmdahl to follow him on foot in the other direction.

They had just rounded the northeast corner, less than fifteen yards from the grand arch of the main gate, when all hell broke loose.

The Lieutenant almost collided with three horsemen who were trying to leave the compound. Perhaps realizing that they were too close to engage with his rifle, he drew his revolver and took aim. There was a flurry of activity as the riders wheeled their mounts around and took off, racing back across the courtyard toward the hacienda. Holmdahl reached the Lieutenant's side a moment later, just in time to see the horsemen halted again, this time by the soldiers sent to cover the back gate.

A pistol shot rang out, and then the air was filled with the noise of battle. The three riders came about and charged once more across the courtyard, making for the main gate, where only two men stood between them and freedom. Holmdahl shrank back behind the wall as bullets from the riders' pistols kicked up gravel at his feet, but the Lieutenant stood his ground like some invincible demi-god.

One of the horses let out a tortured squeal and reared up as a bullet pierced its belly. The rider of a second horse cried out as a round from the Lieutenant's ivory-handled revolver shattered his arm.

Suddenly, a storm of lead sizzled through the compound. The soldiers stationed at the back gate were shooting at the riders, unaware that the Lieutenant was also in their line of fire. Most of their rounds struck the wall, throwing up a cloud of adobe dust that further compromised visibility, leaving the stalwart Lieutenant little choice but to retreat to Holmdahl's side, where he crouched down and began reloading the chambers of his revolver. Holmdahl did not fail to notice the look of pure ecstasy on the other man's face.

As soon as there was a lull in the incoming fusillade, the Lieutenant darted forward again, rushing headlong into the smoke and dust, and was nearly run down by the third horse. Once more, he stood his ground, firing point blank, hitting the horse's flank. As the animal collapsed, the rider tried to leap free, but his foot tangled in a stirrup.

The Lieutenant charged forward, brandishing his pistol. "Come on, you sorry son of a bitch," he roared. "Get up. Die like a man."

Holmdahl breathed a curse at the senseless display of bravado and charged through the gate, his rifle leveled. The Villista pretended to be having difficulty getting his foot free, and then quick as lightning, drew his revolver and took aim. Holmdahl and the Lieutenant fired at almost exactly the same instant, killing the man before he could loose a shot.

Neither man saw the last rider until it was too late. The horse erupted from the choking dust cloud and slipped through the gate behind them, running like the hounds of hell were nipping at its heels. Holmdahl wheeled around, put the man in his sights, took a breath, and then calmly pulled the trigger. A hundred yards away, a puff of red mist bore testimony to his marksmanship. The rider slumped forward and slid out of the saddle, falling in a heap on the ground.

With that shot, the battle came to an abrupt halt. The Lieutenant stood triumphantly over the fallen Villista, breathing fast, the revolver in his fist trailing a wisp of smoke. Finally, he raised his eyes to his men. "We're going to search this place from top to bottom. Bring everyone outside. If they're unarmed, don't lay a hand on them. But if they have a weapon, shoot them dead."

As the officer led a contingent into the house, Holmdahl bent over the Villista that both he and the Lieutenant had fired on. It would be impossible to say which man's bullet had killed him, but Holmdahl was content to let the other man take the credit. He had enough notches in his gun already. Holmdahl was more concerned with who the man had been in life. Was this one of the Dorados? One of Villa's Golden Men?

A shout came from one of the hacienda's upper story windows. "There's one. Making a run for it."

Holmdahl looked up and saw a soldier pointing out across the field. He breathed a curse as he saw the man the Lieutenant had winged in the first moments of the battle making a break for it. He raised his rifle and put the man in his sights, but just as quickly lowered the weapon. It wasn't just the thought of shooting a man in the back that stopped him. Two of the men were already dead, and whatever they had known about Villa's stash of gold had gone to hell with them. Maybe the third man knew where the gold was kept.

He broke into a sprint and caught up to the man in just a few seconds. Already weak from the pain of his injury and loss of blood, the man was half-staggering, but when he heard the pounding of Holmdahl's boots on the rocky ground behind him, he pushed himself a little harder. The effort proved costly. Before he made it ten steps, he stumbled and went sprawling headlong.

"Give up," Holmdahl shouted as he closed to within ten yards. "You don't have to die."

The wounded Villista rolled over to face him, hands raised in surrender. Holmdahl saw two things in that instant. The wounded man was none other than General Julio Cardenas himself, and hanging from a rawhide cord around his neck was a golden coin.

Holmdahl was so transfixed by the coin, he did not realize Cardenas had drawn his pistol until he heard the report and felt a hot rush of gases and gun oil peppering his face. Stunned, Holmdahl leveled his rifle and fired without even thinking. Cardenas' bullet, despite being fired at close range, somehow missed its target. Holmdahl's did not. His shot punched through Cardenas' forehead, killing the revolutionary leader instantly.

For several seconds, Holmdahl just stood there letting the fog of battle dissipate and wondering if he had just made an enormous mistake. He would have preferred not to kill Cardenas, not before questioning him at any rate, but knowing the man's reputation, he doubted any other outcome was possible.

His eyes fell to the gold coin at the dead man's breast. A hard pull snapped the rawhide in two. Holmdahl idly turned the coin over in his hand, letting his fingers caress the images stamped in the gold. On one side, an eagle, wings spread in flight. On the other, the familiar likeness of Lady Liberty. It was an American double-eagle, a twenty dollar gold piece.

"Now where the devil did you get this?" he murmured.

With the coin clenched in his fist, he headed back toward the hacienda. It wouldn't be long before the Villistas they had spotted in Rubio learned of Cardena's death and came in force, looking for revenge, but Holmdahl wasn't thinking about the possibility of another fight.

Pancho Villa was paying his bodyguards with American gold. That was the secret the old gringo had told the Lieutenant about, and that meant the coin in Holmdahl's hand was just the tip of the iceberg. There was more gold out there, and Holmdahl was going to find it.

CHAPTER 1

I am going *to die.*

The thought ricocheted through Juan Garza's head, like a premonition of the bullet that he knew would soon make it happen. He heard Miranda whimpering beside him and squeezed her hand. "We're going to be all right," he promised. "Just don't look at their faces. Don't give them a reason to hurt you."

She nodded, clinging to the false hope. What else could any of them do?

Everything had happened so fast. When the bus had stopped at the police roadblock, Señor Ortiz had assumed that it was just another shakedown, and with a fistful of five hundred peso notes, had stepped out to pay the bribe that would let them continue on their way.

But something had gone terribly wrong. Only a moment after leaving the bus, Ortiz had been shoved roughly aboard, followed by three policemen brandishing assault rifles. Ortiz, bleeding from a gashed forehead courtesy of a rifle butt to the face, had pleaded with the officers and then begged the students to give up their own money to pay the policemen off, but his supplications fell on deaf ears. The head policeman shoved Ortiz down the aisle, then jammed his gun into the driver's back and told him to turn the bus around.

That was the moment when Juan knew they were all going to be killed.

"Why are they doing this?" Miranda said. "Our parents cannot pay a ransom."

It was true. While they were better off than many of the *campesinos* from the rural outskirts of Juarez, none of them would have been able to afford to go to university but for the largess of a wealthy industrialist who saw their education as an investment in the future of the region. Perhaps the corrupt policemen believed their benefactor would come through with the ransom, but this did not feel like a kidnapping.

The bus seesawed back and forth, the driver clearly so rattled by what was happening that the simple task of executing a three-point turn had become an impossibility, but after a few attempts and a few more harsh threats, the bus was heading back down the highway, away from the border and back through the city.

One of the officers waved his gun toward the seating area. "All of you, get down. If I see your face, I will shoot you."

Juan pulled Miranda down, covering her with his own body, for all the good that would do either of them. She trembled beneath him, sobbing quietly. He felt like crying too, but bit the inside of his cheek to stave off desperation. He had to be strong for her sake, no matter what happened. If they somehow made it through this, she would remember how fearless he was, and would tell the tale to their children and their grandchildren. And if they did not?

Well then, at least he would die as the kind of man that she would be proud of, and her last thoughts would be of his courage.

The ride seemed to go on forever, though Juan's wristwatch told him that less than half an hour passed before they left the paved road behind and headed slowly along a dirt road with potholes and ruts that jolted the bus and its passengers violently. The dust of their passage filled the interior, becoming a choking haze, the motes illuminated by the late afternoon sun. Finally, after another twenty minutes of this, the officer in charge ordered the driver to stop.

"Everyone stand up," he continued, shouting down the center aisle. "Go out one at a time."

Juan gave Miranda what he hoped was a reassuring squeeze, then stood up. He kept his gaze downcast, hoping that a show of subservience and a conscious effort to avoid making eye contact—or identifying their captors—might buy them some leniency. Still holding Miranda protectively, he made his way down the steps, off the bus, and joined the queue of his fellow students… His fellow hostages.

The ground underfoot was dry and dusty, but a surreptitious glance showed green fields stretching off in one direction—south, judging by the position of the sun—and a drop off into a ravine or valley to the other. As he was marched away from the bus, he managed to sneak a quick look ahead and saw that they were now being guarded by four men wearing street clothes with ski masks covering their faces.

Narcos, Juan thought. *The police are working with one of the cartels.*

He heard a loud hiss behind them as the air brakes of the bus let go. Overcome by curiosity, Juan risked a quick backward glance and saw the vehicle pulling away, carrying the three renegade police officers along with it.

"Juan," Miranda whispered. "What's going to happen to us?"

"Shhh." It was more an attempt to soothe her than a warning to be quiet. "Everything is going to be all right."

But his every instinct told him otherwise. *We are going to die. I am going to die.*

Their captors said nothing. They just gestured with the rifles, urging the line of students to keep moving until they were all standing at the precipice Juan had earlier noticed.

That's the Rio Bravo, he realized, staring over the international border at the green and gold fields of Texas. *Why would they bring us here?*

They had been on their way to El Paso on a cross-border excursion when the bus was intercepted. Did their captors want them to now attempt to sneak across? Perhaps these men were *narcotraficantes* who intended to use them as drug mules? But surely there were easier ways to smuggle drugs into America.

When the shots came, a long, loud ripping sound like a string of firecrackers all going off at once, Juan almost didn't believe what his ears were telling him. He jerked around to see if the masked men were firing into the air, perhaps trying to intimidate them….

Miranda's hand was torn out of his own, and even as her screams filled the air, Juan felt something white hot pluck at the fabric of his shirt with such force that he was spun around. He collapsed involuntarily, stunned by the realization that he had just been shot.

The burst of gunfire ended as quickly as it had begun. Juan tried to lift himself up, raise his face out of the dirt in order to demand an explanation from the masked men, but when he pushed against the ground with his arms, a lance of pain shot through his ribs and stole his breath away.

A shot—a single staccato report—broke the temporary stillness, and only as its echoes died away did Juan become aware of the voices. Sobbing, pleading, crying out in agony…talking.

"It's done. Let our friends know that the time for destiny has come at last." A low voice. Someone talking on a phone. "No, just say it like that. Destiny. Tell them we need—"

Another gunshot obscured the rest of the utterance, and one of the whimpering voices was silenced. Juan heard the man with the phone resume speaking. "Tell them we need the Patton item from Vienna. As soon as possible. I don't want to have to do this a second time."

The gun barked again, closer now, and Juan finally realized what was happening. The gunmen were killing the wounded. Killing his friends.

Miranda!

He almost reached out for her, but then stopped. If he moved, they would know he was alive and put a bullet in his head.

But…Miranda!

Tears began to well up in his eyes. *I cannot help her now. I can't even help myself.*

Another report thundered in his ears.

The realization that he was going to die, no matter what happened, focused his awareness. Miranda was probably already dead, but even if she was not, he would accomplish nothing for her by simply letting it happen. He had been hit, his right upper chest was on fire with pain, but his lucidity suggested the wound was not immediately life threatening. Yet if he didn't do something, the next one definitely would be.

Another shot, even closer, broke him out of his inertia. He heaved himself sideways, rolling without attempting to rise, and propelled himself over the precipice.

"Hey! We got a runner!" The shout was followed by another report and Juan felt the tremor of a bullet striking the earth right beside him. The near miss galvanized him to move even faster. He scrambled forward awkwardly, fighting the pain of his wound, and without intending to, started rolling down the sloped embankment. More shots, more misses.

"Let him go."

The voice silenced the guns, but Juan did not attempt to stop his downhill plunge. After a few seconds, the dizzying roll ended with a splash into the lukewarm river. He thrashed to get his head above the surface, but as soon as he got his feet under him, he dove out into deeper water and started swimming. His side ached with each overhead stroke, but he did not relent until he felt his knees dragging on the far shore.

He tried to rise, to push himself up out of the mud, but a shot of pain made his arm give out and he fell forward, face first into the shallows. The next attempt was more successful. He lurched up onto the bank and started running.

With solid ground once more underfoot, he risked a glance back to see how close the killers were, and was astonished to discover that he was not being pursued.

They have guns. They don't need to chase me.

The realization that he was still within the range of their assault rifles…that perhaps they were waiting for him to wash up on the other side so they could dispatch him at their leisure, kept him moving.

No shots came.

He kept running anyway. They had killed all the others. There was no reason at all to think he would be spared. But as his panic began to subside, so also did his energy. He stumbled, fell, tried to rise but fell again. He barely felt any pain from his wound or much of anything at all. His arms and legs felt numb. He tried to move them but nothing happened, or if something did happen, he couldn't sense it. His vision had become a shrinking tunnel of darkness.

At last, he understood why the men had not pursued him. The only thing he had accomplished by running was to deny himself the quick release of a bullet in the brain. Instead of dying with Miranda, he would meet his end here, alone.

A faint rumble filled his ears, and as it grew louder, he heard also the sound of crunching gravel. An automobile.

They've come for me after all, he thought. *At least I will not die alone.*

The noise continued to grow louder, but then inexplicably stopped. A moment later, there was another strange noise and then a sardonic voice. "Don't move. You're under arrest."

The last word dissolved into a guffaw, and then another voice joined in. "Think we're too late?"

"Nah. He just passed out. Dehydrated probably. Come on, let's throw him in the back. He can be somebody else's problem."

Juan was faintly aware of hands closing around his arms, lifting him off the ground. These men weren't with *narcotraficantes* who had killed the others. They were speaking English.

I crossed the river…the border. They're Americans, probably Border Patrol officers.

"He's bleeding."

"Damn, chico. What the hell?"

The men continued talking as they manhandled him into their vehicle, but Juan was no longer paying attention. As the darkness rose up to claim him, his thoughts returned to something he had overheard before making his escape.

The time for destiny has come at last.

He had no idea what that meant. It was not the significance of the comment that had seized his curiosity, but rather the actual words themselves. It had not registered in the chaos of the moment, in fact, it was only when he heard the Border Patrol agents talking that he realized what had been so odd about that overheard statement.

The men who had shot Juan and killed Miranda and the others, had also been speaking English.

CHAPTER 2

Carpathian Mountains, Romania

Billy Sievers waited for the artificial blizzard thrown up by the helicopter's rotor-blades to dissipate before leaving the relative comfort of the converted shipping container. He let his AR15 hang from the sling draped over one shoulder and kept his hands buried in his pockets for warmth. As happy as he was to see the helicopter, with its cargo of food and sundry items to replenish their stores, he would have preferred it happen on somebody else's shift.

He tried to be philosophical about it. The sooner the supplies were off-loaded and stowed, the sooner he could get out of the chilly night air, and back into the warmth of the ops shack where he could return to his Top Gear marathon.

As he trekked toward the now idle aircraft, the front door opened, and the passenger got out. Normally, that would have aroused Sievers' suspicions. The guys from Air Services never got out of their birds, much less offered to help unload. But he had been told to expect a visitor, and this evidently was the guy.

Only it wasn't a guy.

Although a heavy parka hid the passenger's upper torso, the skin-tight thermal leggings below the hem left no doubt about the gender of the visitor. Sievers could see just enough to tell that the passenger was female, athletic and toned, but curvy in all the right places. His imagination took care of the rest.

He stood up a little straighter and slowed his pace to his best approximation of a saunter. "About damn time they sent us some entertainment," he called out, flashing a lascivious grin.

The woman's head turned in his direction, giving him a glimpse of the face beneath the fur-lined hood. He immediately noticed that the woman's skin was the color of milk chocolate.

Sievers had zero problem with that.

Her dark eyes studied him for a moment, then she licked

her full lips slowly and gave him a broad smile. "Oh, sugar, you have no idea."

An electric tingle surged through his body. "I like the sound of that."

She closed the remaining distance, stopping just a couple feet away, hands resting on hips that were cocked seductively to the side. "You got a name?"

"Billy…uh, Bill Sievers."

"Well, Billy Boy, I'm actually here for a different kind of business, but maybe after I've taken care of that, I'll show you my idea of a good time."

Sievers definitely liked the sound of that. "So just what kind of business have you got here?"

The woman smiled again. "I'm here to see your ghost."

Tamara Broderick savored the moment when Sievers realized that he had stepped in it. The look on the man's face was almost worth the indignity of tolerating his lewd stares and heavy breathing.

Her declaration would probably be enough to cool his ardor, but behind her confident smile, she remained wary. EmergInt, the mercenary outfit—private security contractor, was the preferred euphemism, but Tam had no patience for political double-speak—that ran the site, employed only former spec-ops types, which meant that Sievers was not merely former military, tough and ruthless, but also very intelligent underneath his somewhat loutish exterior. If his hormones got the better of his good sense and he decided to try something, she would have to act quickly and decisively to end the threat.

Tam was no pushover. In her former role as a special agent of the Federal Bureau of Investigation, an undercover assignment working for a ruthless bio-engineering firm had culminated in a deadly confrontation in the Amazon rainforest. That had led to her current assignment, heading a special division of the Central Intelligence Agency, tasked with hunting down and destroying an international conspiracy known as the Dominion. Tam believed in leading from the front, so she trained hard and fought harder. Krav Maga, Jiu-Jitsu, Tae Kwon

Do, and old-fashioned street brawling were only a few bullet points on her resumé, not to mention the many scrapes she had gotten into in the field. She probably had more combat experience than Sievers, but he was bigger and stronger. She hoped it wouldn't come to a fight, but if it did, he wouldn't be the first man to discover, to his chagrin, that she wasn't defenseless.

Sievers stared at her for a moment, then adopted a more professional demeanor, albeit with more than a hint of underlying aggression. "I'll need verification."

Tam bit back a scathing retort. Funny how he was only now remembering to ask about that. The truth of the matter was that the mere fact of her presence was all the verification he needed, but strictly speaking, this was the procedure. She reached into the pocket of her parka and brought out a small square of pasteboard upon which the recognition code—a code that changed every twelve hours—was printed. She passed it over to Sievers, who inspected it with meticulous care, then took a similar card from his own pocket and compared the two.

He finally lowered the cards and with an almost disappointed sigh, gestured to the row of shipping containers behind him. "This way."

The containers were arranged side by side with no gaps between them. At a glance, the only unusual thing about them was the mere fact that they were lined up in an alpine valley on the Transylvanian Plateau, hundreds of miles from the nearest port facility, but when Sievers guided her through a metal door set in the end of the nearest one, she saw that the exterior façade was just that—a façade. The shipping containers were actually modular suites, equipped with electricity and running water. Originally designed for use by the military, the temporary modules could be easily secured and transported almost anywhere in the world—either by truck or heavy-lift helicopter—making them ideal for forward operating bases, temporary housing for roughnecks working remote oil fields, or as was the case here, for operating an ultra-secret "black site." This site was just one of nearly a hundred off-the-books, CIA-sanctioned, privately-operated detention facilities for "ghosts"—a catch-all term for suspected terrorists, enemy combatants, or anyone else deemed too dangerous to be allowed the due process of law.

The existence of black site facilities was one of the worst kept secrets in the intelligence community, but as was often the case, the leaked rumors were part of a disinformation campaign designed to mask the full extent of the program. In her role as a CIA staff operations officer, Tam was a member of that select group of people who did know the truth, and while she had serious reservations about the legality, not to mention morality, of the program, this was one instance where the system would work to her advantage.

Sievers led her into what looked like a police station interview room. The décor was strictly utilitarian—a table, a few flimsy looking folding chairs. Tam did not fail to notice a large dark stain on the plywood floor in one corner of the room.

Water damage, and not from a leaky roof.

"Wait here." Sievers turned back through the door, leaving her alone in the room.

She drew back her hood and did a slow turn, noting the location of the surveillance cameras, then took a seat at the table. Sievers returned a few minutes later, accompanied by two other men. One of them appeared to have been cast from the same mold as Sievers: shaved head, muscle bound, with a holstered pistol on his belt. His bleary-eyed and slightly irritated expression led Tam to believe that Sievers had woken him up to provide additional security for the prisoner escort.

The other man was the prisoner himself, tall and thin almost to the point of gauntness, with an unruly mop of brown hair and an equally wild beard. His coveralls, which might once have been bright orange but were so grimy and threadbare that it was difficult to say what color they were, seemed to hang off his spare frame. Yet, despite the appearance of frailty, the man moved with a languid self-assurance that belied his frail state. When he saw Tam, he hesitated for a fraction of a second, eyebrows raised in a look of recognition. Sievers steered the prisoner into a chair on the opposite side of the table, and then stood directly behind him, poised to spring into action at the first sign of trouble.

Tam raised her eyes to meet the big man's stare. "Can you give us some space?"

Sievers returned a perturbed frown but moved out from behind the table, taking a station near the door with the other mercenary. Although she knew there were probably microphones hidden in the room, she nevertheless waited until Sievers was out of earshot to address the prisoner.

"Been a while."

Gavin Stone returned a wry smile. "Imagine my surprise at seeing you here."

"I wish I could say the same thing." She leaned forward and held up a pack of cigarettes. "You still smoke? I thought you might want these."

"I never…" Stone's look of confusion passed quickly, and he took an eager breath. "I never thought a pack of coffin nails would look so good."

He reached out with both hands—Tam realized only now that his wrists were bound together with a plastic zip-tie—but Sievers rushed forward and snatched the pack from Tam's grasp. He opened it, shook some of the cigarettes into his hand and then peered into the half-empty packet. When he found nothing amiss, he deposited everything on the tabletop in front of Stone, who had drawn his hands back, calmly folding them in his lap, and was regarding his captor with a bemused expression. As Sievers shuffled away, Stone turned his attention back to Tam.

"You didn't come all this way to facilitate my bad habits." He narrowed his eyes, as if by doing so, he might read her thoughts. "Last I heard, you were FBI."

"I made a lateral career move. I'm with the Company now."

Stone seemed genuinely surprised by this news and a little disappointed. "And given our prior relationship, they thought you might be able to convince me to cooperate."

Tam shook her head. "Actually, I'm here about something else. I'd like to offer you a job."

"A job? With the CIA?" Stone settled back in his chair.

"This should be good."

"I'm heading up a special operational task force called the Myrmidons."

"That sounds impressive," he replied, his tone indicating that he thought it was anything but.

She recalled now that, despite his extraordinary intelligence, Stone's body of knowledge was surprisingly limited. "You always were terrible at Trivial Pursuit. The Myrmidons were legendary warriors who fought under Achilles during the Trojan War."

"I suppose that makes you Achilles." He smirked.

"Something like that, but my heels are stilettos. Feel free to take that as a double-entendre." Her steely gaze told him she was not joking.

"And who are your Myrmidons at war with?"

"The Dominion."

Stone's manner became serious and just a little somber. "Ah, the white whale."

"They're real, Stone. No one doubts that anymore. You heard about what happened at Key West? Norfolk? That was the Dominion's doing."

He pondered this for a moment. "And what is it you think that I could do for you?"

Tam fixed him with a stern look. "Are we seriously going to have this conversation? I'm offering you a chance to do something meaningful with that brilliant mind God saw fit to give you. And a ticket out of this place. Unless you're afraid you'll get homesick if you leave."

"Norfolk was... what, over a year ago? It's so hard to keep track of time in here. I'm guessing this task force of yours has been around for a little while. Obviously I wasn't your first round draft pick. What's changed?"

Tam couldn't help but smile. This was Stone's gift, the ability to look beneath the surface. "There were some personnel issues. I had to let some people go."

Stone nodded as if he understood, and Tam was grateful that he didn't ask her to elaborate. "Good help is hard to find. But you didn't answer my question. What's changed?"

"Yesterday, a bus full of university students was hijacked in Juarez, Mexico. They were taken out into the boonies and killed…executed. Except for one student who escaped. He managed to make it across the Rio Grande where he was picked up by Border Patrol. Once they realized that, A—he wasn't a run-of-the-mill illegal, and B—he was bleeding out, they were able to put together what had happened."

"Drug cartels?"

"That's what the survivor thought at first, but there was a discrepancy."

"A discrepancy?"

"The survivor overheard one of the killers making a phone call. In English. He only remembered a few words, but it was enough for the NSA to isolate the call." She gave Stone a sidelong glance. "You understand the intricacies of electronic eavesdropping, right?"

A faint smile. "I'm vaguely familiar."

"The call was sent from a cloned cell phone, so there's no way to know who was directly responsible for the killings, but the recipient was a suspected Dominion intermediary. That's when I was called in."

"The Dominion is working with Mexican drug cartels? Strange bedfellows."

"There may not be a direct relationship. The Dominion may only be interested in causing instability. The fallout has already started. Mexico has been a powder keg for years. There are widespread protests and a lot of comms traffic among revolutionary groups. President Mendoza's reaction has been…." She groped for a word.

"Half-assed?"

She frowned. "I'm trying to cut back on the vulgar language, but I suppose it's as good a word as any."

Stone considered this for a moment. "You don't think this has anything to do with drug cartels."

Tam nodded, once again impressed by his swift insight. "The call we intercepted included a message. 'The time for destiny has come.'"

"Destiny?"

"The caller was very specific about that. Our best guess is that it's the code name for a new Dominion operation, but that's all we have to go on right now. That and one other thing. The caller said it was imperative to retrieve 'the Patton item from Vienna.'"

"And do you know what that is?"

"My chief researcher, Avery Halsey, has an idea about that, but…" She rolled her eyes in the direction of the mercenaries. "I'll give you the full briefing later. If you're in, that is."

Stone grinned. "Well, it's an offer I can't very well refuse." He turned his gaze to the pair at the door. "Did you hear that, gents? I've got my walking papers."

Sievers looked at his partner. "You know anything about that?"

The other man shrugged. "First I've heard of it."

Sievers addressed Tam. "I guess you don't know how this works, ma'am. We've got a contract. We don't get paid until he gives up…information. Which means he's not going anywhere until we get it. Period."

Tam affected an indignant expression, although this wrinkle was not entirely unexpected. In order to maintain the illusion of deniability, the CIA had very little actual involvement with the black sites. In strictly legal terms, extraordinary rendition—the practice of arresting a suspect without cause, denying them their day in court, and spiriting them away to a secret prison on foreign soil—was not much different than kidnapping. Since the actual management of the black sites, from housing the ghost prisoners to conducting "enhanced interrogations"— another euphemism which turned Tam's stomach—was controlled by EmergInt, any CIA officials called to testify before congressional committees could claim, without perjuring themselves, that the Agency had no knowledge of secret detention facilities or what went on in them. Unfortunately, that also meant that she had no real authority to effect Stone's release. Even though her boss, the Deputy Director of the National Clandestine Service—for all intents and purposes, the number two guy at the Company—had given the go ahead to recruit Stone, that would mean little to these mercenaries.

There was only one way Stone was going to leave his prison.

She turned back to Stone. "Are you going to tell the nice men what they want to know?"

Stone raised his bound hands in a helpless gesture. "Sorry, Tam. It's the principle of the thing. But I do appreciate you thinking of me. And the cancer sticks, too."

He retrieved the pack from the tabletop and began sliding the loose cigarettes back inside, one at a time as if it was some kind of three-dimensional puzzle he was intent on solving. "Don't suppose you brought matches?"

Tam took a disposable lighter from the pocket of her parka. She held it up for Sievers to inspect, but the mercenary merely waved indifferently, so she slid it across the table to him. He picked it up, brought one of the cigarettes to his mouth, and then holding the lighter awkwardly in both hands, lit up and blew out a large cloud of smoke. "Stop in again if you're ever in the neighborhood."

Tam studied his face for some hint of compromise. It wasn't there. She shook her head sadly. "You and your principles. Fine. You're on your own."

He gave a rueful smile. "I always have been."

She pushed away from the table, turned, and headed for the door without another word. Sievers opened it for her and followed her out into the darkness.

"Ex-boyfriend?"

"Just an old family friend," Tam replied. It was more than she wanted to reveal to the mercenary, but now that the plan was in motion, she had to be very careful about what she did and did not say. "I thought I could convince him to talk, but…" She shrugged.

"You should stick around," Sievers said. "Maybe he'll come to his senses."

"You'd love that," she muttered, then in a more conversational tone, added, "That's not likely to happen. He can be very stubborn, as I'm sure you've discovered. And I have other places I need to be."

CHAPTER 3

Stone remained seated as Tam exited the interview room. He pretended to relish the cigarette though he was careful not to inhale, lest a coughing fit betray him. He had never actually smoked a cigarette before and had no idea what effect the tobacco would have on him. Just gathering the smoke into his mouth and blowing it out in a cloud around his head was making him a little woozy. He would need his wits about him to survive what was coming.

Sievers followed Tam out the door, leaving Stone alone with the hulking John Bowers. Many of his captors possessed a penchant for cruelty—it was probably a prerequisite for the job—but among the team that had kept and tormented him for the last ten months, Bowers was by far the cruelest. Without the outlet of his work, the man probably would have been a serial killer.

The click of the door latch was Bowers' cue to move. Stone had no doubt that Bowers intended to make him pay dearly for the visit with Tam. The carrot of freedom which Tam had dangled before him would seem even more desirable—and his apparent decision to refuse it, all the more foolhardy—once Bowers brought down the stick, both figuratively and literally. Stone kept looking forward but followed the man's approach in his peripheral vision.

Doing his best to appear oblivious, Stone lifted the cigarette to his lips and feigned another drag. Bowers raised his right hand, cocking it across his body to deliver a backhand blow, not hard enough to hurt, but just enough to knock the cigarette away and demonstrate his contempt for the helpless prisoner.

Not quite helpless.

As Bowers hand came down, Stone calmly ducked under the swing, and in the same motion lashed out with his foot, jamming it into the side of Bowers' leg, just below the knee.

There was a sickening crack as cartilage snapped, and the leg folded at an unnatural angle. Bowers howled and groped reflexively for the injured limb, but quickly recovered his wits and reached instead for the gun holstered at his hip.

Stone was faster.

He knew that he could not defeat Bowers in a sustained struggle. After nearly a year of living on subsistence rations, subjected to constant physical and psychological abuse, he felt as weak as a toddler. Even under the best of circumstances, he could not hope to best someone with Bowers' size and ability, but he had one advantage over the mercenary. For ten months, he had watched the man, studied his movements, his behaviors, his personality. He knew about the old knee injury, which caused Bowers to limp ever so slightly, from time to time. He knew how Bowers would react to a surprise attack, and how long it would take for him to remember to go for his gun.

Bowers was an open book to him. All his captors were. He knew what they would do in any given circumstance even before they did. That knowledge had made it possible for him to endure the worst of their torments, to keep both his psyche and his secret intact. He could have used the knowledge to escape, but given the remoteness of the location, he knew he wouldn't get far. Not without help.

The sort of help that Tam Broderick was offering.

Under the pretense of lighting the cigarette, Stone had used the flame to soften the plastic zip-tie binding his wrists, and now only a sharp twist was required to break free. He threw himself onto Bowers, pinning the mercenary's gun arm to the floor with one hand, and delivering a savage punch to Bowers' exposed throat with the other.

Bowers forgot about his gun, forgot about everything except the desperate need to breath. Both of his hands went to his throat, clutching it in a futile effort to draw a breath. Stone knew that he had only bruised the man's windpipe and that the effects would last a few minutes at most, so he deftly unholstered the pistol and slammed it against the side of the man's head. Bowers went limp.

Stone methodically untied the unconscious man's boots and drew them off, and then took his trousers as well. A search of the pockets produced a bundle of zip-ties held together with a rubber band, and he used one to secure Bowers' wrists behind his back.

Only then did he open his left hand to reveal the tiny flesh-colored lump of plastic that Tam passed over to him along with the cigarette lighter. He rolled it between his fingers for a moment, then pushed it into his right ear canal.

"Slick move with the cigarettes," he whispered. "Turns out, they were bad for his health."

"Nice." The electronically reproduced voice was tinny in his ear. Female. Youngish. Trace of a So Cal accent. Clipped consonants. Asian-American, but not first generation. Definitely not Tam Broderick. "Listen up. If you want to make it out of here alive, you need to do exactly as I tell you."

"Who are you?"

"Go outside. Now."

He glanced down at his feet, which were shod in cheap rubber flip-flops. "Can I at least put on—"

"No. No more questions. The surveillance cameras are recording everything you say and do. If you keep talking, they'll know you're getting help. Now get moving. I'll explain everything once you're out of that room."

"Yes, ma'am," he muttered.

He opened the door a crack and peered out into the darkness. He couldn't make out Tam and Sievers, but there was no mistaking the noise of a helicopter turbine engine coming to life. The aircraft would be ready for take-off in a minute, perhaps less. Somehow he would have to get past Sievers and—

"Don't worry about the helicopter," the voice told him. "Head for the woods to the south."

"South?" He stared up at the night sky, trying to find Polaris.

"Turn left out the door. Go! Now."

The turbine noise built to a fever pitch, and then the sound of the rotor blades beating the air joined the tumult. A stiff breeze raced through the compound, pushing a flurry of loose snow. The helicopter was taking off.

Stone hesitated. Blind faith did not come easy to him. He relied on his observations, on patterns of predictable behavior that were far more reliable indicators of trustworthiness than vague promises of assistance. It wasn't that he did not trust the voice coming from the ear bud. The woman was clearly working with Tam, and Stone trusted Tam implicitly. The problem was that he had no clear sense about whether or not his mysterious guide could deliver on the promise of freedom.

A total of eight men were assigned to the secret detention facility. Two of them worked primarily in an administrative capacity while the others, including both Sievers and Bowers, functioned as all-purpose muscle. The latter group worked a rotating schedule which meant that, at this late hour, everyone else was probably in bed.

Asleep? Impossible to say. The helicopter's arrival might have awakened some of them, but the twice-weekly flights were a routine occurrence, hardly worth getting up for.

Once Sievers realized that Stone had overpowered Bowers and made a run for it, the alarm would sound, and it would be only a matter of seconds before the entire camp started hunting him. They would find his tracks in the snow....

The breeze from the rotors would hide his footprints, at least as far as the edge of the woods.

He took off running, ignoring the snow that intruded between his toes. He reached the treeline just as the helicopter's take-off noise reached a climax and began to subside.

"I see you. Keep going. I'm fifty yards from you."

Fifty yards? The tree boughs blocked out the scant illumination of starlight. He could not see five yards, much less fifty. *She's got night vision.*

"Keep going. Getting warmer, warmer." She coaxed him onward like they were kids on the playground.

"Warmer? Seriously?" Stone's toes were already numb, and the ache of cold was rising up his ankles. "You do realize I'm practically barefoot."

"The sooner you get here," the woman replied, without a trace of sympathy, "the sooner you can warm up. I'm at your eleven o'clock. Twenty yards. Hurry."

He adjusted course and started counting his paces. When he got to eighteen, the same voice issued from out of the darkness. "Stop. I'm right beside you. Hold out your hand."

He did and a moment later felt something in his outstretched palm. "Night vision goggles," she explained. "Put them on and this will go a lot faster."

His cold fingers fumbled with the device, but after a few seconds he succeeded in donning the goggles and switching them on. There was a flare of green light and then his surroundings lit up. The ground was strangely dark, the cold earth giving up precious little infrared light, but he could now easily distinguish the surrounding forest, as well as the petite form of his guide, though that was about all he could see of her since she was dressed head-to-toe in black.

"Here." She thrust a dark bundle in his direction. "Put this on."

He unfurled the bundle and saw what appeared to be a pair of insulated coveralls. He slid into them without further urging, and immediately felt warmth radiate through his limbs. It was like wearing an electric blanket.

"Battery operated heater," the woman said, handing him a pair of insulated boot liners. "These, too. Now maybe you'll stop griping about how cold your little piggies are."

"Thanks." Stone was grateful enough that her sarcasm did not even bother him. The radiant heat from the boot liners felt like hot needles stabbing through his nearly frozen feet, but he ignored the sensation. Coping with pain was a skill he had mastered during his time at the black site. "I'm Gavin Stone, by the way. But I guess you already knew that."

"Kasey." Her abrupt manner was indication enough that there would be no further small talk. She stepped to the side and pointed to something that Stone had initially dismissed as a small tree. He now saw that it was actually a strange contraption that looked a little like a toy helicopter sitting atop tripod legs that looked like they had been salvaged from a collapsible ironing board. "Have a seat."

Stone stared blankly at the thing, noting a small molded

plastic chair, similar to a toddler's booster seat. "What the hell is that thing?"

"A GEN H-4 personal helicopter," Kasey replied, impatiently. "And it's taking off in about thirty seconds, with or without you."

"Personal? As in one person? There are two of us."

"It's rated to carry four hundred and eighty-five pounds. About fifty of that is fuel. So unless your skeleton is made of adamantium, I think it can handle the two of us."

"Ada…what?"

"Just sit down."

Stone resignedly sank into the chair. The tubular metal framework flexed and wobbled with the addition of his weight. "Uh, I don't think this is—"

Kasey abruptly sat on his lap. Weight certainly wasn't going to be an issue. She was probably ninety pounds, soaking wet, but she plopped down hard enough to silence his protest. She reached down to either side of him and drew up the halves of a long nylon seatbelt which she secured around her midsection, cinching it tight. Stone felt her grind into him even harder.

"And I didn't even have to buy you a drink," he remarked.

"Don't get any ideas. You're not my type."

"I don't think I want to meet your type."

"When I fire up the engines, they're going to come running. We have to be off the ground before they get here. You need to stay perfectly still so I can fly this thing, got it?"

"I'll just shut my eyes and go to my happy place."

He did exactly that. The warmth from the heated garments had all but erased the memory of the miserable trek through the snow, and for a few fleeting seconds, he was happier than he had been in a long time.

His tranquility was shattered by a strident mechanical roar. The H-4's power plant, which was only about eighteen inches above his head, sounded like a leaf-blower giving birth to a Harrier jump jet. The torque from the engine start-up vibrated through the flimsy-looking frame, and if not for the restraints holding him in place, he probably would have bolted.

The twin counter-rotating rotor blades began to cut the air

above him, slowly at first, but picking up speed until there was just a single blurry disc. The engine noise grew louder, but for a long time, too long it seemed, nothing else happened. Then, with a violent shudder, the H-4 began to rise. Stone felt a primal panic as the ground beneath him fell away. The aircraft tilted crazily, swinging them back and forth, and it took every ounce of self-control Stone possessed to remain still.

Even though he knew better, Stone glanced down. They were hovering just a few feet above the tree-tops, still bobbing back and forth, as if Kasey was trying to figure out which direction to go. He could see the blocky modules of the detention facility, still too close for his liking, and movement in the trees as his former captors raced to investigate the source of the noise.

Kasey must have seen it too, for, at that instant, she flexed her body, contorting against Stone's immobilized form and the aircraft and started to move. The forward motion smoothed out the vibrations and Stone felt a rush of frigid air on his face as they swooped over the forest. There was an eruption of noise behind them, multiple gunshots, barely audible over the whine of the engines, but none of the bullets found their mark, and after just a few seconds, they were well out of range.

Stone's initial terror quickly gave way to something more like the thrill of skiing a black diamond run. The mini-copter had rudimentary controls. Steering, lift, and forward motion relied on the leverage of the pilot to tilt the rotor disk, which meant that flying the machine was more like surfing or hang-gliding than operating a machine. The prospect of crashing was never far from his thoughts, but his fear was tempered by the raw excitement of defying gravity, not to mention the literal freedom from his tormentors.

The latter was, he knew, not a foregone conclusion, but the odds against being recaptured, at least in the near term, were good. There were no roads leading to the black site, which meant no chance of any ground pursuit. Word of his escape would already have gone out, but the questionable legality of the black sites was their Achilles' Heel. The contractors would not be able to enlist the help of Romanian authorities or involve legitimate American intelligence interests since doing so would expose what was going on. Indeed, they would have a powerful incentive to keep the incident a secret as long as possible, managing the search for the fugitive with their own resources. Moreover, Tam Broderick had a plan, which meant she was already several steps ahead of them.

At least, he hoped so.

Kasey kept the craft low, hugging the terrain. More than once, Stone thought he felt treetops brushing against his boots. A couple times, Kasey threw the mini-helicopter into a sharp bank, narrowly avoiding collisions. The constant peril was enough to keep Stone on the razor's edge between white-knuckle fear and heart-pounding exhilaration, at least until the battery in his suit heater went dead. After that, he was able to measure the passage of time by the chattering of his teeth.

At least ten more minutes passed before he glimpsed the lights of a city in a distant valley, some fifty miles away. Judging by the rush of wind against his face, Stone guessed they were barely hitting highway speeds. He was mentally bracing himself for an hour of frozen hell when Kasey swung the craft to the south, away from the city. A few minutes later, they began descending, following the slope of the plateau but headed toward no destination that Stone could discern. It wasn't until they were almost on the ground that Stone saw the clearing, a flat rectangle several hundred feet long, and just wide enough to accommodate a small airplane or a helicopter like the one that sat idle near the middle of the landing strip.

They spiraled down to land about a hundred feet away from the helicopter. Kasey made it look positively easy, reaching out with her toes at the last second to make contact with the ground as easily as stepping off an escalator. She relaxed the throttle, and the H-4's frame settled with equal grace.

Kasey unbuckled the safety belt and slid off Stone's lap, freeing him to move. He struggled to rise on rubbery legs, at once grateful to be back on terra firma, and ready for another ride on the crazy little machine.

A light came on inside the helicopter, bright enough that Stone had to remove his night optics. Two figures got out of the larger aircraft and headed to meet them. One was a tall, lean man with dark hair trimmed to a military buzz. Stone got the sense that he was an athlete, probably basketball or track. The other passenger was Tam.

"Enjoy the ride?" she asked when she got closer.

Stone grinned. "You always did have the best toys, Tam. That's one of the things I always loved about you."

"Ouch, with the L-word. Okay, introductions all around. You've already met Kasey Kim."

Stone glanced over at Kasey, who had also removed her night vision goggles and was busy disassembling the H-4. As he had surmised, under her short wedge-cut hairstyle, she had Asian features; Korean, judging by her surname.

Tam gestured to Tall Guy, who had gone over to assist Kasey. "That's Greg Johns, my second-in-command. He'll be flying us from here to the airport in Bucharest. Once we get there, Kasey will make you look presentable."

Greg rubbed the bristle on his scalp. "Kasey's our resident beautician. If she ever leaves the Company, she'll have to open her own salon."

Kasey shot Greg a venomous look, but Stone sensed nothing mean-spirited in the exchange.

Tam turned to Kasey. "Any problems?"

Kasey shook her head. "Nope. It handled like a dream."

"I meant with your passenger."

Kasey laughed. "You mean other than him being so clingy?" She shook her head. "We got away about as clean as we hoped, but they're probably already trying to figure out where we went."

"They won't give up," Stone said.

"No," Tam replied. "I don't imagine they will. You know, you could save us all a lot of grief by just giving up the data. And don't give me any bullsh…" She stopped short for just a second, then went on. "About your principles. The data you stole could cause a lot of problems if it ever fell into the wrong hands or went public. Life or death problems. It's one thing to risk your own life for principles, but there are innocent lives at stake."

"Trust me, Tam. No one is in any danger. At least not from me. The real danger is how quickly people are willing to give up their freedom in response to fear. Or for the sake of convenience, which is even scarier."

"I told you not to give me any of that." Tam shook her head. "But that's none of my business."

"No?" Stone stared at her sideways. "Well, you've gone to a lot of trouble to get me this far. What do you want? You know, I could never figure out what's going on in your mind. That's a rare thing. It's the other thing I love about you."

"You're gonna really love this, then," she said, breaking into a grin. "Gavin Stone, you're under arrest."

CHAPTER 4

Vienna, Austria

The hotel room looked more like a college dorm room after an all-night cram session than a suite in a luxury hotel on the historic Ringstrasse. The dining table was piled with books, a few tourist guides but mostly historical reference material, as well as trays with the remains of the previous night's dinner and a litter of empty paper cups.

It was not the European vacation Avery Halsey had always dreamed of, but as often happened when she was deep in a research project, she was too caught up in reliving the past to worry about what was going on around her.

A knock at the door brought her back to the twenty-first century, but only just. "It's unlocked," she shouted. "Come on in."

There was a click as the door opened and then another a few seconds later as it closed again. "Avery honey, we're going to need to have a talk about basic security precautions."

Avery started at the sound of the unexpected but familiar voice of Tam Broderick. "Sorry. I thought you were room service bringing the coffee I ordered."

She turned around, somewhat embarrassed at the reproof but mostly relieved that Tam and the others were back, safe and sound after their excursion to Romania. Her mood darkened a little when she realized that there was someone else with them. She did not recognize the tall, thin man with the buzz cut, neatly trimmed beard and generally haggard appearance. His clothes—khaki chinos and a navy blue polo shirt—hung on his gaunt frame, giving him the appearance of a homeless derelict or an Old Testament prophet, cleaned up but still lost in the wilderness of his own mind.

"I see you found him."

Tam nodded to the man. "Avery, this is Gavin Stone.

Stone, Avery Halsey, our resident historian and researcher."

Stone inclined his head in a sort of bow, then met Avery's eyes. "Relax, Miss Halsey. Your job is safe. I'm here under duress."

Avery gaped at him. "How did…" She shook her head in astonishment. Although secretly bothered by Tam's insistence that they needed to bring in an outsider—even if he was an old acquaintance of Tam's—she had been careful to hide her displeasure. Had Tam picked up on it anyway?

Tam gave Stone a sidelong glance. "I can take you back if that's what you really want. I'm sure EmergInt will be more than happy to take you in again."

Without answering, Stone strode forward and dropped into a chair on the opposite side of the table from Avery. "You said there's coffee coming? I hope you ordered a whole pot."

"Don't pay him any mind," Tam said. She gave Avery a long appraising look. "And I hope you didn't get the idea that I brought him in to replace you."

Avery cocked her jaw sideways. "Well…"

Stone leaned forward, fixing Avery with an unusually intense stare. "She's telling the truth. Tam has complete confidence in you. Besides, I'm no researcher."

Avery studied him for a moment, then turned her eyes to Tam. "Then why *is* he here? I mean, I know you two go way back, but it just seems to me like the last thing we need is the kind of baggage he's bringing along."

"That's taken care of," Tam said. "As for the rest, you're just going to have to trust me. Catch him up on what we know. It's been a long night, and I need to grab some shut-eye. We'll reconvene at 1400."

Before Avery could offer any further protest, Tam departed with Kasey and Greg in tow, leaving her with only Stone for company.

"Canada, right?"

She stared at him. "I'm sorry?"

"You're Canadian." He peered at her as if expecting to find confirmation written across her forehead. "East Coast. Halifax?"

"What, is this some kind of Sherlock Holmes parlor trick?"

"I'll take that as a 'yes.' And no, not really a trick. I have an ear for accents. You can tell a lot about where a person is from by the way they pronounce the word 'coffee.'"

Avery frowned. She did not have an accent. At least she was pretty sure that she didn't. But Stone had been on the money. She did indeed hail from a small town about fifty miles south of the capital of Nova Scotia, but she had made a real effort to neutralize the broad vowel sounds that were so often associated with the region. As a junior college history professor, and then subsequently as the Myrmidons' research specialist for the last year, she knew she wouldn't get any respect if she sounded like a backwater fisherman's daughter.

"Is that your special talent then? Master of accents? Or maybe it's your ability to be super-condescending?"

Stone leaned back in his chair and stretched. "No. I don't have any special talents."

Avery's instincts said otherwise. Tam had not told her much about Stone, and despite the fact that Avery *was* a crack researcher, she had found very little real information about him. She knew that he was the only scion of a wealthy Virginia family—in addition to being rich, his grandfather and great-great-grandfather had been famous explorers in their day—but as near as she could tell, the only noteworthy thing Gavin Stone had accomplished was to single-handedly infiltrate the American National Security Agency's ultra-secure computer network, and help himself to reams of data detailing their controversial, and not entirely legal, domestic surveillance program.

Exactly what was in the data, or why Stone had pilfered it, was anyone's guess. Avery assumed he was some kind of whistle-blowing hacktivist, but he had made no attempt to release the data, nor had he offered it up in exchange for his freedom after being captured and whisked off to a secret CIA detention site. He was either a criminal or a vigilante—maybe both—and while Avery felt a certain admiration for what he had done, her sense was that he had done a good thing for a bad, or at the very least ambiguous, reason.

None of which explained why Tam felt he was worth the bother.

To cover her discomfort, Avery got up and went over to the room phone. "You hungry?" she asked him.

"Absolutely famished."

"Me too." She dialed the front desk and canceled her room service order, then turned back to Stone. "Let's go. I need some air."

His eyes narrowed suspiciously. "I'm not sure Tam wants me wandering off."

Avery shrugged. "What's she going to do, arrest you?"

He gave a mirthless laugh. "She already did that."

Stone took a sip of coffee and allowed the hot liquid to roll around his mouth for a moment before swallowing. "Perfect. You know, the Viennese truly perfected the art of coffee."

"Of course I know that," Avery replied. "I'm a history professor. And I've been here for a couple days. That's why I picked this place."

"This place" was Café Sperl, an elegant old coffee house, situated in a white brick triangle building just a few blocks from the hotel. According to the sign, the café had been in business since 1880, and it certainly looked like it. The décor and furnishings were like something from a museum. It wasn't hard to imagine Strauss or Mozart sitting at the café tables or in one of the plush upholstered booths, sipping coffee or eating *apfelstrudel*. High arched windows looked out over the street, and dark mahogany paneling lined the back wall, beneath sconces that probably once burned with gaslight. The effect of both the hot coffee and the décor was amplified by the wintry weather outside. Although bitterly cold, the snowdrifts that lined the streets made the city seem like something from a fairy tale and imbued the warm interior of the café and its offerings with a sublime, almost supernatural quality.

"Did Tam really arrest you?" Avery asked when he set the cup down. "I thought you two were old friends."

"The arrest is just a formality," he explained, intentionally avoiding the implicit question in her latter statement. "As long as I'm in federal custody, so to speak, the US government won't treat me as a fugitive. I don't have to worry about my picture going out to every CIA station in Europe, and I can go anywhere Tam wants to take me."

"Seems like a big hassle. Why don't you just give back the data you stole? Wipe the slate clean?"

"You're very direct."

"It saves time."

Stone took another sip of coffee. He could already feel his pulse quickening with the infusion of caffeine. Ten months of going without had diminished his tolerance for the stimulant. He would have to pace himself. "I assume you think you know what it was that I… *stole*."

"Something to do with the NSA domestic surveillance program. Don't get me wrong. I don't think it's right for the government to be spying on its citizens, but you broke the law. Two wrongs don't make a right."

"Did I break the law? The legal system is predicated on the notion that the accused must be proven guilty in court. So if I broke the law, why haven't I been given my day in court?"

"They can't put you on trial without revealing top secret information," Avery replied, matter-of-factly. "It sucks, but you left them no choice."

Stone smiled. "Are you so sure that's what really happened?"

"You're saying it's not?"

Stone set his cup down. "Tell me about Destiny."

Avery frowned but accepted the change of subject without protest. "If you know that much, then I have to assume that Tam has already briefed you. We intercepted a cell phone call—thanks to the NSA's surveillance protocols, incidentally—to a suspected Dominion operative. The call mentioned 'destiny' and indicated that there's something here in Vienna that they need. Something related to General George S. Patton. You know about him, right?"

"I recall seeing a movie about the man," Stone said. "But it was ages ago."

Avery arched an eyebrow in surprise. "Seriously? Tam

made you out to be some kind of super-genius."

"That was generous of her. I told you, Miss Halsey—"

"It's Dr. Halsey actually," she snapped, but then immediately softened her tone. "But I guess if we're going to be working together, you can call me Avery."

"Avery, then. But as I was saying, I'm not a researcher. That's your job, and I would be delighted to hear what you've been researching."

Avery regarded him with her storm gray eyes. Stone could tell that she was an intense person, driven to accomplish whatever task she set her mind to, and not someone who accepted change without a fight. She was attractive, but Stone sensed that she was the kind of person who saw her looks as an impediment to her goals instead of an asset. It was not an unwarranted concern, he knew. Misogyny was endemic in academic circles where the 'old boy' mentality prevailed, and successful women were often accused of sleeping their way to the top. He could tell that her ambivalence toward him stemmed from the perception that Tam had brought him into the equation because of a lack of confidence in Avery's abilities. The truth was much more complicated, but nothing he could say would disabuse the young historian of that notion.

"George Patton," Avery said, "was quite probably the most brilliant and aggressive military strategist in World War II. He led the campaign that broke the German Army in North Africa, and then went on to liberate Italy. He was a prickly character though, and that got him into a lot of trouble with Allied command. The Germans knew that he was the best and believed that he would lead the war effort in Europe, which is why the Allies started using him to divert attention away from their real operation. Ultimately, that deception was probably the key to the success of the D-Day invasion."

Stone nodded, indicating that she should continue.

"The idea of being side-lined didn't sit well with Patton, and he managed to get back in the fight. His forces were among the first to reach Berlin, but by that point in the war, it wasn't so much a battle with the Germans as it was a race with the Soviets for control of Eastern Europe. After Hitler was defeated, Patton was briefly appointed military governor of Bavaria, but he ruffled too many feathers and was relieved of command. That would probably have been the end of his military command, but before he could return to the States, he was killed in a car accident."

"Bavaria? Not Austria?"

"At the time, Vienna was under Soviet control. Patton didn't get along with the Russians very well."

"So what's the Vienna connection to Patton?"

Avery stared at him again, the apprehension in her eyes giving way to curiosity. "First, tell me why Tam brought you aboard. What exactly is it that makes you worth all this trouble? Are you a computer guy? A hacker? 'Cause I already have a guy for that."

"That's good to know. No, I don't think that's what she has in mind for me."

"Well, what then? You're not getting anything more from me until you 'fess up."

Stone managed a grin to hide his discomfort. "Tam really didn't tell you?"

"She said that you would bring a unique set of skills and perspectives. She also thought you would be a lot more useful working on our team than rotting in a CIA detention facility."

"Ah." Stone took a sip from his cup. "Well, I have picked up a few skills over the years—"

"Like hacking?"

"Among other things."

Avery did not relent. "She said you had a unique ability to see what most people miss. What was she talking about?"

Stone fiddled with his coffee cup. "It's not easy to explain. Most people think it sounds crazy."

"Believe me, I can handle crazy."

"I'm good at recognizing patterns."

"Uh, huh. So are the people in Mensa. You'll have to do better than that."

"Maybe I should be asking you. I'm sure there's no shortage of available personnel. So why would she pick me? You must have some ideas about that?"

Avery frowned. "Well, there aren't as many qualified candidates as you might think. The Dominion has a pretty long reach. When Tam set up the Myrmidons, she limited recruitment to people that she was sure hated the Dominion as much as she did. My brother, Dane, worked with her for a while last year to help take down the Dominion in America, but being a secret agent wasn't really his thing. Tam thought it would get easier to find qualified people after the terror attacks, but things actually got worse. We got infiltrated by these guys calling themselves the Norfolk Group. After she cleaned house, we were pretty much down to a skeleton crew. That's when Tam decided to bring you in. She trusts you, obviously, and that's probably the most important thing. But aside from being able to recognize patterns and avoid answering questions, what are you good at? Are you ex-CIA? Is that it? Is that how you two know each other?"

Stone did not answer for several seconds. Then, he met her gaze. "I'll tell you, but first, tell me something. Why are you one of Tam's Myrmidons? Why are *you* fighting the Dominion?"

"Because they're evil. They're as bad as the Nazis. Hell, the local branch—the Heilig Herrschaft—*are* modern-day Nazis. They want the same things Hitler wanted. Racial purity, religious oppression, global domination. Someone has to take a stand against them; it's as simple as that."

"It's never as simple as that," Stone said, almost too softly to be heard. "But those are noble reasons, I'll grant you. Why do you think *they* want those things?"

"The short answer? They're psychopaths. I meant that in the literal, clinical sense."

Stone nodded enthusiastically. "Exactly. The people who are driven to create something like the Third Reich or the Dominion…they are wired differently than the rest of us. Who knows what causes it? Nature or nurture? Maybe something happens, a genetic switch gets thrown, the conscience gets turned off, and presto, you've got yourself a Hitler or a Mengele."

Avery crossed her arms. "You aren't going to answer my question are you?"

"I told you. It's hard to explain. And my conversational skills may have become a little rusty." Stone took another sip of the coffee. "Are you familiar with the hypothesis that our universe and everything in it is actually a holographic computer simulation?"

Avery just stared at him as if he had grown a second head.

"You did say you could handle crazy," he reminded her.

"Uh, you mean like in the Matrix? We're all plugged into a big computer, living out a virtual reality."

"Nothing so banal." Stone managed a smile. "Have your historical studies taught you much about the history of computers?"

Avery shrugged. "I know that there were mechanical computers—like adding machines—long before the twentieth century."

"Right. When most people think computers, they think electronics, but a computer is any device that carries out logical computations. The moving parts of the computer must follow the mathematical rules of logic. The universe behaves the same way. We can observe these mathematical operations in everything from the movement of galaxies to the behavior of atoms."

"Okay. I get that. Math is everywhere. How does that make everything a hologram?"

"Think about it. What is reality?" He rapped on the table. "What is stuff made of? Atoms, right? We could take it down a couple more levels, but that's good enough for our purposes. The most abundant element in the universe is hydrogen. It's a simple atom, one proton, one electron—a positive charge and a negative charge. Hydrogen atoms collect because of gravity, and when they reach a certain critical mass, the atoms start fusing together to form helium atoms, and a star is born. Basic high school science, right?

"At a certain point, the process continues with helium fusing into other elements. The stars eventually explode as supernovae, scattering the elements across the universe to become gas clouds, asteroids, and planets. All the matter in the universe—all the stuff—comes from that process.

"The important point is that it's all mathematical. The gravity that draws atoms together, the critical mass necessary for fusion to begin, how long the star will burn before it goes supernova—these are all mathematical operations, not random events."

He could see that he was losing her, so he decided to change tack. "Do you have a coin?"

She dug a one euro coin from her pocket and slid it across the table. Stone picked it up and looked at the image stamped on the front—the likeness of Wolfgang Amadeus Mozart. "If I flip this in the air, what will happen?"

"It will land, either heads or tails up."

"Any other possibilities?"

She shrugged. "Anything is possible. It could land on edge, but that's really unlikely."

"We can't reliably predict whether it will land heads or tails, but if we flip it exactly the same way, we should get the same results. Why don't we?"

"Because you can't flip it exactly the same way. There's always going to be a slight variation."

Stone nodded. "The science of studying the effects of those slight variations is called chaos theory. You've probably heard of it but the name is misleading. There is no such thing as chaos in the mythological sense. We call it chaos because full awareness of all the possible variations in a complicated system is impossible. For us at least. But with a sufficiently powerful computer, capable of detecting all those minute variables, we could predict the outcome every time." He flipped the coin in the air and deftly caught it, slapping it down on the back of his left hand, covered with his right. "Heads."

He uncovered it without looking and showed it to her.

"Luck," she said, dismissively. "You had a fifty-fifty chance of getting it right."

"There's no such thing as luck. Only a confluence of variables that have been in motion for about fourteen billion years. The universe itself is the computer, working out the inevitable program of its own existence. Everything that has happened in the entire universe, and everything that will ever happen, is the predictable result of a mathematical progression that began with the Big Bang."

Comprehension began to dawn in Avery's eyes but was just as quickly replaced by disbelief. "Wait. Everything?"

"Everything." He held up the coin. "The atoms that make up this, and the atoms that make up me, and the table, and you and this coffee shop, are all the result of a chain of events that was set in motion billions of years ago."

"You're talking about fate. Predestination."

Stone shrugged. "Those are philosophical terms. I prefer 'deterministic.'"

"I don't buy it. Maybe stars and planets behave like clockwork, but living creatures aren't predictable."

"Why not?"

"A little thing called free will. We do things because we choose to, not because we've been programmed to."

"Are you so sure?" He pointed to her coffee cup. "Why did you order coffee instead of tea?"

"I was in the mood for coffee. If I had been in the mood for tea, I would have ordered tea."

"And what controls your moods?"

Avery opened her mouth to answer, but closed it without saying anything.

"Our moods, not to mention everything else that happens in our brains, are the result of chemical interactions. Chemicals that are made up of elements that were created in stars. Those chemicals react with each other according to very precise mathematical rules. Complex rules to be sure, but not as random or independent as we fool ourselves into thinking. What we call free will is really just us convincing ourselves that we wanted to do something that we were going to do anyway."

"No. You're wrong. I can choose to do something that I don't want to do. I might order tea just to spite you. Can you predict when I'll do that?"

"Not yet. But if I observed you long enough, I'd be able to predict most of your behavioral choices with above average accuracy. It's easier, of course, when the subject doesn't know they're being observed, but even then, it's not impossible."

"You're really serious, aren't you? You think that everything since the Big Bang has been leading up to this. You and me, practically strangers, sitting in a coffee shop thousands of miles from our homes, talking about…this?"

"In a word, yes. Everything that occurs happens because it has to. Because that's the only way it could have happened. I know that's pretty mind-boggling, but it can be proven mathematically."

Avery shook her head, unconvinced.

"Well," Stone went on. "I did tell you it would sound crazy. Just knowing—or I should say believing—something is true does not automatically make it useful. But if you know how to look for it, you can see the evidence for it everywhere. I've gotten pretty good at recognizing the pattern, and once you do that… well, it's a whole different kind of computer hacking."

"Tam knows you believe this stuff?"

Stone made see-saw motion with his hand. "She knows what I can do with it."

"Then tell me this. Why bother breaking into the NSA? If we're really living in a…what did you call it…a predetermined universe, then why bother? If we're all just slaves to the machine, doing what we have to do, what's the point of even living?"

"I can see that this is upsetting you, but you did ask." Stone rotated his coffee cup in a series of precise quarter turns. "So, I've told you about my *special talent*. Now it's your turn. What is the Dominion looking for in Vienna?"

Avery's expression did not soften. "Don't you already know? Can't you predict what I'm going to say next?"

"It doesn't work like that. To even make an educated guess, I would have to have a lot more information." He paused a moment. "What I can tell is that on some level, you know that I'm right. You've always believed that everything happens for a reason."

"How did…" Avery caught herself and closed her mouth defiantly.

Stone didn't need confirmation. "To truly predict everything in the universe, you would need to be outside the universe, which is why the idea that it is all a simulation being run by an extra-dimensional being—God, for want of a better word—makes a certain kind of sense. On some level, most of us already know it's true."

Avery sighed. "There's only one thing in Vienna, relating to Patton, that the Dominion could possibly want. And it's even got the word 'destiny' right in the name. The *Heilige Lanze*, also known as the Spear of Destiny."

Stone's hand froze on his coffee cup. "The spear that was used to stab Jesus during the crucifixion, if you happen to believe in that sort of thing."

"It's not the real Spear of Destiny," Avery said quickly.

"No, of course not. And you know that how exactly?"

"It doesn't matter. The point is, the Dominion thinks it's real. They're obsessed with finding mystical relics. If they're looking for anything here, that's got to be it."

"The Spear of Destiny." Stone shook his head. "And to think I was worried about sounding crazy."

CHAPTER 5

El Paso, Texas

Guillermo Esperanza paced stiffly about the waiting room of the University Medical Center, the concern on his face masking the rage that burned under the surface. He had been waiting for nearly fifteen minutes, but while he was not a patient man, the reason for his ire had little to do with the delay.

"Guillermo?"

He turned in the direction of the voice, meeting the earnest gaze of his business associate and confidant, Roger Lavelle. "May I see him?"

"Just for a moment." Both men were bilingual, but Lavelle, a Texas native, used Spanish in deference to his friend. Although their acquaintance had begun as strictly business— Lavelle's El Paso-based company liaised with Esperanza's organization to facilitate both trade and educational opportunities across the border—they had become fast friends over the two years they had worked together. "He's in stable condition physically, but as you can imagine, he's quite shaken. And the DHS agents have requested that you not ask any questions about the incident as it might interfere with their investigation."

Esperanza nodded irritably. Lavelle led him through the door to the private suite where Juan Garza was being treated, or more precisely, being held in protective custody. Although the horrific crime, to which he was the only witness, had occurred across the border in Mexico, the American authorities were nonetheless being very deliberate in their investigation. Esperanza wondered if their concern stemmed from an interest in seeing the wrongdoers punished, or a fear that the violence might spill over the international boundary as it had in the past.

Esperanza's interest in the young man's well-being was deeply personal. Although he did not know Garza, he felt a kinship with the young man. Esperanza had come up in the same rural environment, faced the same challenges and ultimately conquered them to become one of the richest men in Mexico. His *maquiladoras*—manufacturing facilities operating in the Free Trade Zone, exporting industrial equipment across the border to the United States—had not only made him a fortune, but were helping to revitalize Juarez, lifting it out of the cycle of drug violence that threatened to utterly destroy, not only the border region, but the entire country. Esperanza had made a promise to himself, many years earlier, that if he ever found success, he would make it his goal in life to share his good fortune with young men and women who, like him, dreamed of being something more, and to that end he had created special educational programs for his workers and their children which would, he believed, stimulate a new era of prosperity for the nation that he loved. The attack, the brutal murder of twenty-two of those young dreamers, was an attack on him as well. Worse, he felt a measure of responsibility for what had happened. His act of kindness had resulted in their deaths.

Garza's hospital bed was surrounded by people—hospital staff and American law enforcement agents wearing rumpled suits. Lavelle had assured him that Garza was not being treated as an illegal and that the young man was safer in the American hospital than he would be back in Juarez, but Esperanza nonetheless sensed an air of hostility—directed both at the young man, and at himself.

Esperanza approached the bed and took the young man's hand. "I'm so very sorry this happened," he told Garza, speaking in Spanish. "I will take care of everything. Make sure that your family is well cared for. All the families."

Garza's eyes were red with grief, but he managed a wan smile. "*Gracias señor.*"

Esperanza's gaze flitted briefly to the American agents before returning to the injured man. "Was it the *narcos*?"

One of the agents cleared his throat, signaling that such inquiries were not welcome, but Esperanza pressed on. "Did they want a ransom? I would have paid anything to keep you safe."

"It was the police."

"The police?" Esperanza was more disappointed than surprised. Police corruption, particularly at the local level, was widespread. But why target these students?

"They never asked for anything," Garza went on, miserably. "They just…"

Esperanza felt a hand on his arm. It was Lavelle. "Guillermo, that's enough. We should go."

Esperanza squeezed Garza's hand again. "There will be justice. I promise it."

He could feel the harsh stares of the American agents like a physical force, pushing him out of the room. He was not the sort of man easily cowed into submission, yet the oppressive atmosphere in the room had reminded him that the violence perpetrated by the drug cartels was only a symptom of the real problem—the disease—that had afflicted his country for too long.

Lavelle caught up to him. "He's in good hands, Guillermo. He'll be okay."

Esperanza made a cutting gesture. "This has to stop."

"I know," Lavelle said sympathetically, and then, as if he had been waiting for the cue to speak, added. "But there's only so much you can do as a private citizen."

It was not the first time Lavelle had told him something like this. The Texan had often encouraged him to seek public office, leveraging his success as a businessman in the political arena, perhaps even seeking the presidency. Esperanza had always demurred, believing that he could do more for his country as a successful businessman than by wading into the morass of government service. This time, however, Esperanza's response was more measured. "Do you think I could really make a difference, Roger? The government is broken. It cannot be fixed. Not by one man."

"If anyone could fix it, it's you. You have widespread support, both in the congress and the general population. Not to mention a lot of friends on my side of the fence. President Mendoza knows it. It's possible that he engineered this incident to send you a warning."

Esperanza's eyes went wide in disbelief. He stopped in his tracks and faced Lavelle. "Surely he would not do something so terrible."

Even as he said it, he knew he was wrong. Mendoza had a reputation for ruthlessness, and even if he was not personally responsible, it was not unthinkable that one of his cronies might have taken the initiative.

Lavelle did not answer the question directly. "You may be right though about the state of the government. Perhaps the time has come for a different solution."

"What do you mean?"

Lavelle looked around as if to ensure that they would not be overheard before answering. "The free trade agreement has served us well as businessmen, but political instability could ruin what we've accomplished. Our prosperity will evaporate if Mexico becomes a failed state. There are many people, on both sides of the border, who believe the time has come for something more…permanent. An end to the corruption and violence. There is a way to make it happen, but it will require great sacrifice."

Esperanza's eyes narrowed suspiciously. "You are not just talking about a presidential campaign."

"No," Lavelle replied in a grave voice. "Becoming president is only the first step."

CHAPTER 6

Vienna, Austria

The Heilige Lanze, or Holy Lance, Avery explained as they left Café Sperl and trekked through the snow in the direction of the Ringstrasse, was housed in the Hofburg, a vast palace complex that contained over twenty museums and galleries, featuring more than a thousand years' worth of art and historical treasures—everything from jewel-encrusted crowns to royal furniture—artifacts from the Holy Roman Empire and the Habsburg dynasty. The Lance was part of the Imperial Regalia, sacred items used in the coronation ceremony, and was housed in the Schatzkammer—the Imperial Treasury, situated just off the Schweizerhof, or Swiss Courtyard, in the oldest part of the Hofburg. Avery had spent several hours in the palace, both in the Treasury, staring at the relic, and in the Austrian National Library, situated in another part of the palace, researching its history and provenance in an effort to determine exactly what the Dominion might have planned for it.

Once inside the palace, she led Stone to the treasure room and straight to the glass case where the Lance rested on a red velvet pedestal, alongside the Imperial Cross, an enormous golden cross-shaped reliquary, which had been designed to hold both the Spear and the other object in the display case, a length of wood purported to be a piece of the True Cross.

"So that's the infamous Spear of Destiny," Stone remarked, peering through the glass. "Not what I expected really. It looks like something from a hardware store. What's with that gold foil wrapping?"

Stone was not wrong. The iron spearhead was in nearly-immaculate condition, naturally black, without a trace of corrosion. It was about nineteen inches long, bound with a web of wire wrappings every inch or so of its length, around a central shaft. The middle of the blade was covered with a six-inch long band of beaten gold. A close examination revealed tiny crosses and doves adorning the spearhead, but it did not really look like a two-thousand-year-old killing weapon.

"The spear has been an object of reverence since at least the tenth century," she explained, "so it's been well cared for. The gold band was added in 1350 by Charles the Fourth. There's a Latin inscription on it: *Lancea et clavus Domini.* 'Lance and nail of the Lord.' That may be the source of the confusion about this spear being the one used at the Crucifixion."

"It's definitely not?"

Avery shifted uncomfortably. There was more to the story of the Holy Lance, but now was not the time. "A metallurgical analysis conducted in 2003 indicates that it probably dates from about the seventh century. It's old, but not quite old enough, although many believe that it may have been recast from a much older blade, so who knows. There is an iron pin affixed to the spearhead which does appear to be an actual nail from first century Rome. It may be that the spear was meant to serve as a vessel for carrying what was believed to be a nail from the True Cross, and over time, this spear became confused with the actual Holy Lance."

Stone continued to stare at it thoughtfully. "So if this definitely is *not* the spear from the crucifixion, why does the Dominion want it?"

"Regardless of its true provenance, there are a number of legends associated with this relic. It reputedly gave Charlemagne clairvoyant powers which he used to win dozens of campaigns on his way to becoming the first Emperor of the Holy Roman Empire. It was widely believed that an army led by someone carrying the Spear of Destiny, as it came to be called, was invincible, but that if the king lost possession of it, he would die soon thereafter. Napoleon sought to possess it, as did Adolf Hitler. In fact, the Spear inspired Hitler's rise to power. He lived in Vienna as a young man and would come here to work on architectural drawings. He wrote in *Mein Kampf* that one day he overheard a museum guide recounting the legend of the Spear, that whoever claimed it would hold the destiny of the world in his hands. When he finally seized power, he removed the Spear from the Hofburg and moved it to Nuremberg."

"I guess that whole invincibility thing didn't work out for him."

Avery shrugged. "The Emperors of old would carry the relic into battle, so maybe there's a literal component too. Regardless, the Allied armies captured Nuremberg on April 30, 1945 and secured the vault where the Spear was being kept at 2:10 in the afternoon. Hitler committed suicide the same day, less than ninety minutes later."

Stone said nothing.

"The Dominion's interest in the Spear may be merely symbolic, just as it was for the Holy Roman emperors. And for Hitler, for that matter."

"Why would they identify it as relating to Patton?"

"Patton was passionate about history. He believed in reincarnation and claimed to have vivid memories of fighting on ancient battlefields. He became obsessed with the Spear and did an extensive study of its history before returning it here. He believed it was once wielded by Emperor Constantine. In fact, a lot of what I've been able to learn about it came from one of Patton's diaries here in the library."

Stone made a thoughtful humming noise.

Avery frowned. Had he spotted some connection that had eluded her? Was there some mysterious pattern that only he could see? "What?"

Stone shook his head. "It seems to fit. So we think the Dominion is going to try to steal it, right?"

"I don't think the Treasury is going to sell it to them."

He turned to face her, a mischievous smile softening the haunted look in his eyes.

"What?"

Stone turned away, scanning the crowd of people in the room until he spotted one of the uniformed attendants. Without waiting for Avery, he approached the man. "Excuse me, do you speak English?"

The man regarded him warily. "*Ja…* Yes."

"My friend and I work for the American government. We need to talk to the head of museum security. It's very urgent."

Avery gasped as the words left Stone's mouth. She grabbed his arm, trying to silence him, but there was no shutting him up.

"What is this regarding?" The attendant's manner of speech suggested that his grasp of English might not be as good as he thought.

"We think someone may be planning to steal the Holy Lance."

The man blinked as if waiting for the punch line.

Avery thought about trying to slip away, but what then? Should she call Tam?

Or should she play along?

"That's right," she said, stepping forward. "I'm Dr. Avery Halsey with the International…umm, Society for the Protection of—"

"What my colleague is trying to say," Stone interjected, "is that this threat is very real and very immediate. There's no time to lose, so if you could just put us in touch with your director of security, we would be ever so grateful."

The attendant mumbled something—probably "wait here"—and then moved off. When he was gone, Avery punched Stone in the arm. Hard. "What the hell was that?"

Stone put on his best "what me?" face. "I'm sorry, but isn't this what we're here for? To stop the Dominion from getting their hands on the Spear of Destiny?"

"No, we're… I mean, yes, but you're going to blow our cover."

"We have a cover?" Stone let the mask of innocence slip away. He motioned for her to follow, and headed back to the display case. "Take a look. Tell me what you see."

She frowned but played along. "You mean security-wise?"

"Not much, right? Shatterproof glass. Probably rigged up to an alarm and maybe drop down doors. Break the glass and get sealed in. Those pedestals are probably weight sensitive, too. Is that enough to stop someone with the Dominion's resources?"

Avery shrugged. "I guess not?"

"Are you asking me, or telling me?" Stone grinned. "There could be more than meets the eye here. Motion sensors, cameras. But none of that is likely to slow down a determined thief."

"And that's why you're warning museum security?"

"Not exactly." He glanced at the exit. There was no sign of the attendant. "Come on. Let's get out of here."

"But I thought—"

"Don't want to blow our cover." He took her hand and led her away. The oddly familiar gesture caught her off guard, silencing further protests. Stone's touch triggered a wave of memories. Her father had held her hand like that. Her father, with whom she had shared only a few precious days a year, stolen moments that were now treasured memories more valuable to her than any of the baubles in the Imperial Collection. Before she knew what was even happening, Stone had led her, unerringly, through the Imperial Apartments and out onto the broad expanse of the Heldenplatz, the open grassy area where Adolf Hitler had once addressed a crowd of Viennese Germans to announce the annexation of Austria.

Avery pulled free of his grip and stopped him there. "Not another step until you tell me what's going on. You saw something in there. One of your patterns, didn't you?"

Stone nodded grimly. "I don't think you need to worry about the Dominion stealing that lance."

"And why not?"

"Because somebody already beat them to it."

CHAPTER 7

Stone maintained a brisk but inconspicuous pace, giving Avery the impression that he was hurrying toward something, rather than escaping the hornet's nest he had no doubt poked in the Treasury. She matched his pace and held her questions until they were back in the hotel room.

"Okay, explain."

"It's just a hunch, but if you'll let me use your computer, I should be able to prove it."

She directed him to her laptop, but instead of letting him take over, she sat herself in front of it and logged in. "What am I looking up?"

Stone regarded her thoughtfully as if trying to decide whether to share a secret. "You said that you have a computer guy, a hacker?"

"Well, I probably shouldn't have—"

"We need to track all communications going in and out of the Hofburg security department. Email, Internet searches, phone calls. Can your guy do that?"

Avery had no idea whether Jimmy Letson could do that, much less if he would do it for her. She had been exaggerating a little in her claim to Stone. The truth was that she didn't really know Letson all that well. He was her brother's friend, a former reporter who had ventured into the untamed frontier of the Internet back in the early '90s and never looked back. Letson had helped her half-brother, Dane Maddock, on several occasions, most recently during the incident where she and Maddock had discovered the truth about the *real* Spear of Destiny. She figured her blood ties to Maddock had to count for something.

To the best of her knowledge, Letson only ever communicated through electronic measures, but he conveyed the impression of the stereotypical computer nerd—a technical wizard, but socially awkward. Surely, he would do a favor for his friend's sister.

She logged into her user account then opened an Internet Relay Chat client and sent Letson a private message. She wasn't sure exactly where he lived; presumably in the United States, but that did not exactly narrow it down. It was almost noon in Vienna, which meant that it was early morning where Letson was. Hopefully not too early.

The chat window flashed an incoming message.

I really shouldn't be talking to you. I know who you work for

Avery grimaced, aware that Stone was looking over her shoulder. She quickly typed her reply.

Come on, Jimmy. I'd never do anything to get you in trouble.

Like you could. I can take care of myself. You should be more worried about your own ass.

Before she could reply, he hastily added:

Watching it, I mean.

Covering it, I mean.

Her grimace slowly softened into a grin.

I'll be careful.

She quickly typed out her request, glancing back at Stone to see if she had hit all the salient points. He nodded, and she sent the message.

Is that all?

She did not respond to the rhetorical question, but a few seconds later, Letson sent her link to a secure directory that was already populated with more than a dozen files. Some were audio files; others were graphical. As instructed, the files Letson had collected were time-stamped after their visit to the Hofburg.

This will keep gathering data until you tell me to shut it down. It's passive. Not likely to trigger any alarms, especially not considering the state of their security protocols, but it would probably be best not to let this go for too long.

Avery looked at Stone. Another nod.

Anything else?

Not right now. I owe you one, Jimmy. Hugs!!!

If all I get is hugs, better from you than your brother.

"Hugs," Stone muttered. Avery could not tell if he was amused or irritated. "Start at the beginning."

Avery clicked the first and a media player popped up in the corner of the screen. She frowned when she heard voices speaking German but then saw that Stone was listening intently. "You speak German?"

He raised a hand to silence her, but nodded. The file, evidently a phone conversation, went on for several minutes. When it ended, Stone pointed to the next audio file. "Play that one."

She did, and then spent several more minutes watching him listen to the incomprehensible exchange.

There was a knock at the door, and then it opened and Tam Broderick, looking considerably fresher than she had a few hours earlier, entered the room. "You kids playing nice?"

Avery's face reddened. How would Tam react when she learned what Stone had done?

Stone was so calm as to be indifferent. "Avery's been filling me in on her theory about the Dominion being after the Spear of Destiny."

The way he said "theory" rankled Avery, but she did not comment.

"You think she's wrong?" Tam asked, arching an eyebrow.

Stone shrugged. "Something about this doesn't feel right,

but I don't have enough information to come up with something better. In any event, I see no reason not to proceed as if she's right."

Tam strode over to join them and peered at the list on the computer screen. "I see you've been busy. What is that?"

"We're monitoring communications from the Hofburg security office," Stone explained. "I told them that someone was going to try to steal the Spear of Destiny."

Tam raised an eyebrow, then turned an accusing gaze on Avery. "He did what?"

"It's an old trick that pickpockets often use," Stone said. "Blend in with a crowd and shout: 'My wallet's been stolen,' then watch how many people check to make sure they still have theirs."

Tam's expression softened. "And in the process they show you exactly where they keep their wallets. Nice. And what have you learned?"

"Their first response to the report of a threat should have been to tighten security. That was this first call. The head of security telling the museum director about our visit. But the museum director isn't worried about it. He tells the security head to double-check the alarms, but you can tell by his tone that he's not worried."

"Why not?"

"Because he knows that the lance in that case is a reproduction."

Avery frowned again. "Are you sure of that?"

"Not completely, but based on the museum director's reaction, I'd say it's pretty likely. This second call is the interesting one though. It's the director calling one of his assistants, asking him to follow up with the authorities to see if the threat is credible." He pointed to another file, further down the list. "That one is the call from the assistant. Play it next."

Avery complied and yet another phone conversation began. Stone listened intently, saying nothing until the short call ended. When it did, he turned to face the others. "I'm afraid you're going to have to rethink your theory."

Avery bit back an indignant reply, and instead said simply,

"Why is that?"

"The Dominion already has the 'real' Spear."

Stone waited until the prescribed two o'clock strategy meeting to fully elaborate on his revelation, but the intervening time was not wasted. By the time Greg and Kasey arrived, he had a much better idea of the deception the Dominion—more specifically, the Heilig Herrschaft branch of the organization—had already perpetrated.

"First off," he said, "I want to thank you all for getting me out of that hellhole in Romania. You all took a big risk on nothing more than Tam's say so, and I want you to know that I appreciate it." He paused, allowing the sentiment a measure of gravity, then continued. "Avery has already told you that the Dominion has an interest in the Spear of Destiny. From what I know about them, which admittedly isn't much, that comes as no surprise. But this will. The Dominion is already in possession of the Spear."

Greg glanced at Tam for confirmation and got it in the form of a nod. "How did they pull that off?"

"It was, or I should say *is* an inside job. The Spear on display in the Treasury is a replica. That's not an unusual practice. Most of the priceless artifacts displayed in museums are. It's the only way to keep insurance costs down. The real Imperial Treasures are kept in a secure vault that isn't on the tour route."

"And just how would you know that?" inquired Greg.

Stone shot Tam a quizzical look. "You really didn't tell them anything about me, did you?"

"You're entitled to your secrets," Tam replied.

"I would never have guessed you'd feel that way," Stone said with a chuckle. He looked back at Greg. "I have some experience with how the insurance industry works."

"Were you a claims investigator?"

"More like a claims initiator."

Kasey laughed out loud. "You're a burglar."

Avery's eyes went wide. "You said—" She didn't finish the sentence but stared at him accusingly. "So all that bull—"

Tam cleared her throat. "Swear jar."

Avery remained undeterred. "—about seeing patterns was just a smokescreen. Breaking into the NSA wasn't some crusade to protect the right to privacy, was it? It was just another job."

"The things I do, and the reasons I do them are two very different things, Avery."

"*You* can go back to calling me Dr. Halsey." She glowered at him but said nothing more.

"To answer your question," Stone continued. "After *Dr. Halsey* and I inquired about the Spear and indicated that it might be at risk, one of the assistant museum directors, a certain Emil Zanger, made a call to a Paul Karcher in Berlin, alerting him to the possibility of an audit and directing him to return the Spear to the vault until the coast is clear. The museum director knows the spear in the display case is a fake, but he doesn't know that the one in the vault is too. Zanger and Karcher are going to switch them back, at least until after the director is satisfied that there's no threat."

"Karcher is Heilig Herrschaft?" Kasey asked, though it sounded like a rhetorical question.

Greg leaned forward. "That call from Mexico was just a couple days ago. They moved fast."

"Based on the tone of this call, I think they've had the Spear in their possession for some time. Years, perhaps. Zanger has remained at his post just for this reason, to put the Spear back as needed."

"If they already had the Spear," Kasey asked, "why the phone call from Mexico?"

"The message said to retrieve it," Tam said. "They didn't specifically say to steal it. Maybe they were just saying that it was time to put it to use."

Stone went on. "There may be an opportunity here to strike a blow against the Dominion. We know that they're planning to return the Spear to the vault, if only temporarily."

"You think that will be our chance to expose Zanger?" asked Greg.

"No," Stone replied. "This will be our chance to steal the Spear."

"Steal?" Greg looked to Tam again. "You're okay with this?"

Tam returned a coy smile. "Can you think of a better way to keep it out of the Dominion's hands?"

Greg shook his head in resignation. "I take it you've already got a plan for how we're going to do this?"

Stone nodded. "I hope you got some sleep. It's going to be a long night."

CHAPTER 8

Greg Johns sat in the lounge of the charter air travel terminal at Schwechat Airport, sipping a cup of coffee and, to all appearances, poring over a sheaf of documents as if trying to draw up a flight plan. The Learjet 60 he had ridden from Bucharest in the early hours of the morning—leased by a CIA shell company and more or less on permanent loan to the Myrmidons—sat hangared nearby. Tam had hired the flight crew to give them all a chance to rest in between stops, but Greg was a licensed and internationally certified pilot, so his presence was not unusual, certainly not enough to arouse the suspicions of the staff. However, Greg was not here to plan his next flight. He was waiting for an arrival, specifically, the arrival of a German industrialist named Paul Karcher.

It had only taken a few minutes of searching to find Karcher, a steel magnate from Berlin. A little more digging uncovered several red flags that supported their suspicion that he was working with Heilig Herrschaft. Stone, who evidently was as adept at breaking into secure computers as he was secure buildings, had used the phone number for Karcher to track the man's movements and discovered that he was already en route to Vienna, flying aboard the corporate jet, which would allow him to bypass security measures.

Armed with Karcher's flight plan, Greg and Tam had raced to the airport in order to get eyes on the man, while Stone and Kasey had returned to the Hofburg to arrange a special welcome for the Heilig Herrschaft operative, with Avery coordinating their efforts from the safety of her hotel room.

Greg checked his watch. It was just after seven p.m. and already dark outside. Karcher's plane should have already landed. He surreptitiously keyed his radio microphone. "Got a twenty on our guy?"

He wondered absently if Avery knew about the old-fashioned ten-code, verbal shorthand designed to facilitate radio communications over an open net. Ten-twenty was radio speak for "advise location."

Brevity codes had mostly gone the way of eight-track tapes and VHS machines, radios too, for that matter, but Greg had come up in that world, and old habits died hard. Though he was only in his mid-thirties, he thought of himself as an old-fashioned kind of guy. An old school patriot who had grown up on '80s action movies and always dreamed of being a secret agent. He had missed the Cold War by a few years but finished his training at the Farm just in time for the War on Terror to kick off.

Avery's reply sounded in his ear bud. "Karcher is on the ground. You should see him any moment." Evidently she had understood.

Greg fumbled with his papers some more, then took another sip of coffee, raising his head just as the doors opened, and three men wearing business suits stepped in off the tarmac. Two of them were grim-faced, burly bodyguard types that appeared to have been sent over from central casting. The third was Paul Karcher, recognizable from the passport photo that Stone had procured during their mission meeting.

Greg was not sure what to make of their newest team member. Tam held Stone in high regard, but everything Greg knew about the man left him wary. Stone had breached NSA security, stolen top secret data about domestic surveillance. That might have made him a hacktivist hero, but Greg knew well how critical such programs were to protecting the United States from terror attacks. The NSA wasn't interested in the day-to-day indiscretions of average Americans; they were watching for keywords that might presage another 9/11. In fact, it was just such a program that had helped them identify this latest Dominion threat, even if they did not yet completely understand it. Stone's personal crusade had the potential to deprive the intelligence community of a critical weapon in fighting terrorists.

And then there was the revelation of Stone's true career—

professional burglar. At least Greg assumed he was a pro. It was not at all unusual for staff operations officers to recruit known criminals as assets since they often had unique expertise and connections, and in a worst case scenario, it was a lot easier to sacrifice a dirt bag if an op went south. But Tam's personal connection to Stone was a twist he had not yet worked out. Tam had risked a lot by going to the black site and facilitating Stone's escape. While they had been very careful to avoid giving the appearance of direct action on Stone's behalf, the private contractors running the site would almost certainly have put two and two together, and realized that Stone's escape right after Tam's visit was no coincidence. It was Tam's neck on the line, not his, but Greg was worried for her. And while he was willing to trust Tam's judgment, that did not mean he had to trust Stone just yet.

Karcher crossed the lounge and headed directly for the exit doors. He carried an attaché case, easily large enough to conceal the Spear. Greg gathered his papers together and moved toward the reception desk, but as soon as Karcher was through the door, he reversed course and made for the exit. He got there just in time to see Karcher disappear into a limousine. As the car pulled away, he memorized the license plate and continued to the parking lot and his own rental car.

"He's not wasting any time," Greg said into his sleeve. "Black limo. He's riding in style." He rattled off the license number.

"Roger," came the reply, not Avery but Tam, who was waiting in another car closer to the edge of the lot. "I see him."

Greg started his own vehicle and pulled out, but made no effort to close the gap.

After a few minutes, Tam reported that the limousine was pulling onto the E58, the main highway leading into the heart of Vienna. No surprise there.

Greg slid into the flow of traffic departing the airport, driving assertively but not aggressively, while Tam reported on the hired car's movements. When he got the chance, Greg accelerated forward, leapfrogging ahead of both Tam and Karcher. They would tag team Karcher all the way to his destination, never lingering in the limo's rearview mirror long enough to arouse suspicion. The odds of being discovered were slim. At night, particularly on this night, with a scattering of snowflakes blowing across the busy highway, one pair of headlights looked very much like another. Ideally, they should have had at least four cars for the surveillance to minimize the chances of being made, but with Avery still tracking Karcher's phone from the safety of the hotel room, they did not need to actually maintain constant visual contact. Still, sometimes the eyes saw what the GPS satellites did not. Karcher might pull off the road unexpectedly, and hand the Spear off to someone else, and that would put the entire operation at risk.

If Karcher's driver suspected he was being tailed, it was not evident in the way he drove. The driver kept a brisk pace but changed lanes only when encountering slower traffic. They followed the highway to its terminus, and then continued on, following a route that was almost exactly the reverse of the course Tam and Greg had used to reach the airport. The limo did not stop until it reached the Heldenplatz, right outside the front entrance to the Hofburg Neue Burg. The Neue Burg, which literally meant "new castle," was the youngest part of the palace, though it was well over a century old.

Tam pulled in right behind him but drove past the limousine without stopping. "I've got eyes on. He still has the package."

Greg turned into the parking area a moment later, just in time to catch a glimpse of their quarry as he moved through the arched gate into the inner courtyard.

"I'm going to follow on foot," he said. He left the car at the edge of the nearly empty lot and strode as inconspicuously as his haste would allow, across the snow-covered ground toward the entrance, where the limousine was just pulling away. He spotted Karcher and his retinue heading up the staircase to the doors. A moment later, they disappeared inside. Greg broke into a sprint, reaching the steps a few seconds thereafter, but the door was locked.

"Lost him. He's inside. Avery, you have the ball."

Avery studied the image on the computer screen, a live feed from the security cameras inside the Hofburg. Karcher, still carrying the attaché case, moved through the frame, crossing through a reception lobby before vanishing from view. A moment later, the picture changed, showing a corridor that Avery had not seen in her earlier explorations of the museum. Karcher was now accompanied by an older man whom she recognized from the photo in his personnel file: Emil Zanger. The pair appeared to be engaged in conversation as they moved at a casual pace down the hallway, and then Karcher once again left the camera's coverage zone. A few seconds later, the screen refreshed with yet another camera's feed.

Before leaving, Stone had hacked into the museum security system and tapped the close circuit cameras. He had also synced the cameras to Karcher's phone so that Avery would be able to track his progress through the museum without having to manually switch between cameras. Stone had been confident that the Heilig Herrschaft operative would keep the Spear in his possession as long as possible, but on the off chance that he handed it off to Zanger or someone else, Avery was ready to disengage the program and track the Spear's movement the hard way. With over two thousand rooms, spread out across several enormous buildings which included not only the museums and the library, but also the seat of the Austrian government, and no way of knowing exactly where the Spear would be taken, that would have been an extraordinary challenge. Fortunately, it appeared that Stone had been right on the money.

She was not sure how she felt about that. She had felt a strange attraction to him during their conversation over coffee that morning. It wasn't exactly physical desire, though aside from being about twenty pounds underweight, the result of ten months' confinement, he was by no means unattractive. Her initial reaction however had been something else. Stone's intelligence and confidence reminded her of her father—the man she had loved from afar even though much of his life was a mystery to her—and her half-brother. Perhaps that was why she had reacted so viscerally to the revelation that he was nothing more than a common criminal. Her objection was not to the illicit nature of his profession per se, but rather the fact that he was squandering his profound gifts. It was, she imagined, a little like discovering that Superman used his X-ray vision to cheat at cards.

At least for the moment, Stone was using his powers for good. He had made breaking into the Hofburg security look as easy as checking his Facebook status, not only accessing the closed circuit television cameras, but also locating complete blueprints of the museum, including a sub-basement level that Avery had not known of, despite several days of exploring the palace and researching its mysteries in the library. Stone surmised that the subterranean levels probably dated back at least a thousand years, to a time when cities like Vienna and palaces like the Hofburg were built to withstand long sieges. Indeed, Vienna had twice been besieged by Ottoman Turks in the 16th and 17th centuries, both times successfully staving off destruction, no doubt in part because of provisions hidden away beneath the palace. The blueprints indicated that the sub-basement had been upgraded in the 1940s, transformed from a mere storehouse into a bunker and bomb shelter. If further modifications had been made since, the plans on file did not show them.

The image on the display changed again. Karcher and Zanger, trailed by the two hulking bodyguards, entered yet another sparsely decorated corridor, one of the dozens that existed only for staff members to move quickly between sections of the sprawling palace complex. At the midpoint of the passage, they passed through an unmarked metal door and disappeared again. Avery waited for the screen to change, but after fifteen seconds, she minimized the window with the camera feed and checked the blueprints which had also been synched to the GPS tracker. The door through which the men had gone led to a stairwell that descended into the sub-basement. There were no cameras in the stairwell, or in any of the underground portion network beneath the Hofburg. After a few more seconds of waiting, Avery realized that dot marking Karcher's location had stopped moving.

"Stone, I've lost Karcher's signal. I guess there's no cell reception down there. He's coming your way."

Stone's voice sounded in her ear bud, the transmissions scratchy with static. "The concrete foundations are blocking the signal. That's going to be a problem for us too. I set up a repeater, but it can't handle too much data."

There was a pause, and then he added. "I see him. We'll take care of the rest. Stone out."

Kasey Kim looked over Stone's shoulder at the seven-inch screen of an iPad mini tablet computer. The glow from the screen was the only light in the musty storeroom where they had been hiding for the last ninety minutes, patiently waiting for their quarry to arrive with the Spear of Destiny. Now it seemed, both the moment and the man had arrived.

Aside from a few exchanges relating to the mission, the time had passed in silence. Kasey was not chatty by nature, and Stone seemed like a lone wolf-type personality.

Probably not used to working with an accomplice, Kasey thought mordantly. There certainly wasn't much for her to do, but when given his choice of partners for the mission, Stone had chosen her. Not only was Kasey fully schooled in a range of skills useful for making covert entry into hardened military and industrial facilities—the museum was a cakewalk by comparison—she was also small, which meant that she could move quickly through tight spaces, like ventilation ducts and wet walls. Her size had been the reason that she had flown the H-4 out of the black site, even though both Greg and Tam were better pilots. She had been able to hide in one of the cargo containers. The ultra-light helicopter, disassembled for transport, had been in another.

She was curious about what made Stone tick, but tagging along with him had sufficiently answered any questions about why Tam had recruited him. The guy knew his stuff.

After a wild shopping spree at an electronics store, followed by a stop at a home hardware store and then lastly a department store where they both picked up some working apparel—all black—they had headed for the palace complex, arriving half an hour before closing time. They mingled with all the other tourists, and then when no one was looking, ducked into one of the restricted hallways and hid in a maintenance closet where they changed into their newly acquired clothes. There was little danger of being spotted; Stone had used his access to the security net to check that the hall was empty and had then looped the feed to conceal their presence. When the palace was empty of visitors, they headed for the sub-basement.

Stone dodged security cameras, bypassed alarms and picked locks so swiftly that Kasey wondered if this was perhaps not the first time he had broken into the Hofburg. She didn't ask.

Security in the sub-basement was a different story. The place was a maze of corridors, the walls concrete in some places, old crumbling brick or bare bedrock in others. Old incandescent light bulbs were mounted in the ceiling, but none burned. Stone and Kasey used night vision goggles and infrared flashlights to navigate. There were no alarms, just doors. Some were ordinary hollow metal doors, of the kind used in most institutional and commercial buildings, but others were secured with heavy-duty vault doors like a bank. Stone inspected several of the latter but made no attempt to breach them. Instead, he busied himself with placing several miniature webcams at strategic locations and then found a hiding place in the storeroom to await Karcher's arrival.

Kasey had made a cursory investigation of the room, but there wasn't much of interest. Just banker boxes full of old records in a language that she couldn't read. No priceless artifacts here. She had shut off her night vision, and waited in near total silence. For an hour and a half, Stone's webcams had shown only darkness. Then the lights had come on and the screen of the iPad had lit up.

The tablet showed a grid of static images from the webcams, except for one that showed a quartet of men ambling down one of the corridors, only to disappear for a moment and reappear in another screen. After a few minutes, they stopped at one of the vault doors and the older man in the group—Zanger—produced a pair of keys which he used to open the heavy door.

"Old school," Stone commented in a low voice. "Museums are the worst…Or for our purposes, the best, when it comes to security. They spend so much just to keep the lights on, they can't afford state of the art."

"Even to protect something as valuable as the Spear?"

"The Spear is only valuable to a certain kind of collector. There are a lot more valuable pieces in this collection from a monetary standpoint. But the short answer is 'yes.' Their one concession to security is the switcheroo with the reproduction in the main case, but that means they have to go low-tech down here. Otherwise, people would figure it out."

Kasey nodded but said nothing more. Stone's confidence was reassuring; she just hoped it wasn't misplaced.

The vault opened, and Zanger and Karcher disappeared inside. "Not a combo?" Kasey asked.

"There are at least a dozen vaults down here. Hard enough to remember one combination. No, keys are better. Two locks per door ensure that no one makes unauthorized visits."

"Looks like Zanger found a workaround."

Stone just nodded. A few minutes later, the men exited the vault. Karcher still carried his attaché, but his demeanor had changed. Where his body language had been confident going in, he now seemed apprehensive, as if being separated from the cherished Spear was causing him physical distress.

Placebo effect, Kasey thought. But then she remembered some of the legends Avery had related to them about the Spear of Destiny, how anyone who held the Spear but then lost it would die soon afterward. *Probably better to let Stone handle it. Just in case.*

As he watched Zanger lead the men out of the sub-basement, Stone was plagued by the feeling that he was missing something. Thus far, the scenario had played out exactly as Stone had predicted, but there were too many unknown variables, too many unanswered questions, for Stone to believe that he was seeing the pattern correctly. It was like walking into the middle of a movie and trying to figure out who the main characters were and what they wanted? He wasn't even sure what kind of movie it was. Drama? Science fiction? Comedy?

There had been no tangible clues to suggest that he was reading the situation wrong. The Heilig Herrschaft had surreptitiously stolen the Spear of Destiny, and they evidently were not willing to risk letting that crime come to light. They were acting like a teenager, borrowing his father's car for the night, and then trying to return it without anyone being the wiser. That reinforced the idea that they saw the relic as a symbol of power, and not a supernatural talisman. But if the Spear was critical to some plot for world domination, why would they care about covering their tracks?

The most likely answer was that their plan was at a critical stage where the discovery of the theft might derail the endeavor. Perhaps they were not quite ready to execute the plan. Perhaps zero hour was yet a few days or even weeks off.

And yet, the message they had intercepted clearly indicated the time for "Destiny" had arrived. There had been a sense of urgency about the request to procure the Spear.

What am I missing?

He knew the answer. Too much. But if the Dominion plan hinged on possessing this relic, then depriving them of it was the only logical course of action.

Only when the lights in the corridor went out did they leave their hiding place. They used flashlights instead of night vision technology now. Stone was relying on his iPad to guide him through the maze to the correct vault door, collecting the miniature cameras as he went.

When they at last arrived at the door, he donned a head mounted flashlight and a pair of glasses with jeweler's loupes attached for additional magnification. The locks on the vaults were at least fifty years old. The design of the doors made replacing, or even maintaining the lock mechanisms virtually impossible. The security of the sub-basement relied primarily on secrecy—only a handful of personnel would even know of its existence—and replacing the vault doors with current technology would expose that secret. That did not however mean that the locks were going to be easy to get past.

He took out his tools, a slim diamond-tipped probe and a homemade tension wrench—a small standard head screwdriver with the tip carefully bent over at a ninety degree angle—and went to work on the left-hand lock. He raked the probe down the length of the cylinder, counting the pins, six in all. They moved smoothly, but he could tell that some of the springs were almost imperceptibly softer than others. He applied slight pressure to the tension wrench and then began teasing the pins one at a time until the lock yielded, and the cylinder began to rotate.

"Need a hand here," he said.

"So you're going to actually let me do something?" Kasey said.

"I didn't bring you along for the stimulating conversation. Hold this tension wrench in place while I pick the second lock."

"Oh. Is that all?" Kasey sounded a little disappointed. She took hold of the screwdriver and held it steady.

"For now." He repeated the process with the lock on the right-hand side. "Okay, on three, rotate the cylinder." He gave the requisite count, and then at the prescribed signal they turned the locks together. There was a click from inside the heavy metal door and a firm pull on the handle was all the effort required to open it.

Stone swept the interior of the vault with his headlamp, revealing a narrow room, lined with spacious shelves which contained wooden packing crates of varying sizes. The boxes were marked with an alphanumeric sequence, but there was no other way to determine the content of each.

"Look for packing material or wood splinters," Stone told Kasey. "They would have had to open the crate and—"

"Found it," Kasey sang out. Stone turned just in time to see her pry the lid off an oblong container about two feet in length, a foot wide and six inches deep. Stone looked inside and saw an exact duplicate of the item he had viewed in the Imperial Treasury earlier in the day. Or more precisely, the original from which that duplicate had been made.

Stone reached for it without hesitation. The real Spear of Destiny—to the extent that a seventh-century artifact purporting to be from the first century could be called "real"—meant nothing more to him than the reproduction. It had no special religious significance to him and possessed no particular aesthetic value…except for the gold band which reflected the beam of his light like sunlight on the surface of a pool.

Despite himself, he found the dazzling display of brilliance to be hypnotic. The inscription—he recalled Avery's translation from earlier, something about the Nail and the Lance— shimmered beneath his outstretched fingertips.

"Stone," Kasey prompted. "Let's move."

He nodded, surprised by his reaction and seized hold of the iron spear head. There was no discharge of holy fire, not even a sense of touching something forbidden. It was just an inanimate hunk of metal. He thrust it into a nylon duffel bag he had brought along for just this purpose, and then slung the parcel over one shoulder.

"Done," he said, though he knew that, in reality they were only halfway to their goal. They had succeeded in acquiring the Spear, but the victory celebration would have to wait until they were safely out of the palace and back on more familiar ground.

He carefully repacked the crate so there would be no outward sign of disturbance, and then led Kasey out of the vault. Their exit was methodical. Stone knew that, with the end of the endeavor almost in sight, it was all the more important to pay attention to details. He gathered the rest of his surveillance cameras, and then they retraced their steps back to the stairwell.

Using the iPad, he brought up the security interface and isolated the alarm for the door leading back into the palace complex. But as he reached out a finger to disable the alarm, the screen suddenly flashed red. At almost the same instant, a harsh claxon sound began to reverberate through the hollow metal door.

"What did you do?" Panic tinged Kasey's voice.

Stone's brow furrowed. As he studied the screen, he could hear the rasp of security gates dropping in the hallway beyond.

Avery's voice sounded in his ear, echoing Kasey's question. "What's going on in there? Did you trip an alarm?"

Tam chimed in as well. "Stone, what's going on?"

He ignored them all, focusing instead on the information being relayed through the security network. An alarm had been tripped, but not by him. He pinpointed the source of the alert. It was coming from the Imperial Treasury. He tapped the controls to get access to the closed circuit cameras, and on an impulse that might have been a premonition, checked the Treasure Room.

There was a haze in the air that might have been static—Stone knew it was smoke—and through it, he could make out the case where the relics of the True Cross were kept.

The case had been shattered and the Spear, or rather the replica, was missing.

Stone felt his pulse quicken. Something was very wrong about this.

Avery's voice sounded again. "The place is crawling with guards now. It looks like they're doing a sweep of the entire palace. There are security gates down all over the place. You won't be able to get out."

Stone continued to stare at the feed from the Treasure Room, trying to make sense of the theft. Was this all a Dominion ruse? A trap set to catch them in the act of stealing the Spear?

The pattern eluded him. He simply didn't have enough information.

The alarm had been sounding for less than a minute. The thief had to still be on the premises. He broke his silence. "Avery, watch the cameras for anyone that isn't a guard."

"Which cameras?"

"All of them. Tam, you need to watch the exterior. There's another intruder in the museum and he's going to be looking for a way out."

"There's only two of us Stone," Tam replied. "We can't watch every exit."

"Watch the places where there aren't any exits. He won't be leaving out the front door."

There was a flurry of noise as Tam relayed the order to Greg, then she spoke directly into her mic. "What about you?

Stone turned to Kasey and nodded in what he hoped was an encouraging gesture. "We won't be leaving out the front either."

CHAPTER 9

Tam Broderick's gut was churning. From her vantage at the edge of the Heldenplatz, she could hear the alarms going off inside the palace grounds. The disturbance had already drawn the notice of passersby out for a stroll in the wintry evening. She could also hear the noise of police sirens, growing louder as they closed in on the palace. Meanwhile, Stone and Kasey were trapped inside, sealed in behind a sequence of heavy steel security shutters that could only be opened manually by the contingent of guards who were already sweeping through the palace. While the situation had not yet reached the point where she could justifiably forego her self-imposed ban on blue language, the trajectory of events was not cause for hope. As Stone might put it, there were too many variables in play right now.

If there was a bright spot though, it was Stone himself. She had known him for years, almost all her life. If anyone could think his way out of a tight spot, it was Stone.

She spoke into her concealed microphone. "Greg, you see anything?"

She had sent Greg on foot to the southeast side of the palace. His reply, when it came, was slightly out of breath. "A lot of people gawking."

"Keep your eyes peeled."

Avery broke in. "Tam, I've got something. There's someone in the library."

"That's not much help. Where is the library?"

"In the Neue Burg wing... right in front of you."

Tam scanned the expansive neoclassical exterior for any sign of activity and after a few seconds, glimpsed a shadow moving behind the columns on the north balcony. She followed the shape—definitely a man—until it reached the far end, only a few hundred feet from her location.

"I see him," she reported.

A burst of static filled her ear, but through the haze, she could make out Stone's voice. "Don't let him escape."

Tam breathed a five dollar curse. The intruder, whomever he was, obviously had the wrong Spear. What difference did it make if he got away?

"Greg. Get back over here." She drew a compact Makarov from a holster at the small of her back and started for the edge of the building. Although CIA officers were discouraged from carrying weapons in the course of normal operations on foreign soil, Tam's crusade against the Dominion had too often escalated into open combat, so carrying a concealed sidearm was now Myrmidon SOP. For her own part, it had been a long time since she went anywhere without the Russian-made semi-automatic pistol.

High above, the shadowy figure had just swung out over the balcony rail. A pair of dark lines trailed beneath him, and as she watched, he leaped out into space, rappelling down to the snowy ground below. The man moved with a smooth, unhurried professionalism, reeling in the rope so that there would be no physical evidence left behind. He was average height, with broad shoulders and a barrel chest. He wore all black, with a ski mask covering his head, and a small pack was slung across his back.

Tam charged forward, drawing a bead on the dark figure. "Keep those hands where I can see them!" She didn't know if the man spoke English, but her stentorian command was unmistakable in any language.

The man stiffened and let the coiled rope fall. His arms came up slowly, empty hands rising to shoulder level, and then he turned toward her. When he caught sight of her, the eyes, barely visible through the holes in the mask, went wide in surprise. Then he started laughing,

"You are a shade too dark to be Austrian police, I think." The voice was gravelly, but there was no mistaking the man's harsh Slavic accent. Russian? "And you are definitely not one of them."

"One of who? The Dominion?"

The man laughed again. "American. CIA, I think, which means you have no authority here. Run along before you get hurt."

She waggled the gun. "This is all the authority I need."

"You would kill me? I think your government would not like that."

"If I couldn't handle the heat, sugar, I would've stayed out of the kitchen. Besides, I don't need to kill you. A round in the knee is a lot easier to explain. So unless you want a permanent limp, how 'bout you take that mask off, nice and slow, and let me get a look at your ugly mug."

The man inclined his head, and then with exaggerated slowness, reached up and peeled back the ski mask. *Ugly mug* was putting it mildly. The man had the battered features of a veteran brawler and a lunar landscape of pockmark scars on his face, but there was a dangerous glimmer of intelligence in his eyes. His lips curled into a humorless smile.

"Are you enjoying Vienna?" He gestured toward the palace behind him. "Is beautiful, tragic city."

"You're talking, but you're not saying anything I want to hear. Let's start with a name."

He ignored her. "Do you think Emperor Franz Josef saw what was coming? Saw that it would all end with him? One day, this is center of world. The next, is a tired nearly forgotten museum. Just like America."

Tam did not like the soliloquy one bit. The man was stalling, trying to distract her, and she knew it.

"You think is your destiny to rule world," he continued. "You don't even realize that sun is setting on American Empire."

"Destiny?" Tam was unable to completely hide her surprise. "Let's talk about that."

There was a flicker of understanding in the man's expression. "Ah, you know this word. Then is not coincidence that you are here."

She lowered her aim a few degrees, putting his left knee in her sights. "Name. Who the hell are you?"

"Makarov," he said. "A good choice. I have one, too."

"I hope you're not stupid enough to go for it."

"I don't need to," the man said.

His gaze flicked subtly to his left. Tam thought it was an attempt to distract her, but a moment later she heard the roar of an engine.

She reacted without hesitation, whipping her gun arm in the direction of the noise and firing two shots in quick succession before her brain could even register the car speeding toward her. As soon as the second shot was loosed she threw herself backward.

Not quite fast enough. The front bumper clipped her foot, spinning her in midair, to send her reeling into a snowdrift. A sharp pain shot through her ankle, and the impact with the ground drove the breath from her lungs.

Behind her, the car slid to a stop. She heard someone shouting—definitely Russian—and a door slammed. The engine revved, and there was a rasping sound as the tires hissed on the wet pavement, then it was moving again, accelerating away faster than Tam could gather her wits. She rolled over, ignoring the pain, fumbling for her Makarov. She aimed at the retreating taillights and squeezed the trigger. The red light winked out. Tam adjusted her aim, walking the rounds lower in hopes of taking out a tire, but an instant later, the car reached the street, slewed right, and vanished.

"Tam?" Greg said in her ear. "Where are you?"

"North edge of the lot," she said, the words coming out in little gasps as she fought to catch her wind. "Bring the car. Hurry. He's getting away."

"On it."

She cautiously rose to her feet. The ankle held her weight, barely, but her dignity was in worse shape than her foot. She muttered another five dollar curse and hobbled in the direction of the approaching car driven by Greg. The tumble in the snow had left her clothes damp and the frigid night air had chilled flesh and bone, causing her to shiver uncontrollably.

"Lord, let me never complain about the Florida humidity again," she muttered as she settled into the passenger seat.

Greg accelerated out of the parking lot and hit the street, a narrow lane that ran along the northeastern edge of the plaza. There was only one way to go—north. Two hundred yards ahead of them a dark shape with only one working taillight was turning west. "I see him," Greg assured her.

Tam keyed her microphone. "Stone, we're in pursuit of the burglar. What's your status? Have you found a way out yet?"

There was no answer.

Greg reached the turn and took it at a speed slightly in excess of what could be called safe. The rented car fishtailed and nearly went into a spin, but Greg deftly steered out of it and a moment later was closing the distance on their quarry.

"Stone, do you read me?" When there was no reply, she spoke again. "Avery, is there any sign of them?"

"No," Avery said. "I think they're in the sub-basement again. But the guards are heading to that section. They're going to be trapped."

Tam drummed her fingers on the dashboard. Stone and Kasey were in trouble. And they had the real Spear, which made it doubly critical to ensure that they were not caught. But what could she actually do to help them?

The Russian burglar, whomever he was, had the wrong Spear, which meant her Myrmidons had already foiled the Dominion's plans, whatever they were. But stopping the Dominion was a defensive game. Catching the thief, or better yet, following him to learn more about the operation, would give her a chance to go on the offensive, perhaps shut the European Dominion down, even as they had the American chapter following the Atlantis incident a year earlier.

She tried the radio again. "Stone, do you read me?" *Talk to me, Stone,* she thought. *What do you want me do?*

He had already told her what to do. Go after him. She didn't know why, but Stone clearly thought it was important. And he had sounded confident of his ability to find another way out of the Hofburg.

I'm gonna trust you Stone. Don't let me down. She turned to Greg. "Go!"

Although her curiosity burned, Kasey Kim was too much of a professional to ply Stone with questions as they ran through the maze of corridors. He seemed to have some kind of plan, and given the circumstances, that was good enough for her. For the moment, at least.

Stone came to an abrupt halt and raised a hand, signaling her to stop. Or be quiet. She wasn't sure which, but figured both were good. He tapped his night vision goggles, signaling her to put hers on, and then switched off his headlamp, plunging their world into darkness.

With her goggles on, she simply watched Stone, waiting for an explanation. A few seconds later, she got it.

She saw the lights first. The night vision optics worked by amplifying available light, so even though the source of the illumination was faint, and made fainter still by the corners and angles of the tunnel system from which it was imperfectly reflected, the green glow was bright enough for her to recognize it for what it was. Then she heard the voices.

"I thought only a few people even knew about the sub-basement," she whispered.

Stone nodded. "Unfortunately, one of those people was in the building tonight."

"You think Zanger sent the guards down here?"

"Thieves are naturally suspicious. He's got to be wondering if this is related to what he's been up to." He motioned down the corridor. "Come on."

Stone padded quietly but quickly through the halls with such confidence that Kasey was completely shocked when the passage through which they were moving ended suddenly at a brick wall. Stone halted and placed his hands on the wall, tracing the mortar seam, as if trying to figure out why the barrier had been placed there.

"Is this new?" Kasey whispered. "Something added after your map was made?"

"Not exactly." He shrugged off the duffel bag and took something from it. Kasey's eyes widened when she saw that he was holding the Spear of Destiny.

"What are you going to do with—Shit!"

With a savage thrust, Stone jammed the point of the old lance into the wall. There was a bright flash in Kasey's night vision device as the iron blade threw off a friction spark on contact. Stone stabbed the wall again, striking it repeatedly. Motes of dust and smoke swirled in the air, glinting in the monochrome display like fairy sparkles from an old Disney movie.

"What the hell are you doing?" Kasey's voice was louder than a whisper, but not nearly as loud as the noise of the impacts. She knew the answer. Stone was trying to chip his way through a brick wall. What she couldn't understand, or even articulate in a question, was why he was doing it, and why he was using the Spear of Destiny as his chisel.

Stone stopped his attack as abruptly as he had begun it, and without looking, thrust both the Spear and the empty pack in Kasey's direction. She stared at it in mute disbelief for a moment, unable to comprehend his intent. The tip of the relic was now blunted and slightly bent, and there were deep scratches in the black iron, but aside from that, it was in surprisingly good shape.

"Take it," Stone said, shaking the items. "I need my hands free."

Kasey took the Spear, remembering her earlier superstitious determination not to touch it only after it was already in her hands.

Oh well, she thought. *Too late to worry about it now. If we manage to get out of this alive, Tam's probably going to kill me for letting him mangle the Spear, anyway.*

Stone lowered his shoulder to the wall and lurched forward, slamming into it like a linebacker hitting the scrimmage. There was a muted thud and an odd scraping sound upon impact. Stone drew back and charged again, and this time, the wall buckled, filling the air with noise and more dust. When he pulled away from the wall, Kasey saw that the place Stone had attacked with the Spear was gone. Now, there was just a dark hole, big enough for her to put head and shoulders through. Stone slammed into the bricks again, and this time the entire wall collapsed, sending him crashing into the darkness beyond.

Stone was on his feet in an instant, though she could barely see him amid the cloud of dust raised by the demolition of the wall. "This way," he said, and then turned and disappeared into the gloom.

Kasey shoved the Spear into the bag and carefully picked her way through the rubble. Beyond the hole, the tunnel continued though the walls were rougher, and the air smelled of dampness and decay. "What is this place?"

"Secret passage," Stone said without looking back. "There are all kinds of tunnels and crypts running under the whole city."

"How did you know it was there?"

"I guessed."

"You…what?"

With each step, the passage became less like something from a medieval fortress and more like a naturally occurring cavern. "The layout made me think that the original underground portion of the palace was originally much more extensive."

Kasey was still mentally stuck on one detail. "You guessed?"

"An educated guess," Stone said, a hint of irritation creeping into his tone. "I was right. Does it matter?"

"When you're taking chances with my life? Yeah, it matters. We could have hidden out in one of the file rooms. Waited for the guards to clear out."

Stone stopped and turned back. With the goggles on, she couldn't judge his mood. "I don't take chances. Maybe 'guess' was the wrong word, but it's easier than trying to explain that I had a high degree of confidence in my logical deduction. Now, I trusted you with my life last night. You need to trust me."

Kasey was tempted to argue that she did *not* in fact need to trust him, but he had not been wrong about the passage. "They're going to find that hole, you know. They'll know where we went."

"Which is why we have to keep moving."

She let out a low growl. "Fine."

The passage opened up into a much larger cavern. The

walls were pocked with niches hewn into solid rock. A warning from Stone to watch her step prompted a look down, and Kasey saw that the floor was riddled with open pits. Kasey looked down into the nearest of them. The bottom of the twenty foot vertical shaft was strewn with old rags and other detritus. It was only after she looked away that she realized what she had just seen. Skeletons.

"I can see why this place isn't on the tour route," she muttered.

Stone did not reply.

A narrow slit in the far wall led out of the cavern. Kasey followed Stone into it without hesitation, but after a few steps, the walls and ceiling seemed to close in around her. The sides of the passage scraped her shoulders, and she felt compelled to hunch forward. Stone, still forging ahead, was bent nearly double.

"Just so you know," she said, "I am not having fun."

"Are you claustrophobic?"

"I didn't think I was until now. Are you sure this leads somewhere? Or is this another guess?"

"This passage wouldn't be here if it didn't lead somewhere," Stone replied.

"That was a dungeon back there. Those pits had bodies in them. It's an old-fashioned maximum security lock-up. What if this just leads to some kind of medieval super-max?"

"I don't think that's very likely." His voice, muffled by the close quarters, sounded funereal. Then, ominously, he stopped.

"What?" Kasey tried to look past him, but his body almost completely filled the passage, blocking her view.

"Another dead end," Stone admitted.

"But you said—"

"It used to go somewhere. Now it's blocked. Something's covering the end of the tunnel. Back up. Give me some room. I'll try to push it out of the way."

There was not enough room to turn around, so Kasey wriggled back a few steps, feeling the confined space all the more acutely. Stone backed up as well, then charged forward, once more using his body like a battering ram. There was a muted thump.

"It moved." Stone repositioned and braced himself against the obstacle, exerting steady pressure instead. There was a faint scraping sound as the object blocking the passage slid a few inches, and then a few inches more. Stone took a moment to catch his breath and then threw himself into the effort again, not relenting until he had opened a gap at least a foot wide.

He stuck his head into the open space, then forced himself the rest of the way through. "Come on."

Kasey slipped through the gap with an almost frenetic urgency, but the relief she expected to feel after escaping the constricting confines of the passage was denied her. What lay beyond the gap Stone had forced was yet another ominous subterranean chamber with no outlet immediately apparent. The room had been carved from bedrock, the barrel-ceiling curving down to meet the floor like an inverted half-pipe. A quick visual sweep revealed an irregularly-shaped floor plan with too many niches and corners to count. Everywhere she looked, she saw box-like shapes arranged with only a semblance of orderliness. Behind her, a stone pedestal with yet another box stood slightly askew, the obstacle that had blocked the passage. Most of the chests were rectangular, but several of them were damaged, permitting a glimpse of their contents or in some instances, spilling them out onto the floor.

More skeletons.

"Ugh. They're coffins."

"It's a burial crypt," Stone confirmed. "Come on. There has to be a way out."

"What if our way in is the only way out?"

He shook his head and made a vague gesture at the funerary containers. "These coffins are too big to fit through that little tunnel."

"But if they sealed the main entrance—"

Stone started forward, deftly threading the narrow aisles between the coffins. "Crypts were used to preserve the bodies of nobility and the wealthy. They're like very exclusive cemeteries. There are dozens of coffins in this room alone. People visit their dead, pay their respects. There has to be access from the surface."

"I don't see fresh flowers anywhere," Kasey retorted. "I don't think anyone's paid their respects to these people in about a thousand years."

"Only a few hundred years actually," Stone admitted. "But unless you'd want to take your chances going back, we should keep looking."

Kasey had no argument for that and resignedly trudged along in Stone's footsteps. They skirted along the left edge of the chamber, venturing down passages that ended—*dead ended*, Kasey thought morbidly—in cul de sacs, or looped back to the main chamber. It was like a suburban neighborhood for the dead. Her hopes brightened a little with the discovery of a tunnel that led to a flight of steps hewn into the rock, but at its summit, they found yet another labyrinth of burial niches.

"How big is the place?" she wondered aloud. "There must be thousands of coffins down here."

"That's a good sign," Stone assured her. "It means this place was in use for a long time."

"I'm unclear on the part where it's a 'good sign.'"

Stone didn't answer.

Another staircase and another level of the crypt, but Kasey was grudgingly forced to accept that Stone's instincts were correct. Many of the coffins on this level were in surprisingly good shape. Some were ornate with elaborate gilt scrollwork or murals—the skull and crossbones motif was particularly popular—painted directly on the wood panels. Several of the coffins were open, revealing mummified bodies in repose, adorned with brittle rags that might once have been silk finery and grinning skulls capped with a weird tangle of hair, like something from a Grateful Dead album cover. Wigs.

Kasey wished she had a little of Avery's expertise on matters of history. Vienna was full of images of people in wigs—statues and portraits of famous composers, actors putting on historical plays in city parks. How long ago had these people lived? Two hundred, three hundred years?

Stone let out a triumphant whoop and Kasey found him pointing to something that was most definitely not two centuries old. A brightly colored plastic chain was stretched across their path, bolted to the walls on either side. A placard hung from the chain, the message displayed on it visible only to someone approaching from the other direction.

"This place *is* on the tour route," Stone said. He stepped over the largely symbolic barrier and continued on, moving at a jog. Kasey allowed herself a sigh of relief and followed, feeling a little bit lighter with every step.

There were more indications of recent activity, including tastefully understated informational placards on easels identifying some of the occupants of the necropolis. Other coffins were marked with numbered paper tents, like exhibits at a crime scene.

Stone raised a hand, warning her to slow down. "We're probably going to come up in an old church or something," he whispered. "I doubt there will be any alarms, but there might be a night watchman. Or the police. If they've figured out where we went, there's a good chance they already know where the tunnel ended. They might be waiting for us out there."

Kasey's burgeoning good mood started to sputter like a damp wick.

Stone spoke again, but not to her. "Tam, do you copy?"

There was a scratch of static in Kasey's ear bud, then a voice, but not the voice of her boss. "Stone?" It was Avery. "Are you clear?"

"We're in an old crypt."

"That would be the Michaelergruft. The Crypt of St. Michael's Church. It's right next to the Hofburg. I didn't realize they were connected."

"Let's hope no one else realizes it," Stone said. "What's happening in the palace? Has anyone left?"

"What?" There was an uncertain pause. "No. I don't think so. Half the place is still locked down. People are going in, but not out."

"Good. Hopefully, that means they either don't know about the passage or aren't able to call out."

Stone continued forward, creeping up another staircase, and Kasey followed. They emerged into a groined vault, partitioned off by a wrought iron gate. Through the bars, Kasey could make out the pews of a church nave and, lining the walls of the expansive structure, dozens of statuary images, angels and saints, looking ghastly in the green glow of night-vision technology.

They crept through the deserted church to an exit door, which Stone eased open. "All clear," he whispered. He took off his goggles, stowing them in the duffel bag containing the Spear, which Kasey was only too happy to hand over. She doffed her own goggles as well. After more than half an hour of staring into the green display, her natural night vision was completely shot forcing her to grope her way through the door like someone struck blind. Outside, the city lights provided enough ambient illumination for her to make out the distinctive baroque architecture of the historic Austrian capital.

"Where are we?"

"St. Michael's Church is northeast of the Hofburg," Avery intoned. "You should see a building with three domes. That's the Old Castle wing. If you skirt around the north side, you should be able to find familiar ground."

"I don't think we want to go that way," Stone said calmly.

"Good point. Okay, there should be road directly opposite the palace entrance. Take it and head north a few blocks. I'll guide you the rest of the way."

"Thanks." Stone turned to Kasey and offered his arm. "Are you up for a stroll through scenic old town?"

Kasey cast a dubious eye in his direction. "Like anyone would believe we're a coup—"

A loud noise, like a balloon popping, cut her off. At almost the same instant, something flashed through the air beside her and struck Stone in the chest. His cry of pain and surprise was almost drowned out by a series of staccato crackling sounds. Stone went rigid and dropped in a heap on the damp pavement.

Kasey whirled to face the source of the unexpected attack, and found a tall, broadly built Caucasian man with a Taser in one hand, twin wire leads connecting the less-than-lethal electrical weapon to the darts protruding from Stone's chest, and a more traditional matte-black SIG P226 semi-automatic in the other. The latter was pointed right at her.

Without a nanosecond of hesitation, Kasey spun on her heel, turning in the direction of the wires. The maneuver brought her in close to the man, so close that he couldn't bring the handgun to bear on her, but just to be sure, she threw a rising arm block to ward off the pistol. She followed up by driving an elbow into the man's gut.

Her lightning quick reaction allowed her to score the first blow, but the big man's quick response was indication enough that she was outmatched in every other way. Her blow staggered him back, but even as he seemed to be retreating, he brought his arms together, enfolding her in a bear hug. She twisted out of his grasp, throwing two more completely ineffectual punches, and then something slammed into the side of her head and for a moment, all she could see was stars.

She retreated blindly, knowing even as she did, that her opponent had a gun and that she was the proverbial fish in a barrel. Sure enough, as the stars started to fade, she saw her opponent thrusting the pistol in her direction.

"Stop!" The man spoke in clear English, with just a trace of a southern drawl. "I don't want to shoot you."

"Good!" She charged again, ducking under the gun barrel this time, and aiming a sweep kick at his knee.

As if anticipating that move, the man pivoted on one foot, turning into her kick and blocking it with his shin. Instead of folding under his weight, his braced leg turned her kick, staggering Kasey off balance. He pounced on her before she could recover, tackling her to the ground, pinning her down. She tried to wrestle free but was simply no match for his strength and size. He got hold of one wrist, then the other, and then she felt hard plastic bands pulling tight, binding her arms together.

The man rolled off her and retrieved his weapons from where they had fallen. He holstered the pistol but kept the electric stun gun in his left fist. "Sorry about roughing you up, sweetheart. You're a hell of a fighter. I'll give you that."

"Cut me loose," she snarled. "And I'll show you a fight."

"Tempting, but I got no beef with you. Hell, we're on the

same side."

Realization dawned. "You were at the black site. You're with EmergInt."

The man gave an almost guilty shrug. "I may be a contractor, but I work for the Company, same as you." He turned to Stone, one finger poised on the Taser's firing stud.

"Then you already know that Stone is in our custody. You have no legal right to take him."

"And you have no legal right to stop me. My contract with your agency says that we're to keep him until he talks. You got a problem with that, take it up your chain of command." He depressed the trigger and sent another five-second long jolt of electricity into Stone's motionless body.

"Stop it!" Kasey protested. "He's already out cold. You don't have to torture him."

The mercenary laughed. "If you think a little zap qualifies as torture, you might be too soft for this line of work, sweetheart."

Kasey took a breath, trying to dial back her anger. "What's your name, cowboy?"

The man let out a chuckle. "Bill Sievers. Pleased to meet you."

"Bill, I'm Kasey. Listen to me. Stone isn't just our prisoner. He's an asset, working with us to stop a very real, very immediate threat to America. You do care about America, don't you?"

Sievers ignored her. Working one-handed, he slipped Stone's wrists into the loops of a pair of plastic flexi-cuffs, and snugged them tight. Only then did he eject the spent cartridge from the Taser, reloading and holstering it. He then slipped his hands under Stone's body and heaved the limp form onto one shoulder. As he rose to leave, he glanced over at Kasey.

"It's been fun, Kasey. Next time you're in Bucharest, look me up. We'll go a few more rounds."

Kasey flexed her arms violently, trying to break free, but the flexi-cuffs on her own wrist did not give. She narrowed her eyes. "Count on it."

CHAPTER 10

Ignoring a red traffic signal, Greg turned the car on to the Ringstrasse. He floored the accelerator to reach the relatively open far lane but once there, the car's momentum sent it skidding onto the tracks of the Ring tram. He glimpsed a flash of yellow in his headlights and cranked the wheel hard to the right, narrowly avoiding a head-on collision with a trolley moving against the clockwise flow of traffic. A few irate drivers honked at him, but once the vehicle was back under control, it was only a matter of a few seconds before they were well away from anyone who had been inconvenienced by his hasty intrusion.

The car with only one working taillight was less than two hundred yards ahead of them, but aggressively switching lanes to get around slower vehicles. If he was going to keep up, Greg would have to do the same, which meant there would be no covert pursuit. He was going to have to run the other car down, maybe force it to stop, and doing so would put a lot of innocent people at risk.

"What's the play?" he asked, without looking over at Tam.

She did not immediately reply, and Greg knew she was probably thinking the same thing he was, weighing the potential for a disastrous outcome against the even greater threat of allowing a Dominion operative to slip away. "Don't lose him," she finally said. "If he gives you a free shot, take it."

"He'll make us," Greg warned.

"He already knows we're here."

Greg nodded, keeping his gaze locked on the distant red light as he swerved from lane-to-lane, braking and accelerating to find gaps in the persistent river of cars and occasionally riding up onto the concrete bed where the tram rails were laid. With each passing second, he felt the initial rush of adrenaline ebb, replaced by the confidence borne of experience. The extensive training in tactical driving he had received came back by degrees and as the trees lining the roadside flashed by, he began to see the situation as a problem to be solved, a game to be won. Nevertheless, in the back of his mind, he knew that victory would require something more than just holding his own. He would have to force the car to stop, run it off the road, and somehow avoid causing collateral damage in the process.

The Ringstrasse curved to the right, heading east, past the University, the State Opera House, and the Vienna Stock Exchange. Greg did not know much about architecture, but the whirlwind tour felt like some kind of crazy time travel experience.

The illusion was shattered when the fleeing car made a sharp right turn onto the broad four-lane highway that ran parallel to the Wien River, and he spied brightly lit modern towers of glass and steel on the far shore, bridges spanning a river crowded with tour boats and commercial vessels. The black ribbon of asphalt ahead was a sea of glimmering red lights, staring at him like glowing eyes, and for a moment, the cyclopean stare of their prey was lost. Greg knew he was still there, somewhere ahead of them, and bore down harder on the accelerator.

"There's a lot of places he can go from here," Greg said. His tone was matter-of-fact, but it sounded like an admission of failure in his own ears.

"He's Russian," Tam said.

He risked a quick glance over at her, found her staring intently through the windshield at the array of lights then brought his attention back to the chase. "Sanctioned or free-lancer?"

"Not sure of his current status, but he's seen some action. Spetsnaz. Maybe FSB. There's a revolving door between the Russian government and the mob, so there's no telling who he's working for. But he's definitely a true believer. Spouted all the usual talking points. 'The sun is setting on the American empire,' that sort of stuff. He even mentioned Destiny."

A hundred yards away, the target vehicle became visible as

the driver changed lanes. "Got him." Greg accelerated forward, closing the gap by half before nudging his way into the same lane. "The Dominion working with the Russians. That's new."

New, but not surprising. With the fall of the Communist Old Guard and the resurgence of the Orthodox Church, Russia had seen its own brand of the kind of religious zealotry that had fueled the rise of the Dominion in America and Western Europe. If anything, under the authoritarian rule of its current president, Russia was already well on its way to becoming the kind of intolerant theocratic dictatorship that the Dominion craved.

Tam just nodded, evidently lost in thought. Ahead the highway split, with through traffic in the leftmost lanes passing under a bridge span while the right-hand lanes rose onto an elevated ramp. Their quarry took the exit, threading between two congested lanes without slowing. Greg saw sparks of friction as the car literally scraped through the narrow gap.

Mindful of Tam's aversion to profanity, he bit back a curse and steered into the slot. There was a sickening crunch as the passenger side mirror was torn out by the roots and pulverized. Greg grimaced but resisted the urge to steer away since there was nowhere to go. Tam, thankfully, offered no reproof.

Noise erupted all around them—horns honking and brakes screeching—as the escaping car cut through the cross-traffic and turned left onto the bridge. Greg, taking advantage of the disruption, punched the gas pedal and slipped through, the intersection closing the gap a little bit more. The other car was less than fifty yards away, with no other vehicles between them, but before Greg could seize the opportunity, they were across the bridge. The other car shot across one intersection and then immediately veered right, down a street that was lined with parked cars and tall brick buildings that looked like apartments. Unlike the main roads on which they had traveled thus far, the pavement here was covered in a partially frozen white slush, broken only by a few tire tracks. A block away, the road passed under an elevated railroad. Greg could see little of what lay beyond, but his sense was that their prey was leaving the more heavily trafficked areas behind.

"Where's this joker going?" he muttered.

"Careful," Tam warned, raising her Makarov. "He might be trying to lead us into an ambush."

They passed beneath the old stone arch that supported the train tracks. There were a few more buildings and parked cars. Beyond that the road vanished into the dark woods of an urban park, but above the treetops, Greg could see brightly colored lights, flashing like the world's biggest Christmas display.

Two hundred feet ahead of them, the single working taillight flared brightly as the driver stepped on the brake, bringing the car to a complete stop. Greg also applied his brakes, pressing the pedal firmly. The anti-lock braking system applied just enough pressure to the brake pads to slow the wheels without locking them up and causing him to lose control. The car came to a halt about fifty feet from the other car, where two men—one on either side—were already getting out, aiming pistols at them.

Tam's door was open before they stopped. She slid out of her seat and went prone on the slushy ground. As the car used up the last of its momentum to coast past her, she came up in a crouch directly behind it and started firing.

Greg hunched low in his seat even as the first rounds started cracking into the windshield. Tam's Makarov barked several times and then there was silence. He raised his head quickly, just for a moment, but long enough to see one motionless figure sprawled out on the ground beside the open driver's door of the other car, and another figure running into the woods.

Tam was up, moving cautiously with her pistol still trained on the fallen man. She was also limping.

"I'm going after him," Greg shouted. He burst from the car and gave chase. The fleeing man had already vanished into the trees, but a series of dark spots in the snow—footprints— marked the route he had taken.

Greg plunged into the woods, his left hand extended ahead of him at eye level to protect his face from an unexpected run-in with a low hanging tree branch, the other gripping his Beretta nine-millimeter pistol. Under the dark boughs, the snow glowed with a faint surreal blue light that offered nothing in the way of illumination but nevertheless showed him the way forward. Over the crunch of his steps and the pounding of his heart, he heard strange sounds, machines and music, screams and laughter. The noise grew louder, even as the woods thinned out, and then, without warning, the trail of footprints ended at a slushy footpath trod by hundreds of other feet.

Greg looked up and discovered the source of both the noise and the crazy lights. He was standing at the edge of a carnival midway, lined with roller coasters, bumper cars, parachute rides and crowded with hundreds, maybe thousands of people.

He quickly stuffed his pistol back into its hidden holster then spoke into the concealed microphone. "Lost him. There's some kind of amusement park here."

Avery's voice came over the line. "Not just any amusement park. You're in the Prater. It's practically the original amusement park. It's been in operation since the mid-eighteenth century."

Greg wondered if that was supposed to mean something, but then he glimpsed an enormous Ferris wheel off to this left, and something clicked. "I've seen this place before. It was in a James Bond movie." He contemplated this for a moment, then added. "I don't think he wound up here by accident. This was part of the plan."

"It's a rendezvous," Tam said in his ear. She was panting, breathless. "He's going to hand off the Spear. I'm headed your way."

Greg scanned the crowd, looking for some indication of a disturbance, someone pushing through the crowd, or anyone who seemed less than thrilled by the energy and excitement of the midway. His gaze came back to the brightly lit Ferris wheel which towered above the park, at least two hundred feet high with red gondolas that looked like train cars.

I could see the whole park from up there, he thought.

He started in the direction of the wheel, walking fast, but not so fast that it might draw the attention of the Russian or any of his accomplices. Several of the rides and exhibits were shuttered—evidently, water rides were less popular in the dead of winter—but there was still plenty of fun to be had by those willing to bundle up and brave the cold. Greg pushed through the milling masses, mostly young people and children in brightly colored winter clothes, and a few minutes later reached the gigantic steel A-frame that supported the wheel ride, which according to the sign, was called the "Wiener Riesenrad." A metal staircase led up to a surprisingly almost-deserted loading platform. Evidently, aside from the view, the ponderously turning big wheel had little to offer thrill-seekers who were primed for the park's more exciting attractions.

He froze as he spied a stocky man with a shaved head, dressed entirely in black, heading into one of the wheel's trailer-sized viewing cabins. Half a dozen other people filed into the cabin with him though none of them seemed the least bit interested in their lone black-clad fellow rider. Greg knew better. There was only one reason why the thief would have boarded that cabin, and it wasn't to take in the view of the city skyline. At least one of the other passengers was there for the same reason.

He keyed his mic. "He's getting on the Ferris wheel. I'm going to follow him on."

"Too risky."

"He doesn't know me. This might be our only chance to identify his accomplices."

"Greg. Wait for me."

Greg ignored the order. He shoved a ten euro note through the ticket window but as he started up the stairs, the attendant closed the door and signaled the operator. Greg struggled to hide his ire. The Russian was almost certainly going to pass the stolen Spear to a Dominion agent in the next few minutes, and the only chance of identifying the co-conspirator was to witness the hand-off.

The wheel rotated slowly, lifting the occupied cabin high above his head. Greg knew what he had to do. The next cabin descended to the level of the platform, and the attendant opened the door for him. Greg took one last look up at the car occupied by the Russian, some forty feet away, and then went in. He had the car entirely to himself, and with no one else waiting to board the ride, once the wheel began moving, it did not stop. The Riesenrad was not built with speed and thrills in mind. Greg had been on escalators that moved faster, but he doubted the Russian would waste any time in handing off his prize.

He left the cabin light turned off to conceal his activities from anyone who might happen to be looking up at the wheel, and opened one of the windows that faced toward the hub. A blast of icy air, much colder than what he had felt at ground level, rushed through the cabin, but the exertion of chasing after the Russian, coupled with the nervous excitement of what he was about to do, quickly counteracted the chilling effect. He squeezed through the opening and hoisted himself up and over the sill, then reached up to the top of the cabin and pulled himself onto the gently curving roof just as the car reached the quarter-turn mark.

The cabin with the Russian in it had already moved above him and was now on the opposite side, so there was little chance of being noticed by them, but that would change in a matter of seconds. Greg low-crawled across the roof to the swivel arm, which extended off the wheel and allowed the car to swing free as it moved through its rotation. The wheel itself was made of steel beams with zigzagging struts and a spider's web of guy wires for additional structural support.

His original plan had been to use the struts like a ladder, but before he could do so, the turning of the wheel gave him an oblique view of the interior of the other cabin. It was lit from inside, and in that brief glimpse, he saw that all the car's occupants were facing away from the view, their attention fixed on the Russian burglar.

They were all working with him.

Greg thought about trying to take a photo of them using his phone but knew the opportunity had already slipped away. His own car was nearly at the top of the rotation, and the other car was already descending. If he wanted a clear picture, he would have to get a lot closer.

He edged out onto the wheel frame, careful to keep his feet

pointing down. The frigid metal was leeching the heat from his skin, the cold working its way into his bones, but he ignored the discomfort and kept moving. In just a few seconds, as the rotation progressed, he would go from being almost horizontal to completely vertical, and it wouldn't do at all to be oriented head-down when that happened. The struts and wires were like the monkey bars on a playground, enabling him to scoot along, adjusting his position easily to compensate for the constant shift in his center of gravity, and in just a few seconds, he reached the support arm for the car with the other riders. Slowly, so as not to betray his presence, he crawled out onto the roof of the car, lying flat to distribute his weight and maintain a good purchase.

A tremor rippled through the cabin as the wheel came to an abrupt stop. The cabin rocked back and forth gently beneath him. The unexpected halt did what contact with the cold metal could not; Greg felt the blood in his veins turn to ice water. Had someone spotted him? He lay motionless, pressed flat atop the curved roof, listening for the shouts that would confirm his worst suspicions, but after about thirty seconds in which nothing remarkable happened, he risked a look down.

A hundred feet below, a young couple was leaving the car at the bottom of the wheel.

Greg let out a sigh of relief and brought his thoughts back to the task at hand. He dared not risk trying to lower himself over the side to look through the windows and thankfully, he did not have to. He fished his mobile phone from a pocket and activated its video camera mode. Gripping the phone tightly between fingers that were already too numb to feel much of anything, he eased his arm out over the edge and lowered it until the camera was pointing into the interior of the car.

From his precarious perch, he could barely see what was displayed on the screen, just a bright image with a few dark shadows visible. If the occupants of the cabin were looking the wrong way, his efforts would be for naught, but if he captured just one or two faces, it might give them a loose thread to tug on and follow back to the Dominion cell behind Destiny. He tilted the camera from side to side, panning the interior for what seemed like several minutes.

The car shuddered again as the wheel started moving. Greg snatched the phone back, fearful of losing his grip on it, and clutched it to his chest for a few seconds. After a couple calming breaths, he tapped the display screen to stop recording and then hit the playback button.

The results were better than he could have hoped for, showing several of the faces arrayed around the stocky Russian. Greg did not recognize any of them but felt certain that facial recognition software would be able to supply at least a few names. There was no audio, but the resolution was probably good enough that a talented lip reader might be able to shed light on what was being said.

The wheel brought the cabin back to the loading platform but did not stop to debark its passengers. Evidently, ten euro bought more than just one rotation. Greg covered the screen to minimize his chances of being spotted by anyone on the ground, but did not stop watching. As the car started climbing again, he saw the objective view shift to one side then the other, capturing more of the faces of the men directly below him. The image then went dark, signaling the moment where he had pulled the phone back up.

Perfect, he thought. Yet, as he was about to forward the recording to Avery, something about the final few seconds began nagging at his consciousness.

The car began swinging again, almost violently, yet the wheel was still turning, and in that instant, Greg realized what was bothering him. The last thing he had seen before the screen went black was a tableau of faces, all of them, even those who had initially been turned away. They were all visible. They were all looking right at the camera.

They saw me.

He looked up just in time to see a dark shape heave itself onto the roof of the cabin. Although it was much too dark to distinguish any recognizable features, the uniformly black clothing confirmed Greg's suspicions. It was the Russian, and he had a pistol.

Greg scrambled back, a reflexive action that almost caused

him to tumble off the cabin roof, but also saved his life. The Russian's gun was equipped with a suppressor—no visible flash and the noise of the discharge was barely audible over the mechanical creaking of the wheel ride—but Greg felt the disturbance of the bullets zipping through the air right above him.

There was nowhere to flee to, nowhere to take cover, so Greg did the only other thing he could think to do. He went on the offensive, springing forward in a low dive that would, he hoped, knock the man off balance, and maybe even sweep him off the car.

As if anticipating the move, the Russian shifted away, and then gave Greg a hard shove. Greg scrabbled for a handhold but his numb fingers found no purchase, and then, suddenly there was nothing at all beneath him.

CHAPTER 11

Stone let out a low groan as Sievers' shoulder drove up into his abdomen. The jolts from the Taser had not rendered him unconscious. The electrical shock weapon was designed to overload the body's own neuro-electrical system, causing all the large skeletal muscles to violently seize, exhausting the supply of chemical fuel in the muscle fibers and leaving a victim in a state of quivering exhaustion, but still wide awake. Stone had heard every word of the exchange between Kasey and Sievers, though he had been unable to offer as much as a whimper of protest.

The effect, thankfully, was short-lived.

"Sievers!" He tried to shout, but it sounded more like a croak.

"Don't worry, boss," Sievers replied. "We'll have you back in your comfy little cell in a jiffy."

"Sievers, listen to me. I'll give you what you want."

"Yep. You surely will."

There was an urgency in Sievers' stride. As confident as the mercenary was, he was obviously in a hurry to get off the street, lest a curious onlooker should take note of the abduction and call the police. Stone could not see where the man was taking him, but knew that there was probably a vehicle waiting nearby. Once Sievers reached that goal, all hope would be lost.

Stone swallowed, willing more life into his nearly paralyzed limbs. There was no way he could take Sievers in a fight, but he did have other weapons in his arsenal.

"Put me down," Stone said, trying to sound calm despite the pressure in his gut. "Let me walk. I won't resist."

Sievers halted. "Why should I believe you?" The man's tone was doubtful, but Stone took the pause as a hopeful sign.

"Come on, Sievers. You hold all the cards. I'm tied up. Even if I tried to run, you'd find me right away. You tagged me, didn't you? An RFID implant?"

Sievers chuckled, and then Stone found himself standing on wobbly legs in front of the big mercenary. "I suppose it's kind of obvious, isn't it?"

"It wouldn't have been that hard for you to figure out that Tam brought me to Vienna, but no way could you have known we'd be coming out of that crypt. A radio tracker chip is the obvious explanation."

"Ain't technology great? Come on, let's get moving." He gestured to a van waiting further up the street, and then Stone felt Sievers' powerful hands close on his biceps and something hard burrowing into his back.

"Sievers, listen. I'm ready to deal."

"No deals."

"You don't understand. There's something big going on here. Something a lot bigger than the stolen data."

"Uh, huh. And you're one of the good guys now, is that it?"

"We may not agree on the definition of 'good guys' but Tam is Company." He narrowed his gaze, imparting more gravity to his next words. "The real CIA."

Ten months of studying Sievers and his fellow contractors had given Stone plenty of insight into the man's personality. He knew exactly which buttons to push. Sievers, a Special Forces veteran, deeply regretted leaving the military to pursue a more lucrative paycheck in the private sector. Stone did not want to insult his patriotism so much as appeal to it. "She's trying to stop something really bad. Like 9/11 bad, and she knows I can help. I think that's important enough that I'm willing to give you what you want if that's the only way to get your cooperation." He paused a beat. "I may not have told you what you wanted to hear, but I never lied to you, Sievers. So I'm giving you my word. Let me help Tam, and when it's done, I'll give you the data."

He read the conflict behind Sievers' eyes. There was apprehension there, but not distrust. Sievers was more concerned about what his employers might do if he acceded to Stone's request, and even that was not as strong as his desire to do the right thing. He was on the verge of relenting when Kasey made her move.

Stone had positioned himself so that Sievers would not see Kasey's efforts to free herself. Working by touch alone, she had managed to unzip the duffel bag and use the Spear to slice apart her flexi-cuffs. Hefting the broad blade like a knife, she stole forward soundlessly and jabbed the tip into the small of Sievers' back. The mercenary flinched at first contact but knew better than to make a more dramatic move.

"Move and I skewer your liver," she said. "How do you like that for a rematch?"

Stone lowered his eyes to meet her gaze. "Kasey, it's okay."

"Sure it is. Get his weapons."

Stone shook his head. "I gave him my word. He's going to help us. Isn't that right, Sievers?"

Sievers registered surprise at the question. "You're serious?"

Stone gave a reassuring nod. "Always. Help us, and everyone wins. Deal? I'd offer you my hand, but…"

"Tell Xena Warrior Princess to take that knife out of my back, and I'll cut you loose."

The man's tone was defiant, almost threatening, but Stone could tell that it was merely face-saving posturing. Sievers was being sincere. "Put it away, Kasey. We're all on the same team now."

Kasey was incredulous. "You don't actually believe him?"

"I do. You've got to trust me on this." Then he added, "Tam would."

Kasey proved harder to convince than Sievers but after several seconds, she relaxed perceptibly. "I'll trust you," she said. "Him, not so much. You hear me, cowboy? Keep it real slow."

With exaggerated purposefulness, Sievers reached into a pocket and took out a Leatherman multi-tool. He gestured for Stone to turn around and a moment later, Stone's hands were free again. He turned back and extended his right hand.

Sievers stared at it with open suspicion then grudgingly took it. "If you double-cross me—"

"I won't," Stone said. "Welcome to the team."

Tam's ankle still hurt but it bore her weight, and the pain was diminishing with each step. That was about the only thing that was going right.

She reached the edge of the Prater amusement park just as Greg announced his intention to follow the Russian onto the Riesenrad. She knew that he had ignored her order to wait. In his place, she would have done the same.

She oriented toward the enormous Ferris wheel, walking at a brisk pace that was only a little slower than the jog that had got her through the woods. The ride towered above the park, a halo of electric brilliance, turning with deceptive slowness against the backdrop of the night sky. Her eyes were drawn to one of the fifteen enormous viewing gondolas, its windows lit up from within. She wondered if it was the car with the Russian. She wondered if Greg had made it aboard.

The wheel stopped to let more passengers on, or perhaps to let them off, and then resumed turning. Because she had focused all her attention on the illuminated car as it revolved, rising like the sweep second hand of a clock, Tam saw what evidently no one else in the park did: a man-shaped silhouette crawling along the rim of the wheel, toward the cabin with the Russian.

"Damn it, Greg." She breathed the words but did not transmit them. Greg didn't need the distraction.

She saw everything. Saw him reach his destination, saw him crawl out onto the roof of the car. Saw the Russian climbing out through his own window, likewise unnoticed by the wheel operator, even as the rotation brought the gondolas past the loading platform.

She saw them fight. Saw someone fall.

"Greg!" She keyed her mic. "Greg, talk to me!"

She had only glimpsed the silhouette for an instant, a man falling—she couldn't tell whom—visible in the gap between two of the cars, and then...nothing.

There was no answer on the radio. She forgot about trying to appear inconspicuous and broke into a run. She was immediately rewarded with a fresh spike of pain in her ankle, but she ignored it, focusing completely on reaching the towering Ferris wheel.

The lit-up gondola reached the top of the circle and began to descend. Tam expected at any moment to hear voices raised in alarm, but the park visitors remained blissfully unaware of the drama playing out above them. In the time it took for her to reach the ride, the wheel completed the revolution, bringing the gondola once more to the platform, but even before it was level with the deck, the door burst open and the occupants began streaming out. The wheel stopped suddenly, the car still more than a foot above the platform. Tam heard someone shouting in German, probably the ride's operator, frantic at this breach of safety procedures but none of the men issuing from the car paid any heed. Tam scanned their faces. She recognized only one: the Russian.

She closed her hand on the butt of her Makarov but did not draw it. The Russian stared down at her as if daring her to shoot, while behind him, his fellow passengers dispersed in every direction, some escaping down the stairs, others climbing over the rail and dropping to the ground. Tam held his gaze, but in the corner of her eye, she could see that he was now empty-handed. He had already made the hand-off.

When it became apparent that she was not going to make a move against him, the Russian raised a hand to his forehead in a mocking salute. "*Do svedanya.*" Then he turned and ran.

Tam made no attempt to stop him. Instead, she raced up the steps to the platform, shouting Greg's name, praying for a miracle, fearing the worst. She peered down into the trough below the metal frame, then stared up at the web of girders and wires that formed the spokes of the wheel.

"Greg!"

"Little help."

The voice was barely audible over the din of rides and music, but Tam caught it nevertheless, perhaps because the words were in English, but mostly because she recognized both the voice and the devil-may-care attitude. She looked around, frantic but hopeful, and found Greg clinging to a horizontal bar that stretched between the two outer rims of the wheel, halfway between two of the gondolas. He had fallen but only as far as the crosspiece, a distance of less than twenty feet, where he was hanging on for dear life.

Tam rushed to the end of the platform. She could see the pain etched across his face. The crossbar had saved his life, but the impact with it had not been gentle. Nevertheless, he was grinning like an idiot.

"Hang on," she called. "I'll get someone."

"Never mind me," Greg croaked. "Go after the Russian."

"Too late. He's long gone." She stepped back as the operator brought out an aluminum ladder which he stretched out across the gap in the platform, directly beneath Greg's feet to form a makeshift bridge. Now that Tam knew he was safe, her relief gave way to a sharper emotion. "Lordy Jesus, Greg, what on earth possessed you? Why didn't you wait for me? You could have gotten yourself killed, and for what?"

He grinned again, and then held up his phone. Fixed in the

display was an image of the Russian. "For this."

CHAPTER 12

After two years of working with Navy SEALs and CIA officers, Avery thought she had gotten over her sense of being an outsider, but as the team straggled in from the night's operations, the old feeling returned with a vengeance. They were all soaking wet and bedraggled. Tam was limping. Greg was hugging his ribs protectively and moving like an old man. Kasey had fresh bruises on her face and both she and Stone were filthy. Worst of all, there was an aura of defeat, the kind of shared misery that she could only pretend to understand.

Their collective appearance was a reminder of the gulf that stood between her and the world the rest of the team inhabited. She was just a computer jockey, a bookworm. They were operators, people who actually went out and did stuff. Even Sievers, the brawny security contractor who had crashed the party and was now watching and listening quietly in an effort to figure out exactly what he had gotten mixed up in, looked more like he belonged in the room than Avery did. She knew, if only at an intellectual level, that her contribution was critical. The general failure of the mission affected her as much as them, but they were the ones who had gotten their asses handed to them.

"Hey," she said, trying to fill the miserable silence. "At least we have the real Spear. That's something, right?"

The others seemed to exchange a glance before Tam, in a patient voice, answered. "Unfortunately, if they don't realize the Spear they took is a fake, they may go ahead with whatever it is they have planned."

"But they must already know. Zanger and Karcher are Heilig Herrschaft."

Stone leaned forward. "We've missed something. Something important."

Avery stiffened defensively. "Really? Because it seems to

me that this is exactly what we expected."

Stone shook his head but instead of answering, got to his feet and went over to the suite's writing desk where he took out a pad of hotel stationery and a pen. "There are more pieces in play than we first realized. Let's start at the beginning." He wrote something and then turned the pad to show everyone. In large letters that nearly filled the page, he had written: "Mexico."

He tore the sheet off and placed it on the coffee table in the center of the room where they could all see it. "This all started with the events in Juarez, right? The massacre of the students, followed by the phone call that mentioned…" He glanced at Avery.

"Destiny," she supplied.

Stone wrote the word down and tore off the page, placing it alongside the first.

"And Vienna," Tam added.

"Vienna and an item related to General Patton," Stone said, writing both words down and adding them to the others to form a row. "Okay. Those are things that we know to be factual. We are working under the assumption that the massacre in Mexico was carried out by a drug cartel…" He wrote something down. "And we suspect Dominion involvement." He wrote out "Dominion" and laid that on the table as well. "Now, tonight we may have added another variable."

Tam nodded. "The Russian."

"Our Russian thief took the Spear replica, which the Dominion already knew it was a fake. What does that tell us?"

Avery spoke up quickly. "The spear Heilig Herrschaft knew it was fake."

"Same difference," said Greg, speaking up for the first time. "They're the German branch of the Dominion."

"True, but we know the Dominion utilizes cellular organization. Maybe the branch responsible for 'Destiny' isn't talking to the Heilig Herschaft."

Stone pointed a finger at Avery. "Good." Then he turned to Tam. "We got lucky when we smoked out Zanger's little switcheroo with the Spear, but as you said, the thief tonight may not realize he has a fake. We need to figure out exactly who he is and what his connection to the Dominion is."

Avery felt obliged to check her email again, even though it had only been a few minutes since her last check, and less than half an hour since she had uploaded the video Greg had shot through the window of the Riesenrad gondola to the CIA for analysis. As expected, there was no response. It might be hours or days before positive identification could be established for the men in the video.

"Is there a Russian branch?" Stone asked.

"None that we're aware of," Tam said. "But that doesn't mean they don't have one."

Stone wrote the word "Russian" on another sheet, then added it to the growing collection.

Mexico
Patton
Destiny
Vienna
Dominion
Russian

He stared at the papers, then moved the individual pages around on the table top, arranging them differently.

Vienna
Patton
Russian
Mexico
Dominion
Destiny

He turned to Tam again. "The phone call about Destiny. Exactly what did they say about Patton and Vienna?"

Avery fielded the question. "'Get the Patton item from Vienna.' That could only mean the Spear."

Stone seemed on the verge of rebutting this, but instead he rearranged the papers, placing "Patton" in the center, and then arranging the others around it. "So, Patton connects to Vienna and Destiny, which in turn connects to the Dominion. Is there anything that connects Patton to the Russian or to Mexico?"

Avery was about to answer when Sievers unexpectedly spoke up. "Both, actually. Patton's first taste of combat was during the Mexican Revolution. He accompanied Black Jack Pershing on the hunt for Pancho Villa, back in 1916. As for the Russkies, during World War II, Patton got in a lot of trouble with Allied command for insulting the Russians. He was convinced that the Soviet Union would be as big an enemy of the US as the Nazis had been. He actually favored rearming former Nazis and leading them against the Soviets. There's a pretty compelling theory that Patton's death was no accident but was actually an assassination carried out by an NKVD agent." When he saw Stone's look of surprise, Sievers gave a sheepish shrug. "Old Blood and Guts has always been a hero of mine."

"I don't buy it," Greg said. "The Allies didn't want to fight the Russians, so there's no reason to assassinate him."

Avery cleared her throat. "Actually, it makes a lot of sense. Patton wasn't very popular with the leadership, but the American people loved him. He was planning to leave the Army and run for President. I suppose if he had done that, he might have gotten his war with Russia, after all."

"He was?" Even Sievers was surprised by this revelation.

Avery nodded. "I don't see how it's relevant though."

Stone's eyebrows drew together in a frown. He stared at Sievers for a moment. "You didn't know Patton wanted to be president?"

The contractor shook his head. "I've read a lot of books about General Patton, but I've never heard that. Doesn't surprise me though. The Army was about to put him out to pasture, and he knew it. Without a war to fight, he had no purpose, and he knew that too. Running for office sounds exactly like the sort of thing he would do. Hell, I'm sure he would have won. If the Russkies knew about that, then they definitely would have had a good reason to ice him."

Stone turned to Avery. "How did you know about Patton's plans?"

"I must have read it somewhere. Probably during my research…" Avery trailed off as a strange cold feeling settled into the pit of her stomach. "Oh, no."

Tam moved quickly, gripping her shoulders. "Avery, honey, what is it?"

Stone answered before Avery could find the words. "There's another Patton item in Vienna, isn't there?"

She nodded, now feeling as dejected as the others had upon returning from their respective missions. "Patton's diary, where he wrote about the history of the Spear. It's in the Library at the Hof."

"I wouldn't count on that," Stone said in a grave voice. "Unless I'm very much mistaken, that diary was the item the Dominion agents requested in that phone call. And what that Russian was really after."

"You can't know that for sure." Avery's rebuttal was half-hearted. She knew he was right.

Stone raised his hands. "Call the library…or better yet, the police. If you can get them to cooperate, I'll bet you money that the diary is missing."

"A book?" scoffed Greg. "I'm not buying it. It's not their style. Besides, they picked the name 'Destiny.' That points to the Spear."

"Pun intended, I'm sure," Stone replied. "The Spear may be a part of this, or it may be a ruse to throw us off the trail, but the diary is the important thing."

"How can the ramblings of an old World War II general mean anything today? What does it have to do with what's going on in Mexico? It just doesn't fit."

"Just because we can't see the connection," Stone insisted, "doesn't mean there isn't one. I suspect that if we could get a look at that diary, we'd find the answer."

Tam faced Avery again. "How 'bout it? You read the book. Did Patton mention Mexico at all?"

Avery half-closed her eyes, searching her memory. "I

skimmed over the parts that didn't relate to the Spear. He rambled a lot. Stuff about ancient battlefields and past lives."

Sievers stood up suddenly. "Are you guys for real? You told me you were trying to stop some kind of terrorist attack. But first you're going on about the Spear of Destiny, and now Patton's diaries? Seriously? What the hell is this, a treasure hunt?"

Avery's eyes flew open. "Treasure. He mentioned something about…" She faltered, the thought slipping away as quickly as it had come.

Sievers rolled his eyes. "For Christ's sake."

Stone raised his hands in a placating gesture. "Sievers, give it a chance." He turned back to Avery. "We need to find out if that diary was scanned. A copy isn't as good as the original, but it might give us an idea of what they're planning. And right now, we know even less than we thought we did."

"I'll ask at the library tomorrow. First thing."

"We don't have time for that." Stone came around the table and sat beside her at the computer. "May I?"

Avery felt another twinge of jealousy. She still had not quite come to terms with what she had learned about Stone, and his abrupt take-charge attitude was not helping. But the real problem was that she had goofed, and he had caught it, and that was a tough pill to swallow.

"Fine." She pushed the laptop in his direction.

Stone quickly found his way into the Austrian National Library online catalog and just as quickly gained administrative access. "The diary was never digitized, but there is a microfilm copy…"

Stone trailed off, lost in his search. Avery leaned over to see what he was looking at, but as she did, she spotted a notification for new email in the corner of the screen. Without asking permission, she snatched the computer back and opened her email. "We got a hit on the Russian." She scrolled through the official looking email, looking for the part that would explain who the man was. "Oleg Samsonov. He's the deputy chief of something called the Economic Security Directorate."

She looked up, sensing that her words had triggered a stir in the air. "Does that mean something? Sounds pretty innocuous to me."

"The Economic Security Directorate is the operations arm of the FSB," Tam explained patiently.

Avery knew what the FSB was. In her earliest memories, they had been known by another set of letters—KGB—and although the political landscape and name had changed, the organization remained more or less the same. They were Russia's FBI and CIA rolled into one, but that was only the tip of the iceberg. As far back as Stalin, the security agency had been the de facto ruler of the country. Most of the nation's leaders, including the current president, had come from the leadership ranks of the KGB and FSB.

"The job of the Economic Security division is to ensure that Russia's economy is protected, by any means necessary," Tam went on. "Espionage, sabotage, assassination… whatever it takes. Russia has only one source of income—oil—and global oil prices have crashed in the last six months. The ruble is in a death spiral. The Russian economy has gone into recession. They need a game changer, something that will increase the demand for oil and weaken foreign currency."

"So it's true," Greg said. "Destiny is a joint operation. The Russians and the Dominion."

Stone, who had been listening patiently, now turned to Tam. "You have to go to Mexico. Right now. That's where it's going to happen."

Greg let out a derisive laugh. "And just how do you know that?" He threw up his hands. "This is crazy. We should be tracking Samsonov. That's our best lead."

Tam silenced him with a wave of her hand and faced Stone, scrutinizing him in earnest. "You know I trust you, but… Give me something to work with."

Stone seemed to consider the request for a moment, but then stood, went back to the coffee table and pointed to the pages he had earlier written. "It's right here. Vienna. Patton." He held up each page as he spoke the words. "We know that was a reference to the diary. We know what the Russian connection is, even if we don't completely understand it. We know the Dominion is involved. The one thing that still doesn't fit is what happened in Mexico." He shook the page emphatically. "The massacre in Juarez happened for a reason. That's the key to this. When we understand why it happened, we'll know what they're trying to accomplish."

Avery felt a twinge of irritation at how quickly Stone had switched gears. "What happened to tracking down Patton's diary? I thought *that* was the key."

Stone answered without looking away from Tam. "She's not wrong. There was a microfilm copy of the diary, but it was donated to the Patton collection years ago. It's currently at the Library of Congress in Washington DC. Avery and I can go there and work that angle while the rest of you go to Mexico. We'll catch up to you as soon as we can."

"I'm not letting you out of my sight," Sievers put in.

Stone pressed on. "Samsonov is the deputy chief of his division, right? That makes him…what, number three in the FSB? And he personally ran tonight's operation. Destiny, whatever it is, is big. Maybe the biggest thing since the Cold War ended. It started in Mexico, and I'm certain that it's going to end there, too. So you have to go there as soon as possible."

Tam nodded slowly. "We'll drop you off in DC on our way south. Kasey, you'll stay with them." She cast a wary eye at Sievers. "If you suspect for even a second that Hot Rod here is going to try to grab Stone and make a run for it—"

"He won't," Stone said.

Avery was pleased that Tam did not seem to share Stone's confidence in the word of his former captor. She was also glad that Kasey would be accompanying her. She didn't trust either man any further than she could throw them. But part of her could not help but be impressed with how quickly Stone had reduced the problem to a series of variables and found the pattern.

Against her better judgment, she was actually beginning to admire him.

CHAPTER 13

El Paso, Texas

The unrest in Mexico City was the lead story of the twenty-four hour news cycle, but Roger Lavelle was more interested in watching Esperanza's reaction to the repetitious coverage than he was in the latest updates. He made no comment, content to let Esperanza draw his own conclusions, and why not? The over-hyped media coverage made the argument far more persuasively than anything he might say.

When the pundits finally came up for air, the Mexican businessman turned to his host and asked the question again. "Do you really believe this is the answer, Roger?"

Lavelle gave a patient smile. "We've known each other for…what? Two years now? Have I ever led you astray? Your country has a problem that's bigger than any one man. You know it. I know it." He paused for dramatic effect. "History knows it, Guillermo. This should have happened long before either of us was born, but it didn't. We have a chance to correct that mistake, once and for all, and for the good of all."

He might have continued on in this vein, but a musical chirp from his pocket distracted him. He took out his phone, read the text message, and then rose from his chair. "I need to see to a matter. And you, my friend, need to get some rest. You, more than anyone else, are going to need it."

My friend.

The lie came easy after two years of saying it, and his partnership with the Mexican had been so profitable that sometimes he almost forgot that the man was most certainly *not* his equal. Esperanza and his people had been put on earth to mow the lawns of people like Roger Lavelle.

He left Esperanza in the company of the talking heads and strolled down the hall to a conference room where his aide, Eric Trent, was working on the mystery of the Patton item. As important as it was to make sure that Esperanza played his part, none of it would matter if they could not unravel the secrets contained in that battered leather-bound journal, and soon. The wheels were already turning. Worse, there had been a troubling breach of security.

Samsonov had been quick to blame them for the slip-up, but Lavelle was not so sure. The Russians were not exactly masters of subtlety, and their vaunted spy organization was like an aging heavyweight champion, long past its Cold War prime.

Still, Destiny had been Samsonov's idea. Maybe the KGB, or whatever they were calling themselves this week, had a few moves left, after all. As audacious as the plan was, what was even more astonishing was the fact that Samsonov had known exactly whom to bring it to.

Lavelle still recalled that first meeting, where Samsonov had shown him the letter, intercepted by Soviet agents seven decades earlier, in which the heroic but irascible General George S. Patton had declared his intention to launch a political career, with the ultimate goal of running for the office of president in 1948.

Winning the presidency on the strength of his war record would be only the first battle in a much larger campaign. Patton had been very clear about his motivations. The Soviet Union was, in his mind, an even greater enemy than the Nazi regime of Germany, and every day that passed would see the Russians consolidating their power and rebuilding their war machine. To defeat them would require more than just strong leadership, but the general had an ace up his sleeve which he believed would make all the difference when the inevitable showdown finally arrived.

Patton had been right about the Soviets, right about the threat of Communism and the eventual decline of American moral character. With a man like that leading America, there would have been no need for something like the Dominion. And while he might not have envisioned the coming of the atomic age or the protracted chess game that was the Cold War, in a prescient moment, Patton had foreseen the possibility that his decision would make him a target.

The letter openly detailed the contents of what Patton called "the Devil's Gift"—neither the letter nor the diary explained why he chose this name—and how he would use it to forge a new chapter in American history, but it did not explicitly state where the object was. That information, if the letter was to be believed, was contained in his diary, written in a code which could only be understood, in Patton's words "by someone worthy of such a destiny." Given the context, there was little doubt that the reference was a play on words, a reference to the Spear of Destiny, with which Patton had been obsessed following the fall of Berlin. Patton rightly believed that the Devil's Gift would hold the key to America's future, and Lavelle felt certain the general would have approved of both the Dominion's aims and its methods.

He wondered how Patton would have felt if he had known it would also mean salvation for the Russians.

He strode into the conference room and found Trent seated at the table, the diary open before him. On his right was a laptop computer, and on his left, resting on a square of velvet, was the Spear of Destiny, disassembled into its component pieces.

Trent was a compact, bookish man in his early thirties, an engineer by trade and one of the smartest men in Lavelle's acquaintance. Lavelle, like many of those who had emerged to take positions of leadership in the Dominion following the roll-up of almost everyone involved in the Kingdom Church, was not a true believer, at least not in the quasi-religious mystical mumbo jumbo that had led Bishop Hadel and the others into ruin. Lavelle and Trent shared the view that the economic and political goals of the new and improved Dominion were of paramount importance, but Trent's inquisitive mind and encyclopedic knowledge base made him the perfect point man for this particular task. As far as Lavelle was concerned, the Spear of Destiny was an interesting historical artifact albeit one with dubious provenance, but not much else.

The look on Trent's face was about what Lavelle expected given the terse text message he had sent just a few minutes earlier.

"What's wrong?"

Trent slid the Spear across the table. "See for yourself."

Lavelle peered down at the relic, unsure exactly what he was supposed to be looking for. Samsonov had told him that the Spear was the key to cracking the code in the diary, and Trent had confirmed this shortly after returning from Vienna with the two items, but Lavelle had no clue as to exactly how the key was concealed.

He looked at the gold band with its legendary inscription, and then at the smaller silver band which had been added by Holy Roman Emperor Henry IV in the eleventh century. Trent had carefully removed both, as well as the black iron nail, allegedly used in the crucifixion.

Trent pointed again, leaning across the table to rest his finger on the gold band. Lavelle looked closer and saw a row of tiny letters stamped upon it.

REPLIK

"God damn it," Lavelle breathed. "A goddamned fake."

Trent nodded. "The museum put this on public display. The real one is probably locked away in a vault somewhere."

Lavelle stared at the replica for several seconds. "If it's an exact duplicate, then it should still work, right?"

Trent spread his hands. "If there's a code key hidden there, I don't know what it is."

Lavelle took out a pre-paid "burner" cell phone and typed in the thirteen-digit string of numbers that would connect him to a similar phone unit on the other side of the world. It took a few seconds for the call to be connected and a few more before he heard a grunt. "Da?"

There was no need to waste time with pleasantries. "It's a fake."

Samsonov easily switched to English. "I have just learned this. There was a second break in, probably the same Americans who tried to stop me."

"How did they find out about it?"

It was not the first time he had asked the question, and Samsonov's answer was no more enlightening. "They are CIA. Who knows how they were tipped off?"

"We need the real Spear to crack the code."

"That is your problem." Before Lavelle could protest, Samsonov continued. "The Americans have the Spear now. If my information is correct, they are on their way to Washington D.C."

"D.C.?"

"There is copy of diary in American Library of Congress. Soon, I think, they will know more than you do. If you hurry, you should be able to catch them and take back Spear."

Lavelle did not like the sound of that. "Hang on. The cloak and dagger stuff is your job."

"I am going to Mexico City to carry out next part of plan."

"There won't be a plan if we don't crack that code. And don't forget, I have to be in Mexico, too."

"Is time to get your hands dirty." Samsonov did not sound the least bit sympathetic. "If you cannot handle this small problem, then perhaps you are not ready for what will come when we succeed."

Lavelle let his breath out slowly, measuring his reply. Without the Russian's help, everything would fall apart. He could not afford to appear desperate or incompetent at this stage in the game.

"Relax," Samsonov said, at length. "You know where they are going. Easy thing to set trap."

CHAPTER 14

Washington D.C.

The flight from Vienna to Washington D.C. took nearly sixteen hours, including refueling stops in Ireland and Greenland, but because they were racing the sun, they arrived just before noon, local time. Or so their hired pilot informed them. Avery was so exhausted that, even absent the change in time zones, her body had no clue what time it really was.

She had tried to sleep during the flight, but even in the relative comfort of the Learjet, sleep and air travel just didn't mix well. When she actually did doze off, she awoke feeling even more fatigued. She had spent the intervening waking periods alternately berating herself for her mistaken assumption about the importance of the Spear of Destiny, and trying to figure out how to redeem herself. There was some connection between the situation in Mexico, and something that Patton might have written about in his diary in the closing hours of World War II, but what it was remained a complete mystery.

She was surprised to learn that the Patton family on his mother's side had inhabited California in the days prior to its inclusion in the territories of the United States, which provided a somewhat tenuous connection to old Mexico. Avery filed the information away and moved onto Patton's adventures with General Pershing during the Mexican Revolution.

That part of the story read like an old-fashioned western, not surprisingly since much of the information she found about the showdown with Pancho Villa's henchman, Julio Cardenas, was on websites dedicated to memorializing famous gunfights of the Old West. In true gunslinger fashion, Patton had carved notches into his ivory-handled revolver, tally marks for each man he had killed.

Or rather, allegedly killed.

Avery quickly discovered numerous contradictions between

the many different accounts, as well as the official military record of the expedition. She wondered if perhaps the key to solving the mystery lay in one of those inconsistencies. Had Patton done something, or perhaps failed to do something, which would have scandalized him in later life, thwarting his political aspirations? Some act of brutality or cowardice that might have tarnished his legend?

She searched her memory again, trying to recall the passages she had read only a couple of days previously. Her mistake then had been to focus only on what she assumed was relevant, but she had skimmed the entire document. Maybe the answer was already there, in her brain.

The four of them—Avery, Stone, Kasey, and Sievers—rode the courtesy shuttle from Dulles International Airport to a nearby hotel, which would serve as their base of operations while in the nation's capital. As they rode along, she became aware of Stone's eyes upon her. She turned to him, raising her eyebrow in a look that she hoped would convey her complete disinterest in having a conversation with him. Either the look was misinterpreted or Stone simply didn't care. "Did you have any luck with your research, Dr. Halsey?"

She shook her head.

"Maybe something will click when you read the diary again."

"Maybe. I'm still not sure how something Patton wrote seventy years ago could possibly make any kind of difference." She cocked her head sideways. "Can I ask you something? Something personal?"

Stone regarded her with a faint smile. "You want to know why I do it? Why I turned to a life of crime?" He wiggled his hands as he finished the question as if to make it seem like a joke.

Avery shrugged. "In a nutshell, yes. You're clearly very intelligent. You could do anything you wanted. You don't even seem like a bad guy. I mean, you're helping us stop the Dominion, so obviously you're not a…" She was going to say "villain," but decided that sounded too melodramatic. "So, yeah. Why?"

To her chagrin, Stone seemed to have his answer already prepared. "I would have thought that a historian, of all people, would understand the importance of not jumping to conclusions."

"You as much as admitted to being a thief. I suppose you're going to tell me it was for some greater good? That you're a modern day Robin Hood?"

"Robin Hood." He rolled the words around in his mouth as if trying to decide whether he liked the flavor. "No. My motives are not quite so altruistic." He studied her for a moment. "You already have the answer. I haven't lied to you about anything. Set aside your prejudices and look for the pattern."

His reply was maddening, but before Avery could frame a response to the challenge, the shuttle pulled up to the entrance of the Dulles Airport Marriott hotel. They disembarked and went inside to the registration desk where Kasey signed in, consigned the duffel bag with the Spear to the hotel safe, and collected the keycards for their rooms. They lingered there only long enough to freshen up and within half an hour, were in a taxi bound for Capitol Hill.

Despite its name, the Library of Congress was far more than just a repository of books for use by the American legislative branch. Arguably the largest library in the world, it contained millions of manuscripts, maps, photographs and other media, housed in four different locations, one of which was situated more than fifty miles away in Culpepper, Virginia. It was the modern equivalent of the Library of Alexandria, a collection of diverse knowledge so vast that several lifetimes would be required to take in the information it contained. Avery would have liked to spend a week simply browsing the collection, letting her curiosity lead her into strange corners of history, but the urgency of the situation did not allow for such indulgences.

A visit to the Library was almost enough to make her forget about the enigma that was Gavin Stone. Almost. Sitting beside him on the long taxi ride into the heart of D.C., she could not help but think about his cryptic challenge.

You already have the answer. Look for the pattern.

The maddening part was that she was giving into it, trying to find some reason to excuse what he was and what he had done. That wasn't at all like her. She preferred uncomplicated men.

Do I? Really? A long string of uncomplicated *ex*-boyfriends suggested otherwise. Not that Stone seemed like boyfriend material.

She shook her head to clear away that thought. The fact that they would be working together was reason enough to figure him out.

Using a variation of Stone's own methods, she tried to assemble a mental list of everything that she knew or thought she knew about the man.

Tam trusts him implicitly, but why? She would have to learn more about the nature of their relationship.

He has stolen data from the NSA.

No, she corrected. *He's been accused of doing that, but I shouldn't assume I have the whole story.* She would have to learn more about that as well.

He admitted to being a thief, or something to that effect, and he had demonstrated his skills in that respect, but that alone was no basis for judgment. She had committed her own fair share of illicit acts which, when taken out of context, would be construed as criminal behavior.

Stone had said something else as well. *I haven't lied to you.*

What hadn't he lied about?

Look for the pattern.

Pattern. The word took her back to their conversation at the coffee shop in Vienna. At the time, it had seemed like so much empty philosophical rhetoric. Chaos theory and predestination. All of reality just one big virtual reality simulation. She didn't buy any of it; what sane person would?

Was that what he had meant? Did Stone really believe that the entire universe was governed by some elaborate pattern of logic and that everything in it was predictable, if only the pattern could be recognized? If so, how did that correlate to his criminal activities?

The taxi brought them to Independence Avenue, and the

entrance to the James Madison Memorial Building, the largest of the three Library buildings on Capitol Hill and the third largest federal building in the D.C. metro area, surpassed only by the Pentagon and the J. Edgar Hoover FBI headquarters. Unlike the classically-inspired Thomas Jefferson Building—the primary Library building—or the Capitol, both of which were just across the street, the Madison building was modern in design, not surprising given that it had first opened its doors in 1980. Nevertheless, it was in its own way elegant. The tree-lined walk to the front entrance featured numerous quotes from the nation's fourth president, espousing the importance of learning and knowledge as essential to liberty and governance. The most impressive feature however was a four-story high bronze relief depicting a cascade of open books pouring down the side of the building.

The effect was somewhat diminished by the utilitarian security queue, with its walk-through metal detector and X-ray conveyor belt. In addition to the requisite security concerns of a public building, the Library also prohibited items that might be used to deface or even steal books and other materials, as well as anything that might prove disruptive. The screening was only a minor inconvenience. They had purposely left behind anything that might have aroused suspicion. Avery imagined that Kasey and Sievers probably felt naked without their guns, but neither of them showed the least bit of discomfort. The CIA officer and the security contractor appeared calm, if a little bored.

They passed through the main entry hall, a monument to the building's namesake, and made their way to the research assistance desk on the first floor to submit a request for the Patton diary microfilm.

"You'll need to obtain a reader identification card," explained the woman at the desk. "You can do it from your phone, or use one of the registration stations. When you're finished, just bring your driver's license to me, and we'll get your card printed up."

Avery was familiar with the credentialing procedure, which wasn't much different than applying for an ordinary library card in any city, but the process presented a hurdle for Stone, who had no official documentation whatsoever. Sievers and Kasey seemed reluctant to produce passports or licenses as well. In the end, it was decided that Avery would go alone into the research area while the others waited just outside.

It took only a few minutes for her to obtain her reader ID, after which she submitted her request for the Patton diary.

"That's only available in microfilm," the clerk explained after processing the request. "You'll have to go to the Microform Reading room across the street. It will be waiting for you when you get there. Your card will give you access to the research entrance. You can get there using the tunnel." She handed Avery a paper map with the route marked in pencil.

"Great," Kasey muttered as they headed out. "More secret passages."

Stone grinned. "We'll try to avoid the dungeon this time."

"And the crypt."

Avery felt a twinge of envy. Although she had enjoyed roaming the galleries of the Hofburg, Stone and Kasey had seen a part of old Vienna that few others even knew existed, walking through history, as it were. *Next time*, she promised herself, *I'm not staying back at the hotel.*

The tunnel connecting the buildings of the Capitol complex was considerably more prosaic, well-lit, with tiled floors and bland, painted walls, spacious enough for them to walk four abreast. At the far end, they ascended an ornate marble staircase that let out onto a balcony overlooking the magnificent Main Reading Room, which lay beneath the vaulted copper dome of the Jefferson Building. The room beyond was a feast for the eyes, as beautiful as anything Avery had seen in Vienna, with marble columns, stacked balconies, and everywhere, art—murals and sculptures. The floor below was arranged in a series of concentric rings of reading tables, and at the center was a desk where researchers could pick up requested materials, delivered by conveyor belt.

"This is where we part company," Avery announced. "You guys may want to go grab a cup of coffee or something. I tend to lose track of time in libraries."

Kasey shook her head. "I think we'll stay right here where we can keep an eye on you, just to be safe."

"There's nothing to worry about," Avery replied. "Besides, the microfilm machines are in a different room. You won't be able to see me."

"Then we'll watch the door."

Avery shrugged. "Suit yourselves."

She made her way down the stairs to the main floor and found the entrance to the Microform Reading Room. The décor was less extravagant than the main reading room, but still possessed a historic flair that Avery found appealing. Microfilm and microfiche had once been the cutting edge of document preservation. The advent of the digital age had made film effectively obsolete, but because the Library of Congress collection of film was so large, the process of scanning all the microform images into digital format would probably take decades, which meant that the old microfilm reading machines still had a role to play.

A research assistant directed her to the machine where the film had already been set up for her. In principle, the machine was not much different than a PowerPoint slide show or ebook, and the large back-lit screen actually made for easier reading than the original, which was a plus given the fact that it was a hand-written document. She started at the beginning, speed reading through the entries. She had to resist the urge to skip ahead or start looking for specific catch phrases and keywords as she had done during her first read-through.

Set aside my prejudices, she told herself.

The diary was more personal in nature than she recalled from her first reading, full of musings on war and history. Patton recounted dreams in which he roamed ancient battlefields and fought as a Roman legionary with Julius Caesar in campaigns against the Germanic tribes that had once inhabited the same lands where his troops and tanks fought in his own lifetime. There were poems, some epic in scope, some dark and foreboding in their contemplation of life and death and the mysteries of the universe. Darkest of all were his premonitions of the future that lay ahead, both for the war-torn world and for himself.

Patton opined on topics ranging from Stalin's brutality to the incompetence of Allied leaders, particularly "Ike" for whom Patton seemed to have only contempt. He spoke of the Germans as a noble warrior race who, despite being beaten, were ready to be forged into an army capable of defeating the Soviets, if only someone possessed the political will to do so, and disparaged the Jews liberated from the death camps as miserable "animals" unworthy of the blood that had been shed to free them.

Avery found the latter sentiment particularly shocking. She wondered how many people, like Sievers, who practically worshiped Patton, knew that side of his personality. Given the fact that the Nazi ideology, most recently embraced by the Dominion, refused to die, the answer was probably a lot more than she wanted to believe.

Could that be the secret everyone was after? Proof that one of America's greatest heroes was a closeted anti-Semite? Such a revelation, while discomfiting, hardly seemed of earth-shaking importance, but she could not dismiss it.

She kept reading, fully immersing herself in the narrative.

The tone changed with his discovery of the Spear of Destiny. This was the part of the document that she had paid the most attention to previously, but her new insights into the man caused her to see it all from a much different perspective. The Spear was not merely an object that had belonged to some of the most powerful leaders in history. It was uniquely tied up in their conquests and, in too many cases, their downfalls. Yet, Patton did not seem to ascribe supernatural power to it. Rather, it was the thread that connected men of greatness, and the fact that it had now come within his grasp seemed only to amplify his sense of his own importance.

He spoke of his own destiny in similarly mythic terms, comparing himself to Julius Caesar, who despite winning every battle, recognized that the greatest challenge would be to forge an empire. Although couched in metaphor and hyperbole, there was little question in Avery's mind that Patton had set himself on a path to transform from military leader to something even greater.

The meaning of the gift, all those long years ago, is now apparent to me. Just as the Spear of Constantine was handed down through the ages, a symbol of God's Will for men of greatness, so too is that forgotten treasure, the Devil's gift to me. I understand now what I could not have imagined then, that the seed, planted in a fallow field and left untended all these many years, is now about to bear fruit.

Treasure. She had remembered that, but the reference was so oblique that she did not think it was meant to be taken literally.

Caesar's ultimate fate was not lost on Patton.

These wars that I have fought are nothing beside the field which I must next take. I will command no armies, and my enemies will conspire in shadows rather than face me. This is not the fight that I have prepared for, nor will victory bring the glory I hunger for, yet I realize now that it is the test for which I have lived. I may fall, but that is not failure. To shrink from this test—that is failure, and by God, I will not fail.

Yet, what if it be God's will that I fall? Will another harvest the seed? I have never spoken of what happened that night, so long ago, when the Devil gave me his last gift. None know of it. It may be that someone will stumble upon it, someone seeking a different treasure perhaps. I have heard that the scout is still tramping about in the desert looking for silver and gold. I have often wondered if he understood more than he let on. What would happen if a man like that found it first? Like any sword, it is only as effective as the man who wields it. In the wrong hands, it could destroy the very thing I hope to create.

It is not for me to decide my own fate, and there are none I trust with the secret. A man should not live as if he is about to die, but I must nevertheless make some provision so that, in the event that Brutus should strike the blow that Pompey could not, the knowledge of this thing should not pass away entirely.

I should not tell of it directly. Let him that hath understanding count the number. The spear will point the way.

Beneath the paragraph was a string of numbers.

29 33 13 108 10 8

Avery's breath caught in her throat. How had she missed this before?

"The Spear will point the way," she murmured, wondering how that was meant to be interpreted. Would the Spear literally guide them to the secret Patton had been keeping, like some sort of magical compass?

Perhaps she had not been completely wrong after all. The Spear of Destiny was the key to solving the mystery.

She willed herself to be calm. The numbers had to be a code of some sort, and the code had to be significant, but it was too soon to declare victory. She had erred once by jumping to a conclusion about the Spear of Destiny, and the result had nearly been disastrous. She took out her phone and called Kasey.

She could hear the tumult of background noise over the line. It was a stark contrast to the absolute quiet of the reading room. The public areas of the Library were more tourist attraction than true library, but she had been so immersed in her reading that she had forgotten that there was a world beyond the walls. She glanced at her watch, noting that it was now after 4 p.m. She had been at this for over two hours.

"Find anything?" Kasey asked without preamble.

"I think so." She spoke in a whisper, not wanting to draw attention to her breach of etiquette in using her phone. "Some kind of number code."

She heard Stone's voice, less distinct but still audible. "Get a picture of it."

Avery frowned. Strictly speaking, photography wasn't allowed, but she knew the prohibition was more of a strong suggestion than a hard and fast rule. She held her phone up to the screen and snapped a photo.

Someone behind her cleared his throat. "Excuse me miss, but photography isn't allowed."

Avery turned, a guilty flush blooming on her cheeks. An apology was on her lips, but before she could utter a word, she froze.

Two men stood behind her, dressed in cheap suits that didn't hide their hulking physiques. Yet, it was not the presence of the two men that started alarm bells ringing in her head, but rather the fact that, aside from the three of them, the room was empty. A chill shot through her, numbing her extremities.

"You're going to have to come with us, miss," one of the men said in an officious tone.

"I don't think so," Avery mumbled. Her first instinct was to protest, to state the obvious. No way were these men library staff. They couldn't make her go with them. Yet, she knew that such responses were merely a form of denial. If she continued to treat this situation as something that she could explain her way out of, the opportunity to escape would slip away.

The men were Dominion, or perhaps Russian operatives. There was no trace of accent, but all that meant was that they were good at their job.

The realization triggered a flood of questions, none of which mattered at this moment. That too was a form of denial—the compulsion to understand what was happening—which might also prove costly. Only one thing mattered now.

She held the phone close, but before she could even think about what to do with it, one of the men ripped it from her grasp. "No phones in the Library," he said, still trying to maintain the illusion of an official role. "If you need to make a call, you can do it from the security office."

She drew in a breath and opened her mouth to cry for help, but the other man, evidently sensing that the ruse had failed, struck like a rattlesnake, seizing hold of her and spinning her around, slapping a hand over her mouth. "If you scream, I'll snap your neck," he growled, abandoning all pretense.

Against every instinct of self-preservation, Avery knew what she had to do. She bit down on the man's hand as hard as she could, and when he reflexively yanked it away, she screamed until her lungs hurt.

CHAPTER 15

El Paso, Texas

It started in Mexico….

Tam Broderick gazed across the narrow ribbon of muddy water that separated the United States of America from *Los Estados Unidos Mexicanos*. Somewhere on the other side of that sluggish river and the invisible international border, twenty-two innocent university students had been massacred, the first victims of the Dominion's latest offensive. A lone survivor had escaped, splashing blindly across the river, carrying a tale of woe and a cryptic message.

The time for Destiny has come.

What did that mean?

"Not much to see," remarked Marcus Waller, Director of Field Operations for the US Immigration and Customs Enforcement division. "Waste of time coming out here if you ask me."

Waller, who had accompanied Tam and Greg to the site, was a handsome African-American man in his mid-forties. His looks were of little consequence to Tam, but the mere fact of his racial heritage counted in his favor, not because it was something they shared, but rather because it almost guaranteed that he was not a Dominion double-agent.

That was about the only good thing Tam could say about him. From the moment they entered his office, he had made no secret of his irritation at the intrusion, parceling out information about the cross-border incident like a miser opening his piggy bank for charity. She assumed the underlying reason for his thinly veiled contempt was jurisdictional protectiveness, but the fact that he was marginally more deferential toward Greg made her wonder if the shabby treatment might have more to do with her gender.

No matter. She had been swimming up that stream all her

life, and in spite of men like Waller, she had done pretty well for herself.

She tolerated the ICE officer's condescension only because she had no idea where to begin looking. They had come here, rather than heading straight to Juarez, because Tam hoped to get a somewhat unbiased American perspective on what had happened. Waller's reluctant assistance would seem magnanimous compared to the stonewalling she expected from the *federales* in Mexico, especially given their reputation for corruption and the very real possibility that law enforcement officers were involved in the attack on the students.

"They took the hostages and brought them way out here," Greg said, evidently thinking out loud. "Why? They could have gone anywhere, but they chose this place. Is there some special significance to that?"

"A lot of illegals come across here," replied Waller. "Maybe they wanted to make sure that someone found the bodies. You know, I could have told you all this over the phone."

"Why would they want the bodies to be found?"

A shrug. "Who knows? They're practically animals."

"You mean the cartels?"

"Sure." The answer was laced with sarcasm. "Look, it's just the way it is out here. Sometimes things heat up a little, and that's bad news, but that's why ICE is here. To keep the wildfires from crossing the river. We got it covered."

Tam rolled her eyes. "Just help me wrap my little ol' brain around this. The drug cartels, for no apparent reason, kidnap a bunch of students at a bogus police checkpoint and drive them all the way out here to the boonies to murder them, *because* they want the bodies to be found. There's no particular reason for it except 'just because.' Have I got that right?"

"Pretty much."

"Why target these students? Was someone trying to send a message?"

"Possibly. The students were part of a program funded by a businessman in Juarez—Esperanza's his name. Guillermo Esperanza. He's a NAFTA success story. Decent enough guy. Trying to make the world a better place. You know the type."

"Would that draw fire from the cartels?"

"Economic stability weakens their power base. People with real jobs aren't as desperate to work as drug mules, or pay *coyotes* to get them across the border."

That was a plausible enough motive if the crime really was the work of *narcotraficantes*, but Tam still couldn't see how the Dominion benefited from it. Still, it was a place to start. "Maybe we should talk to this Esperanza guy."

"Good luck with that. You'd have better luck getting an audience with the pope."

"Why is that?"

"He's become a bit of a celebrity over there. Especially after this. A lot of people seem to think he'd make a good president." Waller shrugged. "Take more than one guy to clean that mess up."

"When are their elections?"

"Not for a few more years. The last election was in 2012, and their president serves a single six-year term. But President Mendoza has been a big disappointment. Corrupt. Ineffective. This latest incident has thrown gasoline on the fire. Things are bad over there. People want him out, and if he resigns or is somehow removed from office, it would be up to their congress to appoint his successor."

Tam glanced at Greg, saw him nod. He was thinking the same thing she was. Overthrowing the government of America's closest neighbor definitely sounded a little more like a scheme worthy of the Dominion—the Russians, too, for that matter—especially if this Esperanza was already in their pocket. The brutal attack on the students could easily have been a false flag operation, a final straw to break the back of the Mendoza administration.

She still could not see how any of it connected to Patton or the Spear of Destiny, but it was a place to start.

Stone would say that it fit the pattern.

CHAPTER 16

Washington D.C.

Up until the moment that he heard the scream, Billy Sievers had remained uncertain about almost every facet of the situation in which he now found himself. He did not doubt that each small group of CIA officers and assets was who he claimed to be, but that fact by itself did not make them trustworthy. If anything, his knowledge of the Agency and its penchant for elaborate conspiracies in pursuit of an agenda that did not always put America's best interests first, actually increased his suspicions. The story of a major terror plot, somehow relating to mythical relics and the writings of a World War II general did not enhance their credibility. The fact that the whole affair had begun with the escape of Gavin Stone, a man who was clearly an enemy of the nation that Sievers had sworn to defend, was also a strike against them. Indeed, he had only acceded to Stone's request in order to keep an eye on him. His colleagues at EmergInt had questioned his decision. His phone had about a dozen text messages directing him to deliver Stone back to the black site, ASAP. He had spent the idle hours wondering why he had not done exactly that.

The scream changed his focus, if only because it appeared to validate at least some of what Stone's friends had told him. He still did not trust any of them, but the cry could only mean that someone was threatening the cute little historian, and that meant the threat was real.

The others—the Korean girl and Stone—exchanged a glance, confirming what they all knew, and then both sprang into motion. Despite his immediate alertness, Sievers was caught off guard by what Stone did next. Instead of heading for the nearest staircase, Stone ran to the edge of the balcony that looked out into the reading room as if hoping to catch a glimpse of what had befallen Avery.

In addition to the ornate railing, an eight-foot tall, transparent, noise-reducing barrier stretched across the overlooking balcony, physically separating tourists in the gallery from those wishing to conduct research in peace and quiet on the floor below. It was immediately apparent from the turned heads and questioning expressions of the people on the floor of the reading room that the scream had been heard, but there was no other sign of a disturbance. Sievers was already starting to turn away in preparation for a dash to the nearest staircase, when Stone did something that left him completely stunned.

Seemingly without even a moment's hesitation, Stone reached up for the top of the curving window and then heaved himself up and over. He dropped down the opposite side, and then as if he had rehearsed the move a dozen times, side-stepped to the end of the balcony. He grasped hold of the ornately decorated capital atop one of the massive three-story high vertical columns and worked his way hand over hand until he reached the central pillar. Sievers saw him wrap his arms and legs around it, and then Stone was gone.

Sievers glanced at Kasey in disbelief. She shrugged then glanced up at the top of the barrier. "Give me a boost?"

"You're not serious."

She didn't ask again. Instead, she ducked around him and, gripping his shoulders, hoisted herself onto his back. Before he could even think to stop her, she was over the window and scrambling after Stone.

Who are these people?

Sievers knew what he had to do. Throwing both caution and incredulity to the wind, he bent his legs and launched himself at the glass partition. It was just like climbing a fence or wall, something he had done hundreds of times in his military career. The only difference was that this was no obstacle course at a training facility. This was a public building in the nation's capital. He tried to ignore the shocked expressions of tourists who had been passing through the gallery. Some of them were taking pictures and videos which would probably go viral on the Internet in a matter of minutes, others simply pointed and stared. Forty feet below him, a smaller but no less stunned audience watched as Stone and Kasey ran across the floor of the eerily silent reading room. Muttering a curse, Sievers made his way to the nearest marble column, mounted it like it was the world's fattest firepole, and slid down, using his palms and the soles of his shoes as friction brakes.

The pillar did not go all the way down but rested upon a similarly imposing plinth of darker stone, at least twelve feet high. He lowered himself down, dropping the remaining few feet to the floor and then whirled around just in time to see Kasey rounding the central desk, heading for the main exit on the opposite side of the circular room.

With the inertia of disbelief finally overcome, Sievers held nothing back. He sprinted across the floor of the reading room, oblivious to the frantic shouts and threats of the staff, and reached the exit just a few steps behind Kasey. He regretted now not having paid more attention to the floor plan. Kasey evidently had; she moved without pause through an anteroom and into the corridor beyond. A couple of turns later, she skidded to a halt in a small room furnished with rows of tables upon which sat bulky looking machines that looked to Sievers like computer monitors from before the days of flat-screen technology. Stone was already there, standing motionless near the center of the room, but aside from the three of them, the place was empty. There was no one behind the assistance desk and no sign of Avery.

"Where is she?" Kasey asked.

Stone's head shake was almost imperceptible, but then he burst into motion again, darting across the room and bending over to retrieve something off the floor. He stood up, holding a smartphone in his hand. "This is hers. They left it behind so we couldn't track her."

"Who left it?" asked Sievers.

"Who do you think?" snarled Kasey.

Stone raised his other hand, silencing her. He tapped the phone's screen a few times, staring at the display, then shoved it into his pocket. "Think," he said, the word seemingly self-directed. "They can't just manhandle her out the door. Too many witnesses." A pause. "No, that's the wrong question.

How did they find us? How did they know we'd be here?"

Sievers had no idea why that was important. The only course of action was to call the cops and lock down the building if it wasn't already too late.

"They might have followed us from the airport," Kasey suggested.

Stone nodded. "They didn't have time to plan this. A couple hours at most, but they knew that Avery was by herself. A target of opportunity."

His eyes were flashing back and forth as the wheels turned in his head. "But why come after us at all? They already have the diary. Do they know we have the real Spear?" He shook his head. "No. Wrong question again."

He looked up, snapped his fingers then ran over to the evidently abandoned assistance desk. Sievers followed and saw that his initial assessment was wrong. The library staffer assigned to the microfilm room had not exactly left his post; he lay crumpled in a heap behind his workstation. Stone stepped over the stricken man, not stopping to see if he was even alive, then bent over the computer terminal on the desktop and started clicking the mouse.

"Stone," Kasey snapped. "You want to share?"

Sievers was glad that he wasn't the only one completely in the dark.

"I'm doing a search of all the reader identification cards issued since we arrived." Stone pointed at the screen. "There. Those are the men who have Avery."

Sievers looked and saw a list of names with accompanying thumbnail-sized photographs. He spotted Avery at the top of the list. The next two cards, which had been issued within a few minutes of each other and just eight minutes after Avery's, belonged to a pair of men who Sievers immediately pegged as wanna-be operators, the kind of guys that were always trying to sign on with EmergInt. Even their names looked sketchy.

Stone was already moving again, running for the exit. "Come on. We can still catch them."

"We don't know where they're going!" Kasey's shout evidently went unheard. Stone was already gone.

Kasey growled a curse and then she too was running. Sievers followed, his confusion and ire growing exponentially with each passing second. The Library complex was a maze of corridors and alcoves, and the men who had abducted Avery could have gone anywhere. They all needed to stop, assess the situation and come up with a strategy, not run around like headless chickens, but Stone seemed to be calling all the shots.

Sievers caught up to Kasey again on the stairs right outside the microfilm room, the same stairs they had climbed after arriving through the tunnel from the Madison building, but this time they were heading back down. Stone reached the bottom mere seconds ahead of them and immediately veered into another tunnel, adjacent to the one they had come in through. A sign on the wall indicated that this passage led to the John Adams Building. The tunnel appeared completely deserted. The Adams building was evidently not as big an attraction as the other structures that comprised the Library.

Stone seemed to gain new urgency as he headed into the tunnel, sprinting like an Olympic athlete, and it was all the others could do to keep up. Sievers' gut was telling him that this was a mistake, that they were running in the wrong direction, that there was no way Stone could possibly know where Avery's kidnappers had gone, but before he could voice these concerns, he spied movement in the distance, perhaps fifty yards away.

Two men, walking briskly in the same direction, clearly in a hurry to reach their destination. With their backs turned, there was no way to tell if they were the two men whose pictures he had seen a few moments before, but they clearly were not carrying a captive Avery between them. Then he realized that one of them was pushing something ahead of him.

A wheelchair!

Of course. They could not have smuggled in weapons with which to threaten their hostage or compel her to cooperate, and trying to manhandle her through the public building would have been equally problematic, but no one would look twice at someone in a wheelchair. In fact, people tended to unconsciously look away as if embarrassed by any display of interest in the disabled. The chair itself was strictly no frills, with the words "Property of the Library of Congress" stenciled across the back; a courtesy wheelchair, available on request for elderly or infirm visitors overcome by the daunting task of roaming the endless halls of the institution on foot. They had probably knocked her out with a sleeper hold, and then simply rolled her into the elevator, ridden down to the ground level, and headed down the lightly traveled tunnel, congratulating themselves on the brilliance and efficiency of their improvisation.

Yet Stone had figured it out in just a few seconds. That, or he was damned lucky.

The man pushing the chair broke into a run, but his partner wheeled around to face them. It was definitely one of the men from the pictures. He struck a fighting stance, fists raised, and waited to meet Stone's charge.

To Sievers' amazement, Stone did not slow. Instead, as he closed with the kidnapper, he cut to the man's left side, grazing the wall and rebounding like a ricocheted bullet. The man made a grab for him, but Stone had timed his move perfectly to avoid such an attempt. The man's hands closed on air, and Stone kept going.

Before the man could recover his footing, Sievers and Kasey closed with him. Sievers slowed his pace, readying himself to meet the man's next attack. He was certain Kasey would follow Stone's example and attempt to evade rather than engage the man who outweighed her two-to-one, but to his complete astonishment, she charged ahead like a guided missile. Then, at the last instant before contact, as the man got his feet planted and his fists up, she dropped to her knees, hunching over into a protective curl, as her momentum carried her the rest of the way. She crashed into his left leg like a bowling ball, with roughly the same effect. The man flipped forward and crashed face down, right in front of Sievers, who had to leap into the air to avoid being tripped up.

Kasey was back on her feet in an instant, sprinting down the tunnel. Ahead, Stone had almost reached the man with the wheelchair. Sievers wasn't sure what his former prisoner planned to do once he caught up. Stone was hardly an imposing specimen, physically speaking. He had incapacitated John Bowers with a couple of lucky shots, but that had more to do with Bowers' overconfidence than Stone's skill. Nevertheless, Sievers drew up short and whirled around to deal with the fallen kidnapper who was already trying to get back in the fight. He cut short those plans with a sharp knife-hand blow to the base of the man's skull.

The remaining man, evidently realizing that escape was no longer possible, abruptly wheeled around, chair and all, to face his pursuers. As expected, the chair contained the unmoving form of Avery Halsey. She appeared to be unconscious, slouched back in the chair and mostly covered by a long blanket, which probably concealed tape or ropes that bound her in place.

Instead of trying to meet the charge head on, the kidnapper bent down behind the unmoving woman and reached over the back of the chair to wrap an arm around her throat. "Back off or she's toast."

The suddenness of the move jolted Avery to consciousness. Her eyes went wide, and she jerked in the chair, but her hands and legs remained fixed in place.

Stone managed to stop a few paces away, but nothing about his manner evinced defeat. "You'll never make it out of here with her. We called 911. Told them to look for the guys with the wheelchair. You might be able to slip out of here before the police lock down the exits, but only if you leave her and go."

It was only a partial lie, Sievers knew. They had not called 911, but someone in the Library surely had, and if the police had not already shut down the whole complex, they soon would.

The kidnapper's bravado was fast evaporating. "If you don't back the hell up, I'll kill her. I swear it."

"Taking her won't accomplish anything," Stone went on. "We can't give you the Spear. It's already been turned over to the CIA. We couldn't give it to you even if we wanted to. It's out of our hands. Your only move here is to cut and run."

Another lie, but Stone seemed to know exactly what to say to produce the desired results. The arm around Avery's neck relaxed if only by a degree or two. The man's resolve was nearly gone.

Stone turned to Kasey. "Let's give him some room to think." He gestured for her to move aside and then nodded to Sievers as well. When they were all pressed against one wall, Stone added, "You might want to leave by another door."

The man's eyes flashed dangerously as he looked at Stone, then at his fallen comrade who lay unmoving in the middle of the passage. Sievers thought there might be a last little bit of steel in him, that he would find his nerve and call Stone's bluff, but then something broke in the man. He shoved the wheelchair toward them like a battering ram, then dashed past as if fearful that one of them might try to tackle him. A moment later he was sprinting down the tunnel, heading back toward the Jefferson Building.

Stone deftly caught the chair before it could crash into him and immediately went to work freeing Avery from her bonds. Sievers saw that they had tied her wrists to the armrests with shoelaces. As soon as her arms were loose, she threw them around Stone, embracing him like a long lost friend.

"It's okay," Stone said, returning the embrace. "You're safe now."

Kasey leaned over her as well. "Are you hurt?"

Avery shook her head then winced. "Ow. Maybe a little."

"Can you walk?" Stone asked.

"I think so."

He pulled her to her feet. "We need to get out of here before the police stop *us*."

"How did you know?" Sievers asked.

"Which part?" Stone replied, not looking away from Avery. When she was standing unaided, he gestured in the direction of the Adams Building. He moved at a fast walk, but not so fast that anyone would give him a second look. The others followed without comment, and Sievers had to jog to catch up.

"All of it. How did you know they'd come this way? How did you know they would use a wheelchair? And how in the hell did you know what to say to make him give up like that?"

"I knew they would use a wheelchair because it was the

only possible way to move someone off the premises against their will without attracting attention. I knew they'd come this way because the Adams Building was close, with fewer witnesses, and has a wheelchair accessible exit with easy access to the street."

"And the Spear? How did you know that's what they were after?"

"They need it to crack the code in the diary," Avery said, her voice sounding stronger.

"And it was the only possible motive for them to come after us. The only reason to take a hostage is for negotiations. The Spear is the only thing we have that they could possibly want, and they've only just realized they need it. They planned this whole thing on the fly, and Avery just happened to be an easy target because she was alone."

"You figured all that out?"

"Things happen the way they do because they can't happen any other way. When you see how all the pieces are positioned, there's only one possible outcome."

Sievers scowled. He had heard Stone say similar things before, though he had never actually seen the man's fatalistic philosophy produce any sort of meaningful outcomes. Stone had guessed right, but what impressed Sievers most was not his accuracy, but his certitude and the quickness with which he had analyzed the situation and developed the correct response. Maybe there was something to it after all.

Avery stopped suddenly. "We can't leave yet."

"We got what we came for," Stone said, handing over her phone. "You snapped a picture of the page with the code."

"What if there's more to it?"

"The code is the missing piece. It will tell us where we need to go."

They reached the terminus of the tunnel and ascended to street level. Avery appeared to have completely recovered from the brief ordeal, and easily kept pace, almost vibrating with frenetic urgency. Sievers scanned the faces of pedestrians moving along the sidewalk, looking for suspicious activity, but if the kidnappers had accomplices waiting outside, they were well-concealed. The quartet hastened to Independence Avenue where Kasey flagged down a cab, promising the driver double the meter if he could get them to their hotel "like a pizza"—in thirty minutes or less—and just that quickly they were on their way.

As the hired car zipped through traffic, Avery began recounting everything she had read. Sievers was only half-listening, his attention mostly focused on checking their six for signs of a tail. While there was no evidence of pursuit, he did not relax his vigilance but he did catch some of Avery's tale.

He was intrigued by the Patton connection, but the idea that the future of the free world might be tied up with some bit of trivia bordered on the ridiculous. Yet, they had been targeted, and that meant the people in the cab with him were not the only ones who believed it. The whole situation was so far outside his normal experience that the only way to cope was to stick to what he knew best.

As they pulled onto the I-66, he took mental note of the other cars merging into the flow of traffic. Their driver, evidently intent on earning his bonus, floored the gas pedal and slipped from lane to lane in search of the path of least resistance. Sievers watched to see if any of the other cars would follow suit. None did.

"Why did he call it 'the Devil's Gift'?" Kasey asked. "Does that mean something? Is it another relic, like the Spear?"

Avery shook her head uncertainly. "I've never heard of anything like that."

Sievers, satisfied that they were not being followed, joined in the conversation. "Patton was a devout Christian, even though he believed in reincarnation. Maybe he had a dream in which he thought the Devil came to him and made some kind of bargain."

"The language is very precise," Stone said. "He said the Devil gave him the Gift, whatever it was. I don't think he was speaking figuratively. At least not about the Gift. Someone that he called 'the Devil' visited him and gave him something. Everything about the surrounding passage suggests a tangible object. Something that is hidden. Something that he allowed to remain hidden, but which he planned to use to launch his political career."

Avery sat up straight. "A buried treasure. He said someone might find it while looking for a different treasure."

"Patton came from old money," Sievers said. "And married into even more. He was already wealthy."

Kasey laughed. "Right. Because rich people know they have enough."

"He was more interested in glory than money," countered Sievers. "Besides, if it *was* a treasure, and money was what he wanted, he wouldn't have just left it there."

"We'll know more once we crack that code," Stone said.

Although he remained skeptical, Sievers felt a growing sense of anticipation as they raced along the busy access road that provided a straight shot to the airport. He wanted to know as badly as the rest of them if only to justify his decision to let Stone continue the crazy quest.

Twenty-eight minutes after leaving the Library of Congress, they exited onto Aviation Drive, but despite the NASCAR-worthy performance of their driver, the journey ground to a near-complete stop less than a mile from their destination. Sievers could see their hotel in the distance, but between them and it was an unbroken line of barely moving cars.

Stone grew increasingly restive as they crawled closer. He craned his head forward, peering over the driver's shoulder to get a better look at what lay ahead.

"Turn us around," he said, his voice filled with grave urgency. "Take us to the airport."

Before anyone could respond, Sievers spied the reason for Stone's abrupt command. Just a hundred yards away, blocking the entrance to the hotel parking lot, was a police car, its top mounted lights flashing red and blue. Beyond it waited at least a half-dozen more patrol cars and unmarked vehicles, all of them casting the same familiar light show.

Something bad had happened at the hotel, and as much as Sievers wanted to believe that it was merely a coincidence, that the police presence was in no way related to what they were doing, he knew better. While they had been foiling the kidnappers at the Library of Congress, another team of bad guys had hit their hotel.

Avery let out a low moan of grief. "Oh, no. The Spear."

Stone shook his head. "They have it."

"What do we do now?"

For once, Stone had no answer.

CHAPTER 17

Ciudad Juarez, Mexico

Although the sun was still bright in the western sky, Tam Broderick and Greg Johns crossed the Paso del Norte International Bridge into Juarez under a dark cloud of defeat. Kasey Kim had called from Washington D.C., and the news was dire indeed.

Tam was relieved that Kasey and Stone had thwarted Avery's abduction, but that was about the only good thing that happened. The Dominion now had everything they needed to set Destiny in motion, and the Myrmidons didn't even know what the plan was. Stone believed that he might have a way for them to close the knowledge gap, but the mere fact that her people had been in harm's way, and in the nation's capital no less, put Tam in a foul mood.

There were, however, two developments that gave Tam reason for hope.

The first bit of good news was that the analysts at Langley had put names to several of the faces Greg had captured on video during his extra-vehicular excursion on the Riesenrad. The men who had met with Oleg Samsonov were Americans— from Texas, no less—in the employ of an El Paso businessman named Roger Lavelle. Tam recognized that name immediately. Lavelle was the suspected Dominion operative flagged in the intercepted phone call that had alerted them to the existence of Destiny. Lavelle had loose ties to the Kingdom Church—the organization that had once advanced the Dominion's agenda in North America—but had escaped prosecution in the roll-up of church leadership following the Atlantis crisis. It was further proof that they were on the right trail. Of even greater interest was the fact that Lavelle's import-export business was closely affiliated with a manufacturing concern on the other side of the river—a *maquiladora* owned by one Guillermo Esperanza.

The second development was that Esperanza had agreed to meet with them.

Tam was still undecided about whether this was a good thing. She had identified herself as a State department investigator—which was almost the truth—conducting a follow-up investigation into the border incident. Tam felt certain that identifying themselves as government agents would trigger a noticeable reaction if Esperanza was Dominion, though she thought this very unlikely. Everything she read about the man confirmed Waller's assessment of the Mexican businessman. A self-made millionaire turned philanthropist, Esperanza seemed more interested in enriching his fellow countrymen than his own bank account. He had actually demurred from seeking political office on several occasions, claiming that he could do more good as a private citizen, and despite his popular success, he had not yet formally declared his intention to seek the highest office in the land. In fact, while he was critical of Mendoza's policies and inaction, he had not joined the chorus of voices calling for the president's resignation.

Tam's gut told her that the businessman was an unwitting dupe in the conspiracy, Lavelle's puppet, and not a willful participant. If she was wrong, if Esperanza was part of the Dominion, perhaps even the architect of Destiny, then she and Greg might be walking into a trap.

Wouldn't be the first time.

The differences between the two cities on either side of the river were not as dramatic as Tam would have expected. But for the border crossing, she would not have guess that they had left El Paso, much less entered another country. Juarez was a modern city, with new construction more in evidence than the old Colonial style Tam had been prepared for.

They drove along the highway, past modern concrete and glass buildings, warehouses and factories. There were a few protesters milling around the border checkpoint, but nothing like the images coming out of Mexico City. Aside from a heavy police presence along the roadside—more ad hoc quick response staging areas than anything else—there was little outward indication that Ciudad Juarez was the smoldering powder keg that might lead to the collapse of the Mexican government, but Tam knew of the city's reputation for violence. The North American Free Trade Agreement had brought prosperity to Juarez, and with the infusion of wealth and growth had come the drug cartels. A too-porous border and the waning power of South American organized crime had made the border town a fertile field for the criminal element to take root, with terrifying results. Juarez, literally a stone's throw from American soil, had a well-deserved reputation as the most violent city on earth.

The wave of terror had somewhat abated from its peak in 2010, at which time there had been on average, four homicides per day. Most of the violence had been the result of rivalries between the different drug cartels fighting for control of the profitable smuggling routes into the U.S. but many of the victims had been innocents, particularly women, swept up in the vortex of brutality. Hundreds had vanished, some sold into slavery, others murdered, their bodies never found.

The chaos had spread outward from the border region like a metastasizing tumor. The so-called Drug Wars had been fought in every corner of the country, with many rural areas completely under the control of the drug lords. In many places, the local villagers had taken up arms, becoming resistance fighters of a different stripe. The situation had degenerated to the point where intelligence analysts in the U.S. Defense department believed that a total collapse of the Mexican government was imminent. That had gotten the attention of the American people, if only because a failed state in Mexico would result in millions of refugees swarming across the river. The response, predictably, had been driven by an impulse toward isolationism and xenophobia, with calls to harden the border and deploy the National Guard.

President Mendoza's initiatives to root out corruption and crush the cartels had been even less successful than the world at large believed. This latest tragedy seemed like the opening salvo in a new campaign of kidnapping and murder, an escalation of violence with the potential to bring about the fulfillment of the

Pentagon's doom-and-gloom-prophecy.

The onboard GPS guided them to Esperanza's factory complex, situated on the Boulevard Juan Pablo II, a six-lane highway—three lanes running in either direction, divided by a tree-lined median—which ran parallel to the border. As they rode along, Tam found herself wondering if the bus carrying the students had come this way. A few miles later, Greg pulled their car into the parking lot of a modern, but generic looking structure that was part office complex, part factory.

Before leaving the car behind, they gunned up—Tam with her Makarov, Greg with an equally compact Glock 23. Technically speaking, the weapons had been smuggled across the border, a very serious criminal offense, particularly in Mexico, but what they had done could hardly have been called smuggling. A reasonably thorough search would have easily found them, stuffed up under the dashboard. Tam knew from experience however that tired border cops had better things to do than scrutinize every car that came through, particularly when there was no hint of suspicious activity.

The factory was humming with the noise of industry, but the side of the building devoted to administration was eerily quiet, as if everyone had already gone home for the day.

"Mr. Esperanza is expecting you," the woman at the reception desk said in English. She rose and came around to guide them to an executive elevator. The ride up was brief; the building only had three stories. They exited into a small sparsely furnished sitting area, but the receptionist ushered them directly through a door at the back of the room and into the office of Guillermo Esperanza.

Like the sitting room, Esperanza's office was a no-frills affair. The furniture—desk, chairs, a sofa along the wall—were about on par with what might be found in a low-rent doctor's waiting room or a budget hotel; adequate, but hardly luxurious. Tam suspected this was not the primary location from which Esperanza oversaw his empire, but rather a place where he could meet with his facilities managers.

The man himself was seated behind the sturdy utilitarian desk. Esperanza looked to be in his early forties, stout with a full head of black hair, combed straight back from a high forehead. His profile reminded Tam of the figures carved on the wall of Mayan temples. He had a weary look about him, but when they entered, he managed a wan smile as he rose to greet them, offering his hand even before speaking. "Welcome," he said in effusive, mildly-accented English. "Thank you so much for coming."

It was an odd thing to say since Tam had been the one to request the meeting. She chalked it up to language differences. She sensed no guile in his manner. If Esperanza was Dominion, he was hiding it well. She beamed back at him like they were old friends. "Thanks for having us. I know you're busy, so I won't take too much of your time."

"My time is yours," he insisted. He beckoned them to sit and settled back into his own swivel chair. "Anything that I can do to help find the…" He paused as if trying to find the right word. "The monsters who did this."

Tam decided to start with that. "We were hoping that you could shed some light on that. Is it possible that this was meant as an attack against you?"

"Possible? I think it is a certainty. The young man who survived—his name is Garza—swore to me that the killers were not members of a drug gang. He told me the killers were police."

This was not news to Tam. Both the Mexican government and the Juarez municipal police department had denied involvement in the strongest possible terms, claiming that the perpetrators had impersonated police officers and established a bogus checkpoint. That was a plausible enough explanation, but it was equally likely that actual, sworn officers had succumbed to the appeal of easy money. Neither scenario however answered the next question. "Why? What did these enemies hope to accomplish?"

Esperanza ducked his head. "They wish to destroy everything I have built. This terror attack, aimed at students, will frighten the young people away from university, making them easy prey for the gangs."

"You said this wasn't the gangs."

"There are many in my country—and in yours—who profit from the way things are. You know this is true."

Tam gave an ambiguous nod. "Anyone in particular? I've heard that you've been very critical of President Mendoza?"

Esperanza's expression darkened, and his tone became grave. "Even if he is not directly responsible for this incident, he has led Mexico to ruin."

The abrupt shift in Esperanza's demeanor caught Tam by surprise. Her intent had been to keep her questions vague, gently probing him to get a sense of the degree of his involvement in the conspiracy, but she sensed an opportunity and decided to take a more direct approach. "Juan Garza, the survivor, overheard one of the killers making a phone call. 'The time for destiny has come.' Does that mean anything to you?"

Esperanza shook his head, the question seeming to skip off his consciousness like a stone across the surface of a pond, but a moment later, it sank in and his eyebrows drew together in consternation. "I did not know of this. Destiny, you say?"

Tam watched him, saying nothing as she weighed his response. The man knew nothing about Destiny, she was certain of that, but the word clearly meant something to him. She glanced at Greg, who had been silent thus far, waiting to step in as the 'bad cop' if the situation warranted.

He returned a faint nod then rephrased Tam's question with more assertiveness. "It does mean something, doesn't it? You've heard that word before."

Esperanza shook his head, but the uncertainty was still there. "I don't understand what it means."

"I think you do."

Tam raised a hand, signaling Greg to back off, and then leaned forward, gripping the edge of his desk. "Mr. Esperanza, we believe that this attack is just the beginning of a terror plot that will threaten the security of both Mexico and the United States. If there's anything you can tell us, even something that might seem insignificant, I urge you to share it."

Esperanza's jaw worked as if chewing over an answer, but then he shook his head again. "I am very sorry, but I know of no terror plot." He sat back in his chair. "You must forgive me.

My schedule has been full of late. I'm leaving for Mexico City within the hour. I will be addressing congress and asking for the removal of President Mendoza. I'm afraid I've given you too much of my time already."

So much for "my time is yours," Tam thought, but let it go without comment. Esperanza was not going to say any more on the subject, not to her at least. His sudden about-face was answer enough.

She stood and extended her hand again, this time proffering a business card embossed with the logo of the State Department. "If you think of anything else, please give me a call."

Esperanza accepted the card but instead of pocketing it, simply placed it on the desk. "Of course. Now if you will excuse me."

The dismissal was absolute, and Tam made no further attempt at conversation. She exited the room with Greg in tow and returned to the elevator where they found the car waiting. As soon as the doors closed, she took an ear bud from her pocket and slipped it into place.

"Think he'll bite?" Greg asked.

"If he does, he better do it soon." She did not need to explain the reason for this to Greg. He was well-acquainted with the limitations of the miniaturized transmitter she had planted in the businessman's office. The bug had a range of just a few hundred yards and only about half an hour of battery life, but Tam had a feeling they would know something long before either was a factor. "I don't think he knows what's going on, but he knows something *is* going on."

For several seconds, she heard only creaks and scratches in the earpiece, the sounds of a person sitting by himself in a room. *Come on*, she thought. *Make the call. You know you want to.*

The elevator car made an unexpected stop on the second floor. The doors opened with a faint whooshing sound that almost eclipsed the electronic tones of someone dialing a number on a telephone.

Because she was so intently focused on her electronic eavesdropping, Tam did not even notice that no one had gotten on the elevator.

"Ah, Tam?"

She raised a hand to silence Greg. "He's calling someone." She pressed her hand to her ear so that she wouldn't miss a word. The bug wouldn't allow her to hear the other side of a phone conversation but she had a pretty good idea who he would call first and what he said would reveal the extent of his knowledge, even if the replies were inaudible.

Electronic music, something with a samba beat, filled the air. *A ringtone.*

For a fleeting instant, she thought Esperanza might have put his phone in speaker mode, but then she realized the noise wasn't coming from the ear bud.

She looked up, the coincidence triggering alarm bells in her head, but it was already too late.

More than a half-dozen men stood in front of the elevator doors. Their ethnicity was not immediately apparent. All were Caucasian, but determining whether they were Mexican, American or Russian, would take more than a glance. Two were wearing what looked like police uniforms, security guards probably, while the others were in plain clothes. Their attire was a hodgepodge, as was the variety of firearms—pistols, rifles, a pump-action shotgun—aimed at the pair exiting the elevator.

A man in the middle of the group, wearing a rumpled suit, was conspicuously unarmed. The musical ringtone was issuing from his breast pocket. Even if Tam had not recognized him from a photograph she had seen only a couple hours before, she would have known immediately that he was the most dangerous of the lot.

She mustered a smile to hide her anxiety. "My goodness, if it isn't Mr. Roger Lavelle."

Surprise flickered across Lavelle's face, quickly replaced by a look of cool contempt. "I don't believe we've been introduced. I was about to say that you have me at a disadvantage, but I guess that's not really true."

"I wouldn't be too sure about that."

"I was told that you might be a problem."

"Who told you that? Your Russian pal, Samsonov?"

There was another ripple of astonishment followed by a tense silence in which the only sound was the phone in Lavelle's pocket.

Figuring the situation couldn't get any worse, Tam decided to dig deeper. "I'll admit, the Dominion and the Russians working together threw us a little. You do know that they're playing you, right?"

Lavelle's face twisted into a sneer. "You have no idea what's really going on."

"No?" Tam shrugged. "You might want to answer that. I think your friend Esperanza has some questions about Destiny."

CHAPTER 18

Washington D.C.

The pattern, Stone thought, was proving damned elusive.

The numbers were a code. The Spear of Destiny was somehow the key to cracking it, but the Spear was gone. A discreet inquiry by phone had confirmed their worst fears. The hotel had been robbed at gunpoint, the safe and several rooms—the rooms that would have been theirs—ransacked.

The loss of their single advantage over the Dominion had left them all stunned and Stone was struggling to reorient himself. The attack on Avery had left him shaken. He should have anticipated the Dominion's response, should have taken steps to ensure her safety, as well as protecting the Spear better. It had all been so predictable, yet he had missed the signs and Avery had nearly paid a very dear price for his mistake.

He closed his eyes, tuning out the hum of activity in the pub on the airport concourse where, in the absence of a better destination, they had gathered to plan their next move. Tuning out his dining companions was a problem of a different stripe. Hardly a word had been spoken since their arrival, but their thoughts were anything but quiet. Stone was no mind-reader. He didn't need to be to pick up the none-too-subtle cues of body language.

Sievers was easy, not surprising since Stone had spent the better part of a year dissecting his behavior. The contractor was struggling to understand the significance of what was happening, but because he was following orders and dealing with compartmentalized directives, the uncertainty of the situation did not bother him as much as the possibility that he might have made the wrong call. The obvious course of action, the one Sievers knew he should take, was to simply grab Stone and head for the nearest EmergInt office. He wasn't ready to do that, not yet at least, but if Stone could not show him that they were making progress, the gravity of that option would eventually be impossible to overcome.

Kasey was harder to read. She was the product of a culture where displays of emotion were regarded as a sign of weakness. Compounding that, she had chosen a career where keeping secrets was the essential life-support system. Yet, he had spent enough time with her to identify her self-control mechanisms. Kasey shielded herself with sarcasm and a self-assuredness that bordered on arrogance. He took her present silence as an indication of how frustrated and out of her depth she now felt. Nevertheless, she sat up straight in her chair, sipping a Coke and surreptitiously checking for any signs of Dominion surveillance, as if she might, by sheer willpower, bring about order out of chaos. Stone sensed that the success of their mission was of less importance to Kasey than not being solely responsible for its failure. She was not, of course. They were in an impossible situation, constrained by too little information and facing an enemy who held all the cards, but to someone like Kasey, that was no excuse.

Avery, who had neither formal military training nor any particular cultural programming, was about as hard to read as a neon sign, but the message was not at all what Stone would have expected from someone who had just narrowly escaped a kidnapping. Rather than retreating into herself, Avery's brain was in overdrive as she wrestled with the mystery of what Patton had called the Devil's gift. Her brute force attack had not yielded any fresh insights, but Stone was impressed with her resiliency. She was made of tougher stuff than she appeared.

"I don't get it," Sievers said, breaking the long silence. "Why try to kidnap her if they already had what they wanted?"

"They didn't have it," Stone replied. "And they weren't certain that we had it. They were waiting for us at the airport. It wouldn't have been difficult to figure out which plane we were on or to get our flight plan. When we landed, they followed us, first to the hotel, then to the Library. Trading Avery for the Spear was the preferred option because they couldn't be sure where we were keeping it. When that didn't work, they had to go with Plan B. Unfortunately for us, it worked."

"We have to get the Spear back," Kasey declared. "We're dead in the water without it."

"What about the kidnappers?" Sievers suggested. "We know what they look like. Shouldn't be too hard to put names to the faces. We track them down, sweat them until they give up their accomplices."

Kasey brightened at this idea, but Stone shook his head. "That will take time that we don't have. We need to get ahead of them."

"And how are we gonna do that if we don't know where they're going?"

"By cracking the code," Avery declared.

"Without the Spear?" Kasey made no effort to conceal her doubtfulness.

Avery caught Stone's gaze and held it. "A code is just another pattern, right? If we start with what we already know, then all we have to do is fill in the blanks."

"We don't know anything," Kasey said, irritably.

Avery grabbed a napkin and a pen and started writing. "This is how you do it, right? List everything you know and figure out what the connections are?"

Stone couldn't help but smile as Avery's list took shape.

Patton
Code
Spear of Destiny
Devil's gift

"What else?" she asked, her pen hovering above the napkin.

"The Devil," Sievers suggested. "Sounds like it was his nickname for someone. A real person."

"Good." Stone was pleased that Sievers taking an interest. He needed the man to be engaged in their current effort, rather than scheming to return Stone to the black site. "But the code is the important thing. It's a message, hidden in those numbers."

Kasey rolled her eyes. "Duh."

Stone smiled. Kasey's sarcasm was also a good sign.

Avery wrote down the code on another napkin.

29 33 13 108 10 8

"Wasn't that Patton's high school locker combo?" Kasey said with a wink to Sievers.

"I'll try Googling it." Avery tapped the digits in, then shook her head. "Nothing. A lot of basketball scores. A substitution cipher would make sense. It's short, but if that's what it is, we should be able to crack it even without the key."

"I doubt it will be that easy. Patton would have known a thing or two about encryption." Stone drummed his fingers on the table. "What did he say? 'Let him that hath understanding count the number. The Spear will point the way.'"

"The first part is from the Bible," Avery said. "Revelation thirteen. 'Here is wisdom. Let him that hath understanding count the number of the beast: for it is the number of a man, and his number is Six hundred threescore and six.' Maybe the numbers are Bible verses? Or Bible page numbers? What if we start with that verse, then count letters."

She navigated to an online edition of the King James Version and looked up the passage. "All right, if I start with the word 'let', counting forward to twenty-nine gives us the letter 'O.' Then 'T.'" She continued counting and writing letters, then frowned at the final result.

O H A A T H

"Maybe I should start at the beginning of the verse."

"Or maybe it's a math problem," Kasey said. "Try adding the numbers up?"

Stone couldn't tell if she was serious, but Avery shrugged and then did just that.

"201?" She looked up to see if that number had any significance to Stone, the shrugged. "Well, I suppose that would be too obvious." She tapped the pen against the sum. "There's a Latin inscription on the Spear. Maybe we're supposed to convert this into Roman numerals. Or maybe the number itself is significant, like in numerology?"

Stone turned to Sievers. "You're the closest thing we have to a Patton scholar here. Was he interested in esoterica?"

"Not from what I've read."

"It's a joke," Stone declared. "Subterfuge. He's got us chasing our tail." He closed his eyes trying once more to focus on the important details and separate out the extraneous. "'The Spear will point the way.' The way to what? Are we looking for a physical location?"

"That would make sense," suggested Avery. "X marks the spot. Go here and find the Devil's gift."

"The numbers could be map coordinates," offered Sievers.

Stone opened his eyes. "Latitude and longitude? Okay, let's try that. Twenty-nine degrees, thirty-three minutes, thirteen seconds, by one hundred eight degrees, ten minutes, eight seconds. That would narrow it down to an area less than a quarter of a mile across. Without cardinal directions, there are four places on earth that match those coordinates."

"I'm on it." She tapped the phone a few times, then studied the results. "First location, roughly twenty-nine north, one-oh-eight east, is in China, about a hundred miles east of Chongqing. There's a massive limestone karst formation there. Caves, sinkholes, natural bridges." She glanced over at Sievers. "Did Patton ever go to China?"

"I don't think so."

"We can't discount it," Stone said. "Based on the surrounding text, I don't think Patton ever laid eyes on this 'gift,' whatever it is, so it could be at any of these locations."

"Not this one. Twenty-nine south is in the Indian Ocean, about four hundred miles west of Australia. Deep water, not much else. Same story in the western hemisphere. Smack dab in the middle of the… oh."

"What?"

"Those coordinates are less than two hundred miles south of Easter Island."

Stone considered this. There were few places on earth more

remote than Easter Island. "A good place to hide something. Where's the last one?"

Avery's excitement reached a new peak. She turned the phone to show them all the results. "Mexico! That can't be a coincidence."

Stone nodded, but the discovery was not a surprise. This was the connection he had known would be there. All this did was confirm that they had correctly identified the numbers as coordinates. But did they hide another secret?

"It's in the Sierra Madre mountain range, in the state of Chihuahua," Avery continued. "That's the same area where Patton hunted Pancho Villa."

"Treasure of the Sierra Madre," said Sievers. "Patton said he was afraid someone might stumble across it while looking for another treasure. People are always looking for lost gold out there."

"The scout," Avery said. "He said the scout was still looking for treasure. I think he was talking about Emil Holmdahl. He was a cavalry scout who accompanied Patton on his hunt for Pancho Villa. The guy was a real character, but tough as nails. After World War I, he spent the rest of his life running guns and looking for Pancho Villa's lost treasure. At one point, the Mexican government accused him of digging up Villa's body and cutting off the head, which he then sold to the Skull and Bones society at Yale University."

"Skull and Bones." Stone wondered how, or even if, that piece fit into the puzzle. With three United States presidents and many other influential politicians and businessmen among their alumni, there were always rumors that the secret group had a much darker agenda. Those rumors notwithstanding, it was true that among their macabre eccentricities was a penchant for collecting the skeletal remains of famous historical figures. The collection, housed in their exclusive hall known as The Tomb, did contain human skulls, though probably not actually the skulls of Martin Van Buren, Geronimo, or Pancho Villa as was claimed.

"Do you think there could be a connection between them and the Dominion? Maybe Holmdahl found something about this gift and passed it on to the society along with Villa's skull. That could be how the Dominion found out about it."

It felt to Stone like a tangent, too many steps removed from the central issue. "We should go to Mexico. Start looking at those coordinates."

"Hang on a sec," Kasey said. "The numbers aren't a code after all? Then why did the Dominion steal the Spear?"

Avery was ready with an answer. "Patton said 'the Spear will point the way.' We assumed it meant that the Spear was needed to crack a code, but it could mean that once we get to that spot, the Spear will somehow show us where to go."

Kasey threw up her hands. "Then we're back where we started. We have to get the Spear back."

Stone shook his head. "I don't think the Dominion has figured this out yet. They think the numbers are a code and that the key is somewhere on the Spear. That's why they were so desperate to get it. The diary, too, for that matter. Right now, we know more than they do. When they finally do figure it out, we'll be waiting for them."

CHAPTER 19

Ciudad Juarez, Mexico

There were eight men if Lavelle was included, but since he did not appear to have a weapon, Greg figured he didn't count. *Seven men then. Okay, that's manageable.*

He took a slow but purposeful step forward, positioning himself at Tam's left elbow. She would understand the unspoken message. *I'll take the guys on the left; you take the guys on the right.*

That the gunmen were not professionals was blisteringly apparent. That did not make them less dangerous. Quite the opposite, it would make them unpredictable. Nevertheless, the inexperience of their captors did give the two CIA officers a significant advantage. Amateurs trusted in their guns like they were a magical totem, believing that the mere possession of a firearm made them invincible. But having a gun, and knowing what to do with it in a highly-charged situation, were two very different things.

Lavelle frowned then took his phone out to silence the insistent ringing. He turned away, but Greg could still hear his part of the ensuing conversation.

"Yes, Guillermo... No, I hadn't heard that... I don't know what it means. Look, I've just arrived. I'm walking in as we speak... We can talk about it on the flight... I'm sure it doesn't mean anything." He mumbled a few more words in closing, then ended the call and returned the phone to his pocket.

"So you are using him," Tam said. Greg knew that she had been privy to both sides of the call. "I thought as much. What's the plan? Setting Esperanza up to be the next president is... what's the opposite of ambitious? It's a minor-league goal. Is that what you guys are? The Dominion farm team?"

She glanced at Greg, her satisfied nod masking a subtle eye movement that said, *Wait for it.*

Lavelle did not respond to the jibe, nor did he even look in Tam's direction. Instead, he turned to one of the gunmen. "I have to get up there. Put them somewhere out of the way until the end of the shift. Then make them disappear."

The man answered with a nod and Lavelle stepped past them to board the elevator.

Greg was expecting the next move from their captors to be a quick pat down, which would uncover the weapons he and Tam carried. That would be the best chance to turn the tables on the gunmen. When one of them approached to begin the search, Greg would strike, overpowering the man in order to use him as a human shield. Tam would be ready to do the same. Despite having their guns at the ready, the other men would hesitate, just for a moment, out of fear of hitting their comrades, but he and Tam would not. It would take all of three seconds.

Except the gunmen did not search them. Either the men had assumed that they could not be armed because of being foreigners, or they had simply forgotten. The latter was more likely, a further sign of their inexperience. The man in charge simply waved his pistol toward a door at one end of the elevator lobby. "Move."

Greg exchanged another meaningful look with Tam. *Not yet.*

Lavelle had not exactly been forthcoming with information. His responses to Tam's questions suggested they were on the right track, but there was still a lot they didn't know. Maybe one of the goon squad would let something more slip inadvertently, so for now the best course of action was to play along, meekly submit to captivity.

If and when the men remembered to frisk them, that would be the signal to act.

The gunmen however continued to keep a safe distance, taking a position behind them, with the exception of the leader who walked beside Tam, his pistol at the ready. Greg was starting to rethink his estimation of their skills. The men evidently knew enough not to surround their prisoners and inadvertently put themselves in a potential crossfire.

The leader opened the door, stepped through, and waved for the others to follow. The door led to a long nondescript hallway, lined with similarly ambiguous doors. They were ushered through the first of these, into a room that was empty, save for a pair of folded-up rectangular tables, and a row of stackable plastic chairs.

"Against the wall," barked the leader. "Sit on the floor and shut up."

Greg, still following Tam's lead, complied without comment, placing his back against the wall and sliding down into a seated position beside her.

The rest of the gunmen filed into the room, taking turns helping themselves to chairs which they lined up against the wall with the door. Tam waited until they were done to speak. "How long until the shift ends?"

Greg expected the question to be met with a fierce demand for silence, but instead the leader simply glanced at his watch. "Forty-five minutes."

Tam nodded like a Buddhist monk contemplating the mysteries of life. She waited almost a full minute before speaking again. "Quite a plan you've got."

The leader frowned but said nothing.

Tam tried again. "So is this all Lavelle's idea, or did the Russians come up with it?"

That elicited a response, but not the one that Tam probably hoped for. "No talking," the man growled.

Tam looked over at Greg. "Forty-five minutes seems like an awful long time to just sit here."

Greg signaled his agreement.

The leader of the gunmen stood up, bristling with aggression, but before he could repeat himself, Tam cut him off with a saucy shake of her shoulders. "You forgot something, sugar."

He gaped at her for several uncomprehending seconds.

Tam looked at Greg again. "I don't believe these guys."

"Maybe we should quit screwing around and just shoot them," Greg replied.

The comment finally provoked the response they had been

waiting for. The gunmen, all of them, almost in perfect unison, jumped to their feet and trained their weapons on the captives.

"If you've got guns," the leader barked, "take them out. Very slowly."

"We don't have guns," Tam replied, innocently.

"Nope," Greg added. "We were just messing with you."

The man was dumbfounded, but one of his fellow goons tried to pick up the slack. "Face down, both of you. Hands behind your head."

Greg made a clucking noise. "Kneeling is better, you know. Easier to maintain control of your subject."

The second man thrust his rifle forward. "Move it!"

Greg did as instructed, but despite the appearance of levity, his mind had gone into full-tactical mode. Their captors had ceased to be men, ceased to be human, and were now merely targets in a three-dimensional physical battlespace. He assigned them each a threat status. The men with handguns rated 'orange.' Those with rifles and the shotgun wielder were red, since the likelihood of being hit by an inadvertent discharge was higher, as was the potential for catastrophic injury. He marked the location and orientation of their weapons, calculating the amount of time it would take for each man to actually aim and pull the trigger, and what he would have to do in order to avoid catching a bullet. He knew that Tam was doing the same.

Two of the gunmen—the ones in uniforms—advanced, holstering their weapons. Greg immediately downgraded their threat status to yellow. A moment later, the men ceased to be threats at all, and instead became assets.

As soon as one of the pair knelt down beside him, Greg went into motion. From the corner of his eye, he could see the line of gunmen reacting. Their movements were reflexive. Sloppy and uncoordinated. This was the moment of greatest risk, where a hasty trigger pull might end both the escape attempt and his life, but the odds were still better than doing nothing and waiting to be taken out into the sticks and executed.

Greg's first course of action was to make sure that, if someone did fire, the bullet would not have a direct path to him. He sprang off the floor in what looked like a dynamic push-up, and settled back into a crouch just behind where the would-be searcher was kneeling. A half-turn put him directly behind the man, and out of the direct line of fire. He wrapped his left arm around the man's neck, pulling him off balance, and with his right, unholstered the man's pistol and thrust it toward the others. Beside him, Tam had accomplished more or less the same with the man who had come to search her.

They were now faced with a choice, one that had to be made almost without conscious thought. If they fired, they would have no choice but to kill everyone in the room. With the element of surprise on their side, Greg knew he might be able to take out two of them before the return fire started. If Tam matched him, that would leave just one active shooter. As a mathematical problem, the odds would clearly favor them over that one remaining foe, but there was a lot of uncertainty in the calculation. What if the noise of the shooting brought reinforcements? What if he and Tam were too slow, or not quite accurate enough with their initial barrage? What if the unfamiliar pistols malfunctioned? A delay of less than a second might prove fatal. And even if everything went perfectly according to plan, the odds allowed that one of them might be injured or killed. Equations like that were easy to balance if no allowances for humanity were made, but Greg's preference was an outcome where both he and Tam walked away without a scratch.

He figured the odds were good that one of the men would try to get a shot off, and if that happened, there would be only one course of action, but he held his fire. Tam did as well. So did the five men across the room.

Greg got the sense that it was a different sort of uncertainty that made them hesitate. They had probably never faced a situation like this before. If they were Dominion foot soldiers, as he suspected they were, then they would almost certainly conform to a certain personality type: legends in their own mind. Wanna-be soldiers who lived in an alternate reality where they were tough alpha-personalities, equating their manliness with the size of their guns. A few might be ex-military, but even those would have largely failed to develop the necessary instincts that would equip them for a situation like this. Staring down the barrel of a gun, facing an enemy who has the advantage, their reptile-brains could only muster one response. They froze, like deer transfixed by the headlights of an oncoming eighteen-wheeler.

"Drop 'em or get dropped," Tam said, coolly.

The gunmen did not lower their weapons, but instead glanced at one another, looking for someone to take the initiative.

"Count of three," Tam warned. "One."

Three counts were good. There was the pressure of a deadline, just enough time to think it through, but not enough to make a careful examination of all the variables.

"Two."

The only problem with the three count, whether in a hostage crisis or disciplining a wayward child, was in the follow-through. Greg knew that Tam was not bluffing, so he tensed his body and curled his finger around the trigger.

"Wait!" shouted the lead gunman. "Let's talk this out."

"Talking beats dying," Tam said, her tone almost unnaturally calm. Greg knew it was an act, but she was a damned good actor. "But the only way I'm listening is if those guns are on the ground. Otherwise…" She shrugged. "Where was I? Two? Or thr—"

"Okay! We're putting them down." The man stooped over and laid his gun on the floor, then rose, hands held high. He nodded for his companions to do the same. Not all of them appeared to be as eager to surrender their weapons, but they all grudgingly complied.

"So far, so good," Tam said. "Now, move over there."

She gestured with the gun, herding them toward a corner of the room that was several steps removed from the discarded weapons. When they were all a safe distance away, Tam released her hostage and gave him a shove in the direction of his comrades. Greg similarly dispensed with his human shield, then quickly moved over to the guns. There was no way he was going to be able to take them all along with him, so instead he quickly field stripped the automatics and semi-autos, removing small but critical components to render the weapons completely useless. The shotgun he kept.

The process took less than a minute, and while he was occupied with that, Tam collected the men's phones. When they were finished with their respective tasks, Tam addressed the group. "Good news and bad news, gents. The bad news, obviously, is that you screwed up. You should probably find a different line of work. You'd really be better off. The good news, of course, is that you're going to get to live long enough to make that decision. Provided, that is, you stay right here and don't try to come after us. I cannot emphasize that latter point too strongly. Stay here, stay alive. Got it?"

There were grumbles, but the men nodded. Greg pulled open the door. Using the butt of the shotgun like a club, he struck the interior doorknob, breaking it off at the stem. As soon as they were both through, he pulled the door shut behind him. "That'll hold 'em, but not for long."

"Lavelle is with Esperanza in the office. If we can catch him there, we'll be able to end this now."

For the first time since their arrival, Greg found himself disagreeing with his boss. "We should get out of here now while we still can."

"We can flip Esperanza. Once he's on our side, we won't need to run."

Greg's concerns were not allayed, but Tam was the boss. He told her so.

As they entered the elevator foyer, Tam suddenly sprinted forward. "Crap! They just left."

She stabbed a finger at the call button but was either a fraction of a second too late or the elevator was in manual mode. The car kept going, all the way to the ground floor.

Greg glimpsed motion behind them and whirled around, bringing the shotgun up. He fired without hesitation, but not before the man framed in the doorway—one of their former captors—pulled the trigger of the small pistol he carried, evidently a backup weapon which the man had withheld during the surrender.

The single round from the handgun creased the air between Tam and Greg, while the blast from the shotgun obliterated their attacker. As the shredded body fell back, Greg saw several more figures in the hallway behind the ill-fated point man.

The twin reports, particularly the thunderous roar of the shotgun, were deafening in the close confines of the elevator lobby. Any hope of a stealthy exit from the building was now dashed. Greg pumped the weapon to eject the spent shell casing and load another cartridge of double-ought buck from the magazine, and then pointed the muzzle in the direction of the doorway.

"Stair!" Tam shouted. "This way."

Greg backed toward the sound of her voice. When no one else ventured out of the hallway, he ducked through the stairwell door before it could close completely. Tam was bounding down the concrete stairs, already halfway to the first floor. She stopped at the foot of the steps and waited for him to catch up before easing the door open a sliver.

Something banged loudly against the door, the force of the impact tearing the doorknob out of Tam's hand. Tendrils of smoke curling away from the pencil-sized hole in the door, along with a cloud of dust and grit from something striking the wall behind them, left little doubt that someone outside the stairwell was shooting at them. Lavelle had evidently brought along additional manpower.

"There're at least three shooters out there," Tam said, still amazingly calm. She had her Makarov out and held at the ready. She edged out for another peek then drew back faster than the blink of an eye, but this time without any shots fired. "They're bugging out. Covering Lavelle's exit."

Greg kept his attention and his weapon aimed at the top of the stairs. There was no sign of their former captors, but that was not surprising since their weapons were mostly useless, and Greg had already shown them how lethal any attempt to rush them would be.

"Moving!" Tam called.

Greg turned just in time to see her head through the door. When her exit did not trigger another fusillade, he hurried after her. Almost as an afterthought, he pitched the shotgun into the niche under the steps. The weapon was great for discouraging close pursuit in the cramped hallways but too slow and unwieldy for what awaited him on the other side of the door. With his Glock in hand, he charged out into the reception lobby, just a few steps behind Tam.

The smell of burnt gunpowder hung in the air, but there was no sign of the shooters, no sign of anyone at all, in fact. The receptionist was probably hiding under her desk—Greg didn't stop to check—but Lavelle and Esperanza, along with whatever security contingent was accompanying them, were gone.

Tam edged through the main entrance door without being shot at, and headed outside with Greg close behind her. In the parking lot beyond, a rust-colored Ford Excursion with tinted windows and a Texas license plate was pulling away. Tam leveled her pistol at the departing vehicle. The moment was eerily reminiscent of what had happened outside the Hofburg palace, only this time, instead of a red-handed burglar—and a Russian agent to boot—the escaping vehicle held a prominent businessman who might very well be the next president of Mexico. Wisely, Tam held her fire, but she was not ready to throw in the towel. Without a word of explanation, she turned on her heel and sprinted out across the parking lot. Greg didn't have to be psychic to know where she was headed, and as he ran to catch her, he holstered his unfired weapon and dug the car keys out of his pocket, clicking the alarm remote furiously, first to pinpoint the car's location for them both, and then to unlock the doors.

They reached the rented sedan at almost exactly the same instant and Greg slid behind the wheel even as Tam settled into the passenger seat. He hesitated for just a moment as he slotted the key into the ignition. What if Lavelle's men had booby-trapped the car?

No way, he thought. *We weren't in there long enough. Besides, they were planning to take us out in the desert and shoot us. No need to wire the car.*

Nevertheless, he held his breath as he turned the key.

No boom.

He put the car in gear and executed a quick three-point turn to get the car turned in the right direction and then accelerated through the parking lot, steering toward the highway. The Expedition was barely visible, heading west. Traffic was relatively light, but Greg had to tap the brakes and wait for a car to pass before rocketing out of the lot and across the eastbound lanes, leaving a cloud of dust and tire smoke in their wake.

"Déjà vu all over again," Tam said.

"No kidding. What do we do if we catch them?"

The question was moot almost as soon as he finished asking it. Further down the road, just past the outline of the Expedition, was a long line of flashing red and blue lights atop cars and pickups with the distinctive black and white paint scheme of the municipal police. Before Greg could react, two of the police vehicles swerved across the median, into the westbound lanes, and cut the road diagonally, blocking traffic behind the SUV carrying Esperanza and Lavelle. The rest continued on their way, drawing closer with each passing second.

Tam muttered a week's allowance of swear words. Whether the law officers were responding to reports of shooting at Esperanza's factory or were secretly in Lavelle's pocket, there was little mystery as to their intent.

"Maybe we should turn around?" Greg tried to match Tam's earlier calm, but there was no hiding the anxiety. When Tam did not immediately reply, he added. "I'm open to other suggestions."

"Do it."

It was not exactly the clear-cut guidance he had been hoping for, but Greg nevertheless stomped the brakes, bumped the gear-shift lever into 'neutral' and steered hard to the left. The tires shuddered against the pavement and, for a fleeting instant, Greg thought the sedan might roll. The view through the windshield changed with dizzying rapidity as the car spun one hundred-eighty degrees, and then the crazy carnival ride ended with them facing back the way they'd come.

The cars that had been directly behind them before the

maneuver were still in the process of reacting, some skidding to a dead stop, others heading for the shoulder. Further down the road, Greg could see more cars and trucks approaching at highway speed, oblivious to what loomed ahead.

Greg slipped the transmission into 'drive' and punched the gas pedal, threading the sedan between the haphazardly scattered vehicles, edging toward the median. Before he could cross over to the eastbound lanes, however, he spied flashing lights from the corner of his eye. The police cars had almost caught up to them. He veered away from the median and kept accelerating, straight into oncoming traffic.

"Still waiting on that suggestion."

Tam stared out the side window for several long seconds before turning to him. "You know, America is right over there."

"So close, yet so far away."

While it was true that the border between Mexico and the U.S. was close in a very literal sense, the nearest border crossing was several miles away, in the other direction, with half the police force of Ciudad Juarez arrayed between them and it. Even if they could somehow elude the pursuing officers and find a circuitous route back to one of the bridges that spanned the river, the actual crossing would require them to wait in line—possibly for hours—during which time the police would be looking for them.

We could ditch the car. Maybe they don't have descriptions of us....

That was too much to hope for. His face was anonymous enough, but Tam's mocha-colored skin was distinctive enough that she would be singled out immediately.

Tam repeated her statement, emphasizing each word. "Right. Over. There."

"I know, but... Oh. You mean... You can't be serious."

She can't be serious, he thought.

As if to answer his rhetorical question, she gave the shoulder strap of her seatbelt a tug to ensure that it was functional. "I always wanted to make a run for the border."

She's serious.

"Okay, then." Greg turned his attention back to the road ahead. Several cars had already pulled into the far lanes, giving them a more or less clear path, but a police car on the other side of the median was racing ahead, the driver almost certainly planning to cut across and block their escape. Greg realized that Tam's suggestion was not merely a good idea, but just about the only option left. He cranked the wheel left, crossed all three lanes and threaded the needle between a pair of semi-haulers that had pulled over, but not slowed down, and hit the far shoulder.

The rental car lurched as it left the smooth macadam and began jouncing over the unfinished dirt at the roadside. They crunched through a hundred yards of underbrush and then were briefly airborne as the car bumped up and over a sun-hardened rut to thump down on another hundred-yard-wide swath of bare graded dirt that formed the buffer zone between the highway and the river bed.

A plume of dust marked their passage, but through it Greg could see the flashing lights of police vehicles chasing after them. He was committed now; there could be no turning back. It took less than five seconds to reach the electronic "fence," an endless line of what looked like streetlight poles, spaced forty yards apart, each one equipped with cameras, microphones and more exotic detection equipment, to alert border patrol agents of imminent incursions. Somewhere in an office on the other side of the river, alarms were going off, and agents were scrambling to get to their trucks.

A literal fence of the chain-link variety rose into view directly ahead. Greg knew that beyond it lay the mostly dry river channel of the Rio Grande—it was called the Rio Bravo on the Mexican side—and beyond that, the United States. He kept the gas pedal to the floor.

"Hang on!"

He thought he heard Tam shout his name, but it might have been his imagination.

The sedan hit the interlocking web of metal at nearly eighty miles per hour. The impact triggered the collision sensors, causing the airbag to deploy from the steering wheel with all the force of a haymaker punch from a heavyweight champ. Greg did not see most of what happened next.

The fence did not break, but it did buckle under the battering ram assault. The car's momentum kept it going, up and over the collapsing fence, launching it—or rather what was left of it—across the concrete river channel. The initial collision had blown out the front tires and demolished the grill. The coil of concertina wire at the top of the fence snagged on the undercarriage, tearing off one of the rear wheels completely and turning the car in mid-air so that it struck a similar fence on far shore broadside. The chain-links caught the sedan like a spider's web, stealing the last of its momentum and holding it fast above the sloping concrete walls of the canal.

Greg sat unmoving for several seconds, trying to reorient himself. The angle at which the car had come to rest was playing havoc with his senses, and the after-effect of being rattled like a peanut in a can didn't help matters any. He glanced over and saw Tam, likewise dazed but with no visible signs of injury.

She looked back at him, eyes wide in disbelief. "Holy... What on earth possessed you to do that?"

"You told me to."

"I told you to run for the border. I figured you'd stop so we could climb the fence, not go all Evel Knievel."

Greg felt an embarrassed flush creep over his face. "Oh. Good to know."

Tam turned away for a moment, surveying their situation, then offered a mischievous smile. "Hey, your way worked, so I'm not complaining. Though I think we can forget about getting our security deposit back for the car."

Outside, a line of white SUVs with flashing emergency lights and the distinctive green stripe of the United States Border Patrol were racing across the packed dirt toward them.

"Looks like we've got a new problem," Greg remarked as the rapid response team surrounded them to form an inescapable perimeter. "I hear they don't look kindly on illegal aliens in these parts. Think they'll ask for our green cards?"

Tam just laughed. "Welcome to Texas."

CHAPTER 20

With painstaking care, Eric Trent inspected every inch of the Spear of Destiny under a large magnifying glass, comparing it side-by-side with the replica, looking for some tiny detail that would unlock the code in Patton's diary. The craftsman who had made the copy had diligently reproduced even insignificant details, the tiny crosses and doves on the flanges that were almost invisible from a distance, the crinkles in the gold band with its Latin inscription.

There were differences to be sure. The real Spear looked like an actual weapon of war, with deep gouges in the black iron. The tip was blunted, probably the result of a killing thrust through some barbarian's studded armor, although, to Trent's admittedly untrained eye, the defects looked more recent. Yet aside from the damage and, of course, the tell-tale markings that identified one spear as a copy, there were no substantive differences between the two.

"'The Spear will point the way,'" he muttered. So far, it had not pointed to anything. They had risked exposure with the failed kidnapping attempt at the Library of Congress and the more successful, though unfortunately highly visible robbery at the hotel, and what did they have to show for it?

Lavelle was pressuring him for results. The rest of the plan was proceeding like clockwork, but its ultimate success or failure depended on Trent keeping his promise to crack the code. He had been so certain that the answer would become immediately apparent once he held the real Spear in his hand. Lavelle's hired guns had more or less accomplished the task set for them, but thus far, the hastily arranged trip to the nation's capital had not borne the expected fruit.

He had been working under the assumption that Patton had made some sort of modification to the Spear when it was in his possession following the capture of Berlin, an engraving perhaps that would illuminate the meaning of the number code. When he had first discovered the craftsman's mark on the replica, he had assumed that Patton's alterations had not been reproduced, but if there was something there, he had yet to see it.

Refusing to admit defeat, Trent laid aside his magnifying glass and turned the authentic Spear over in order to remove the decorative gold band. As he carefully peeled it apart, something fell out and landed with a metallic clank on the tabletop. That had definitely not happened when he had disassembled the replica. He laid the Spear aside and stared at the object that had fallen from the Spear, but before he could fully process the significance of it, his phone began to vibrate with an incoming call. He did not recognize the number, which probably meant that it belonged to one of the burner phones his team was using.

"Hello?"

"Watchdog, here."

Watchdog, Trent knew, was the man assigned to shadow the four CIA people, who at last report, had been loitering at the airport, to all appearances, drowning their sorrows in drinks at a pub on the concourse. "Go ahead."

"They're bugging out. Just boarded a flight to Houston."

"Houston?" Houston was a major hub, so there was no reason to believe it was their final destination. Trent knew that the rest of their group had gone on to El Paso, where they had nearly thrown a monkey wrench in the works by approaching Guillermo Esperanza in Juarez, and subsequently eluded Lavelle's attempt to disappear them. The obvious explanation for the flight to Houston was that the CIA people were trying to regroup, but Trent could not dismiss the possibility that they had somehow cracked the code. "Follow them. I want to know where they're going."

"Already bought my ticket. I'll let you know where they're heading as soon as we land."

Trent ended the call and pondered his next course of action. If the CIA people had cracked the code, then the obvious move was to shadow them to the destination. He disliked the idea of allowing them to get close, especially when he didn't know exactly where they were going, but until he could solve the cipher in the diary, he was just spinning his wheels here.

Satisfied that things were finally moving, even if by a more circuitous route than he would have liked, Trent returned his attention to the object that had fallen from beneath the gold band.

It was a small disc of metal, glinting the same hue as the band. A coin.

He studied the image on the face, the likeness of a woman—a goddess, he decided—with a torch in one hand and a tree branch in the other. Behind her, radiating lines simulated a sunrise, or perhaps divine glory. It was an ancient likeness, yet the coin itself was only a century old. He knew this because stamped in the lower right were four digits: 1910.

It was an American twenty-dollar gold piece, known more commonly as a 'double-eagle.'

A triumphant grin spread across Trent's face. The coin, by itself, offered no insights to help him crack the code, but its very presence, concealed here within a relic that was at least twelve hundred years old, confirmed everything the Russian had told Lavelle. Patton had placed the coin there, surreptitiously marking his ownership, albeit a very temporary one, of the Spear of Destiny. Yet, the coin itself held greater significance. The date stamp, while not constituting definitive proof, was consistent with the story Samsonov had revealed. The coin was almost certainly part of a cache given to Mexican revolutionaries sometime before the year 1916, when Patton would have learned about the prize he called 'the Devil's Gift.'

The coin meant the story was true. The Devil's Gift was real, and it was everything they hoped it was.

He gathered up the pieces of the Spear, along with the coin, and stowed them in a duffel bag. He would have plenty of time to resume the search for the code key once he was in the air, en route to Texas, but he no longer felt the oppressiveness of the deadline looming overhead. One way or another, the Devil's

Gift would soon be in his hands, and Destiny would become reality.

CHAPTER 21

Chihuahua, Mexico

It was only when she stepped off the plane at General Roberto Fierro Villalobos International Airport that Avery realized she had spent more than half of the preceding forty-eight hours in the air. It had been two days since she'd slept in a bed or had a hot shower. Her body was definitely feeling the former, and her nose was acutely aware of the latter. The others seemed immune to the hectic pace; it was probably business as usual for them.

Aside from being tired and grungy, Avery was also more than a little anxious about the current political climate in Mexico. In the wake of the Juarez student massacre, the State Department was strongly advising Americans to avoid travel, particularly in areas off the regular tourist routes. Remote and rural, Chihuahua was exactly the kind of city that might conceal anti-government or criminal elements, the kind of people who would think nothing of abducting foreign tourists for ransom or simply making them disappear altogether. Avery felt quite sure she had already used up all her luck when it came to being kidnapped. The conspicuous presence of men in camouflaged combat uniforms armed with assault rifles did not allay her concerns. They were probably federal police or military troops, but their very presence only underscored the danger they were facing.

The others seemed unfazed by this. Avery hoped this meant her worries were unfounded, but after what had happened at the Library of Congress, no place was truly safe. She did take some small comfort in the knowledge that Kasey and Sievers were both armed. Before leaving D.C. Kasey had procured traveling documents for them all, including credentials identifying her and Sievers as FBI agents with international carry permits.

Avery's hopes of an overnight stay in Chihuahua were quickly dashed. Within half an hour of arriving, they were on the move again, traveling in a rented Toyota RAV4 along Mexico's Federal Highway 16. She understood that time was in short supply, and that a night wasted in relative luxury might cost them the race, but that did not mean she had to like it.

Staying on the move did have one advantage, however; a moving target was a lot harder to hit.

The closest landmark of any significance to the target coordinates was an archaeological site called Cuarenta Casas. Avery thought she was well-versed in pre-Columbian antiquity, but her research on Cuarenta Casas had come as a real surprise. The forty houses from which the site took its name were actually adobe structures, built into caves like the cliff dwellings of the American southwest by the Paquime culture, which had been contemporaneous with the Aztecs further to the south, and the Anasazi to the north. The culture had declined in the fourteenth century, but caves had been occupied as late as 1520, which meant that, despite their remote location, they had never been lost. The caves would have been the perfect place for someone—Patton's mysterious 'Devil'—to hide a treasure in the early years of the twentieth century.

The road trip through the Mexican countryside was similarly at odds with her preconceived notions. She had expected rough dirt roads lined with dilapidated shacks and weathered adobe houses, and people wearing sombreros and serapes, riding burros everywhere. The reality was far more prosaic. The federal highway was a well-maintained four-lane divided road that sliced through mile after mile of farm country, nestled in the gently sloping foothills of the Sierra Madre Occidental range. Kasey remarked that it was not much different from a drive up the I-5 in California. It was one of the few times that she, or in fact that any of them spoke. Everyone, it seemed, was alone with their thoughts. It was only when they stopped for fuel that Avery was reminded that she was in a foreign country, and only then because the signs were in Spanish.

Avery napped a little, then took her turn behind the wheel,

driving for an hour before letting Sievers take over. Somewhere between hours three and four, the road became two-lane highway but it was not until they were about thirty miles north of a place called Ciudad Madera that the going finally became a little more rugged. Even then, the dirt roads that climbed into the mountains were not dissimilar to back roads Avery had traveled in her native Nova Scotia. The weather was cool but dry, and the roads were, for the most part, firm enough that they did not need to make use of the Toyota's low-range four-wheel drive.

A sign on an unlocked gate informed them that the site was closed for the winter, but they continued on to the road's end, where more signs identified the trailhead leading to the Cuarenta Casas archaeological preserve. They hiked along the trail to the base of a long plank staircase leading up the cliffs, where Kasey, after consulting the Garmin Epix wristwatch-style GPS unit she had picked up at an airport gadget shop before leaving D.C. announced, "We're here. More or less."

"So what do we do now?" Sievers asked. "It's not like we even know what we're looking for."

Avery looked to Stone, wondering if he had cracked the riddle during his long contemplative silence—he had said the least of any of them during the road trip—but he did not seem to be paying attention. He was gazing, with an indifferent expression, at the cliffs high above them, where the Paquime had built their dwellings in shadowy scalloped recesses. Finally Avery herself ventured a guess. "The diary said the Spear would point the way. My brother came across a clue like that once, and he solved it when he realized he had to look in the direction a certain statue was pointing."

Sievers raised a skeptical eyebrow. "Your brother does this cockamamie stuff too?"

Avery put her hands on her hips. "That's right. After he left the SEALs…" She paused for dramatic effect. "He became a professional recovery expert." She thought 'recovery expert' sounded more respectable than 'treasure hunter.' "He's found stuff you wouldn't believe."

Sievers merely shrugged.

"Anyway," she went on, "it's a spearhead, right? Maybe we're supposed to affix it to something—like the shaft of a spear, and whatever direction it points is the way we're supposed to go. If it's something like that, then we don't even need the actual Spear. We just have to find where it should go."

She glanced at Stone, hoping for confirmation, but he gave no indication he had even heard her. Instead, he continued to stare into the distance, as if her suggestion did not even merit comment.

Kasey was more direct with her criticism. "I don't know. That sounds a bit too *Raiders of the Lost Ark* for me."

"Well, if you've got a better idea, I'm all ears."

"Sorry, got nothing. I suppose we can look around. Maybe we'll find a sign that says, 'Spear of Destiny' goes here. At least it will give us something to do while we wait for the Dominion to show up."

"Did Patton come here?" Stone said, not looking away from the cliffs.

Avery, still feeling a little defensive, immediately replied. "This was your idea."

Stone finally turned to face her. "That's not what I mean. This is the right place. But we don't know if Patton ever came here, do we?"

"He fought Julio Cardenas near Rubio. That's less than a hundred miles from here as the crow flies."

Stone accepted this with a slight nod. "All right. But that would have been in 1916, more than thirty years before he would have the Spear of Destiny in his hands. And we know that he was killed shortly after that. He would never have had a chance to come here and set things up with the Spear of Destiny."

"So what are you saying?" Kasey broke in, sounding only slightly less annoyed than Avery felt. "Did you get the clue wrong?"

"Maybe." Stone's gaze kept wandering, as if the conversation could not hold his interest, but Avery recognized the eye movement as indicative of both recollection and creative processing. This was what Stone did best, sorting through the raw data, looking for the connections that others missed. She had been trying to do the same with her suggestion, but evidently had missed some critical piece of evidence.

Set aside my prejudices, she reminded herself.

"Patton wasn't talking about the Spear of Destiny," she said. It was more a question than a statement. She was thinking aloud, testing the plausibility of the idea simply by putting it into words, but as soon as she said it, she knew it was true. "There's another spear here. Maybe not a real spear... Maybe a rock formation, or a petroglyph."

"Patton said the Devil came to him." Stone might have been talking to himself. "The Devil gave him a gift. The gift is a secret, left here like a seed planted in a fallow field. The Devil told him how to find it. Told him, 'Go to Cuarenta Casas." This place is the starting point. Patton could have gotten these latitude and longitude coordinates from any map."

"The Devil told him about the 'spear,' whatever it is," Avery said. The ideas were flowing now. She was seeing the problem in a whole new light. "Possessing the Spear of Destiny made Patton remember that."

"'The Spear will point the way.' It's misdirection. Anyone who didn't know him would think the diary *was* talking about the Spear of Destiny, but he meant something else. A spear that points the way..."

"A compass points north," Sievers offered.

Stone's eyes stopped moving. He faced Sievers. "That's it. He gave map coordinates with no cardinal directions. Anyone who recognized what those numbers meant would also know that the 'spear' is a compass needle. It's so simple."

Sievers straightened, looking very pleased with his contribution. "So from here, we just go north?"

"Well, that sounds easy enough," said Kasey. She looked skyward, marking the location of the sun, then turned until she was facing in a northward direction and looking right at the cliffs of Cuarenta Casas.

"Not as easy as it sounds," countered Sievers. "Standard military reporting requires direction *and* distance. North could mean anywhere between here and the North Pole."

"Maybe that's where we're supposed to go," Kasey said with a smirk. "The gift must be in Santa's workshop."

Sievers ignored the comment. "There's also the question of whether we're supposed to follow true north or magnetic north."

Avery frowned. "There's a difference?"

"True north is the earth's axis. All maps are aligned to true north because it's a fixed location. Mostly, anyways. But compasses point to magnetic north, where the earth's magnetic field is the strongest. Depending on where you're standing, there can be several degrees of difference."

"It will be magnetic north," Stone put in. "The spear points the way. He's talking about a compass needle."

"No problem." Kasey began pushing buttons on her wrist GPS. "I can set this to find magnetic north."

"Problem," said Sievers. "The magnetic north pole is constantly moving. It's moved several degrees in just the last decade. There's no telling how much it's moved since 1945."

"Or 1916," added Stone. "If Patton was merely relaying the information he was given, 'Go to Cuarenta Casas and head north,' then he might not have taken that into account either."

Kasey looked at her watch. "I wonder if this thing can adjust for that."

Sievers was not finished. "There's also the question of geomagnetic anomalies. Iron ore deposits can mess with compass readings. Most maps adjust for that in the declination, but your GPS will almost certainly give a different reading than a regular ferromagnetic compass from the early twentieth century."

Kasey dropped her hands to her sides in disgust. "Well, that's five hundred bucks wasted."

Stone stared at the device on her wrist. "We need a compass. A real one."

"I told you," Sievers countered. "Magnetic north has changed."

"Maybe, but if there is an iron deposit here, something specific to this area, then that won't have changed, right?"

Sievers considered this in silence.

"Well, I don't have a *real* compass," Kasey said, with more than a trace of sarcasm. "Maybe we can get one at the gift shop when it opens."

"I can make a compass," Sievers said. "That's basic elementary school science project stuff."

"Do it," Stone said, his tone no longer speculative. "We'll compare your results with Kasey's GPS. If they're the same, we can rule out local magnetic anomalies. Then all we have to do is estimate how much the pole has shifted over the last century."

"Right," griped Kasey. "That's all we have to do."

"It's guesswork, but if we can't figure it out, then neither can the Dominion, so it's a win for us."

They returned to the RAV4 so that Sievers could gather what he needed to fashion a field expedient compass, which consisted of a few items salvaged from the communal trash bag and a needle from a travel-sized sewing kit Sievers took from his backpack.

"You brought a needle and thread?" Avery asked.

"I never go anywhere without 'em."

"In case you pop a button?" Avery asked.

"Something like that." He grinned as if he'd made a joke. "To make this work, we'll need to magnetize the needle by rubbing it against a magnet."

"Did you bring a magnet, too?"

"Several of them actually. The magnets in the door speakers would be perfect, but I don't want to have to tear the car apart to get at them." He rooted in his backpack again. "I think I may have something that will work in here."

A moment later, he was disassembling the ear bud of a pair of headphones. When the plastic shell was cracked to his satisfaction, he began repeatedly sweeping the sewing needle across the exposed miniature speaker, always moving in the same direction. "The old Army survival manual says you can magnetize a needle by rubbing it against a piece of wool," he said, after a few seconds. "But that doesn't actually work. You need a real magnet to make a magnet."

"Good to know. Just in case you're not around next time I need to make a compass."

When Sievers was satisfied that the needle was magnetized, he placed it on a piece of polystyrene foam torn from a food container. He then filled a paper cup with bottled water and set the foam with the needle in the center of the cup. When he let go of it, the needle began to rotate as if someone was gently blowing on it. Sievers waited until it stopped moving, noted the direction the needle was pointing, and then tapped the foam to start it spinning again. A few moments later, the needle was again pointing in the same direction.

"Voila."

"Nice work, MacGyver," remarked Kasey. "The good news is that your Boy Scout contraption agrees with the GPS magnetic. That should save time."

"Hang on to it, Sievers," Stone advised.

Sievers nodded and carefully poured the water back into the bottle. "What's the declination?"

"Magnetic north is about eight degrees east of true north." Kasey held the GPS so they could all see the topographical map displayed on the small screen. "If we head in that direction, it will take us cross country over these hilltops. Not much there really. And we still don't know which way the compass would have pointed a hundred years ago."

Stone stared at the little map for nearly a minute. "We have to consider the human factor. Patton, and whomever it was that told him about this, didn't have access to precise satellite maps and navigational aids, but he must have believed that those two clues—starting point and compass direction—were all anyone would need to find it. If we follow magnetic north and keep our eyes open, maybe we'll see what they saw."

Equipped with fresh water bottles and a buffet of granola bars, they blazed their own trail up to the hilltop and began walking. The cool air and sparse vegetation made for an easy trek despite the altitude—at more than a mile above sea level, Avery found herself quickly growing winded—but the unvarying terrain held little promise for finding clues in the landscape.

After about a hundred yards, Stone suggested checking their position against the makeshift compass. Sievers dutifully decanted some water into the cup and placed the needle. It rotated half a turn and then came to rest pointing at a forty-five degree angle to the left of their direction of travel. Sievers raised a suspicious eyebrow and then repeated the process, with the same results.

"Looks like we've got ourselves a magnetic anomaly," he declared. "Could be a big deposit of iron ore."

"That's not north," Kasey said. "Are we just going to wander around and hope we get lucky?"

"The spear will point the way," Avery murmured.

Stone nodded. "Let's see where it points."

Kasey, outvoted and pessimistic to begin with, assented without further protest. The new course took them down a moderately steep slope to the bottom of a draw and then back up the other side where Sievers took another compass check. This time the needle pointed in almost the same direction as Kasey's GPS.

Stone turned around and studied the landscape they had just traversed. "We passed it," he said, unequivocally. "Back this way."

He was halfway back up the hill when he came to a sudden stop. Avery reached his side a few seconds later and immediately saw what had arrested Stone's attention.

To call it a cave entrance would have been an exaggeration. It was more of a vertical hollow, mostly covered over with years, perhaps even centuries, of sediment that washed down the hill. But the accumulation could not completely hide the opening—barely larger than a rabbit hole—that disappeared into the hillside.

"Sievers, try the compass here."

Sievers did, and the result was astonishing. The needle did not merely orient toward the depression, but actually began drifting across the water to bump against the side of the cup. "Okay, definitely some kind of big magnetic anomaly there."

"This is the place," Stone said, confidently. "We need to dig this out."

"You think there's something buried here?" asked Avery.

"It looks more like the entrance to an abandoned

mineshaft," Sievers said.

"Seriously?" complained Kasey. "Why does everything have to be underground?" Then as if to laugh it off, she turned to Sievers. "Don't suppose you know how to MacGyver a Coke can into a backhoe?"

"Nope. Might be able to do something with a tire iron from the car, though."

"Maybe we should consider coming back tomorrow," Avery said. "With some real tools. It's going to be dark in a couple hours."

"I think it's going to be dark in there no matter what," Kasey muttered.

"I brought a MagLite," Sievers said.

"Of course, you did."

Stone turned away from the mine entrance, an eager gleam in his eye. "This is what we came for. The answers are right in there."

"And they aren't going anywhere," retorted Kasey.

"We aren't the only ones looking for it."

"He's right," Avery said. "We should at least try to dig through."

Sievers, looking as if he had known all along this was a decision they would reach, said simply, "Be right back."

The tire iron proved to be a very effective pick-axe, loosening the soil enough that it could simply be scooped out of the way. It took less than an hour to widen the hole at the top of the depression enough for Sievers to shine his flashlight in and verify that the tunnel opened up beyond the cave-in. He kept digging until it was big enough for him to crawl through, and then proceeded to do exactly that.

He was no tunnel rat. In fact, tight spaces freaked him out a little. His assertiveness was a sham to cover for what he saw as an embarrassing weakness. It was a strategy that had served him well in other panic-inducing situations.

After a short crawl through the freshly dug passage, he slid down a slope of accumulated debris and into a cramped tunnel hewn into solid rock.

"It's a mineshaft all right," he called over his shoulder. He played the light down the length of the passage. Wooden support frames had been placed at intervals, but the beams looked ready to crumble into dust at the slightest disturbance. Cobwebs shrouded the corners and Sievers saw animal spoor. Rats, or some other sort of rodent, had made a home of this place long after the ore had played out.

A faint shuffling noise warned that someone was coming through, and indeed a few seconds later, Stone emerged from the dugout tunnel. Avery came next, almost jittery with excitement at the prospect of exploring the old mine and finding the mysterious treasure that, to all appearances, lay concealed somewhere within. She brushed past the two men and headed deeper into the mine, almost to the limit of the cone of illumination cast by Sievers' single miniature flashlight.

Several minutes passed before Kasey finally came through. After straightening up and brushing the dirt off, she scowled at the others as if daring them to make a joke about claustrophobia. Sievers knew exactly how she felt.

"Hold old do you think this place is?" Avery asked as she ran a hand along one of the support beams. Little puffs of wood dust rose from her fingertips like smoke.

Sievers winced. "That's probably not a good idea. And to answer your question… Old. A couple hundred years, maybe."

Avery drew her hand back but did not appear to be the least bit apprehensive about venturing deeper into the excavation.

Sievers had explored a few caverns in his lifetime, as well as crumbling ruins in Afghanistan and Iraq. The mineshaft was nothing like those. It reminded him more of a crawlspace beneath a house—cramped and miserable. He could not imagine what life had been like for the miners, toiling forward a few inches at a time, dragging out rocks by the bucket full for months on end, just to procure a few ounces of silver or gold. The ceiling was low, barely high enough to allow him to walk upright, and the air was thick with the smell of damp earth and mildew.

The shaft was not perfectly straight but meandered left and

right, probably following the course of the ore vein. After about a hundred feet, it opened up into a larger chamber, with upright support pillars and some rickety-looking scaffolding positioned along one wall. As they entered, a low, groaning noise filled the air and a stream of dirt began to trickle from the ceiling right in front of them.

"Officially not liking it here," Kasey whispered.

Sievers swept the area quickly with his light, locating two more tunnels that led off in different directions, then scanned the area below the scaffold platform. The area was strewn with heaps of loose rock and litter from random cave-ins, along with broken tools and scraps of wood, detritus not worth packing up to the surface. Then the light fell upon something that he did not expect, and he froze in shock and horror.

"Is that…?"

It was. Resting at the base of the wall and staring back at them was the unmistakable outline of a human skull.

Avery hurried forward, as if finding skulls in dank abandoned holes in the ground was the most natural thing in the world for her, and knelt beside the skeleton to which it was still attached. Sievers and the others approached also, but with slightly less enthusiasm. Stone seemed distracted, peering into the darkness of the adjoining tunnels and sniffing the air experimentally.

As Sievers overcame his initial surprise, he saw the remains with more clarity. The skull, yellowed with age, was not completely intact. Several of the front teeth were missing, and there was an irregular hole, about the size of a quarter-dollar coin, in the top of the cranium. The skeleton was dressed in dark clothes, possibly a suit, though the garment was so ragged from the passage of time and rodent predations that it was impossible to say with any certainty. The object clutched in one bony hand, however, while covered in a scale of rust, was instantly recognizable.

"That's a gun," Avery said, confirming his observation. She knelt over the skeleton, this time taking care to touch nothing, and studied the tableau like a crime scene investigator. "I think he…"

She trailed off, unwilling to formalize the observation, but Sievers had already put the clues together. The missing teeth, the top of the skull missing, the gun in hand; the man had died from a self-inflicted gunshot wound. A suicide.

Her visual inspection complete, Avery now reached out, gently tugging something out from under the skeleton's left arm. It was, Sievers saw, an old-fashioned valise bag. The boiled leather had been gnawed at the corners, but was otherwise intact, as were, presumably, its contents, though when Avery tried to loosen the buckle holding it closed, the strap snapped off in her hands. She shrugged and then with only a little more caution, pried the case open. "Bring the light over here."

Sievers approached and shone his light down into the interior of the valise. There was a glint of metal reflecting in the deepest recesses, but what immediately caught his attention was a folded sheet of parchment positioned intentionally so that anyone opening the bag would immediately encounter it. Avery picked up the paper and carefully unfolded it.

The page was covered with meticulously precise lines of flowing script. The writing looked like a long continuous line, mostly flat but for little peaks to indicate individual letters. "What is that? Arabic?"

Avery laughed. "Seriously? It's cursive. This is how people used to write before text messages."

"You can read that?"

"In my line of work, you have to be able to read old handwritten letters." She continued reading silently for several seconds. When she got to the end, she let out a gasp. "I'll be damned."

CHAPTER 22

June 24, 1916

> *Dear ?*

> *How strange? I cannot think of a single person to be the recipient of these, my final words. It was a mistake to have dared live as long as I have—a mistake which I will forthwith correct.*

> *I do not know why I have persisted so long. Perhaps if I were the misanthrope so many believe me to be, I would have retired from this struggle long ago. Alas, I believe I have lingered this long, long enough to see my sons buried, and all my friendships turn to dust, in the futile hope that my admittedly pessimistic appraisements might be proven false.*

> *Enough about that. Of all the words I have written, I care the least about these, but there are a few matters to which I must attend before I end the journey.*

> *It has been a month since I visited the young cavalryman near Rubio. (If you are the man I think you are, then it is you who reads this now). I shall say now what I did not have the time or inclination to say then.*

> *Three years ago, when I made known my intention to travel south and observe the war in Mexico, I was approached by none other than the president himself, and asked to conduct secret negotiations with Villa and Carranza, the generals of the Revolution. I fulfilled my duty in good faith. The generals, particularly that brute Villa, did not, which left me in a quandary. Should I complete my mission and return to Washington with the signed agreement? Would it make any difference at all? I believe it certainly would not to a man like Villa—All he knows is how to shed blood.*

> *This is the problem that has occupied my thoughts in the months that have followed, and now, at the end of my journey, the answer yet eludes me. Perhaps you who read this will be more decisive than I.*

> *So there. It is done. I have finished my last duty, and now I must depart for another unknown destination. Farewell.*

> *Sincerely Yours,*

Ambrose Bierce

"Ambrose Bierce," Avery repeated the name after finishing the letter, but could tell from the blank looks she received that no one recognized it. "The writer, Ambrose Bierce. 'Occurrence at Owl Creek Bridge'?"

"That kind of rings a bell," said Sievers, hesitantly.

"Ambrose Bierce wrote ghost stories in the late nineteenth century. Owl Creek Bridge was probably his most famous. It's a short story about…well, I don't want to spoil it for you, but let's just say it's Twilight Zone stuff. Which is sort of weird when you consider that his disappearance is one of the world's great unsolved mysteries."

"Until now," Stone pointed out. "Is he our 'Devil'?"

Avery nodded. "Bierce got his start working at a newspaper as a printer's apprentice. The unofficial title for the job was 'printer's devil.' He was also a satirist. One of his most famous works was a collection of satirical definitions that he called 'the Devil's Dictionary.' He was kind of a cantankerous old guy. I think he liked that nickname."

Another ominous groan filled the chamber, but this time even Kasey seemed to barely notice.

"Back in 1913," Avery went on, "Bierce traveled to Mexico to observe the revolution. Or at least that's what everyone believes. It sounds like he was actually some kind of secret peace envoy for President Wilson. He sent a few letters from Mexico, then just vanished. Everyone assumed that he was killed by Villa's men. He was very critical of the revolution. He agreed with their cause but felt that the fighters were little more than bandits and murders."

"But he was actually hiding out here the whole time," Stone said.

"In 1916, Villa's forces escalated and started carrying out attacks across the border. President Wilson retaliated by sending General Pershing's Punitive Expedition—"

"Which Patton was part of," Sievers put in.

"Which Patton was part of," Avery confirmed. "It sounds like Bierce felt some kind of connection to Patton. I'll have to do some research on that. So he comes out of hiding, travels down to meet with Patton and gives him…what exactly?"

"The Devil's Gift," Stone muttered. "Bierce didn't actually give Patton anything, but he did tell him about it. The agreement he negotiated. The secret mission for President Wilson. That's what this was all about."

"Why would the president choose this Bierce guy?" asked Sievers. "I mean, you said he wrote ghost stories."

"He was also a journalist, a war reporter, and a veteran of the Civil War. He had very strong political opinions and wasn't afraid to publish them. And he had close ties to the newspaper giant William Randolph Hearst. He would have made an ideal envoy because of his celebrity status."

"So he tells Patton about his mission and the deal he made with the revolutionaries," Stone said. "Tells him about this place. Then he comes back here and… finishes things. Patton, for whatever reason, decides not to tell anyone about it. Thirty years later, he realizes that he can use it to become president, but before he can do that, he gets killed."

Avery nodded again. "And now the Dominion is after it."

"And the Russians," Kasey added. "So what exactly is *it*?"

Avery laid the letter aside, delved into the valise, and took out a formal-looking presentation portfolio of black or possibly navy blue dyed leather, embossed with the seal of the United States. She opened it and scanned the document contained within. Unlike Bierce's low profile script, the writing on the parchment in the portfolio was elegant and easy to read, the work of a professional calligrapher. "It's a treaty," she announced "'A Treaty between the United States of America and the sovereign States of Northern Mexico.'"

"A treaty?" said Sievers. "We weren't at war with Mexico in 1913."

"It's not a peace treaty," Avery explained, as she began skimming the document. "It's a…Oh!"

She lowered the portfolio slowly, as if its contents were some volatile chemical compound. In a way, that wasn't far from the truth. "This is going to blow your mind."

"Then speak up miss," said a new voice from the mouth of

the chamber. Avery was abruptly plunged into darkness as Sievers swung his light toward the source. Its beam illuminated the faces of three strangers.

No, not quite strangers. Avery recognized one of them from the Library of Congress, one of the men who had tried to abduct her. All three held pistols and looked ready to use them.

"Go on," said the man in the center of the group. "We've come all this way. I want to know if it's everything we've heard it is."

CHAPTER 23

El Paso, Texas

Although he had not formally placed them under arrest, Director Waller made it abundantly clear that Tam and Greg would not be going anywhere for some time. At one point, early on, he had threatened to place them in the general population—where most of the illegals rounded up by the border patrol were kept awaiting deportation—but Tam knew this was a bluff. Waller wanted them where he could keep an eye on them, because as irritated as the Customs officer was, he also knew that a dark storm was brewing to the south, and he was sea-wise enough to know that it would eventually blow his way. His "guests" were part of it, and even though he was not happy about what they had done, he knew that there was probably a very good reason for it. So, instead of consigning them to an overcrowded holding facility, Waller put them in a conference room, under constant supervision, and there they stayed, in a sort of administrative limbo. Waller had not even let them make a phone call.

Yet, somehow, a phone call had been made. Shortly after three in the afternoon, the door to the conference room opened and an innocuous looking man—Caucasian, mid-forties, average height and build, brown hair parted on the right and combed down flat, wearing a tasteful, but inexpensive gray suit—entered the room.

Tam recognized him instantly and jumped to her feet, ignoring the throb of pain that shot through her bruised extremities. "Sir."

"Sit down, Tam." The man turned and closed the door firmly behind him, then strode to the table where she and Greg had been sitting. He did not sit down, but instead placed his hands on the back of a chair, as if in need of support. He stared at Tam for several long seconds before speaking again. "Christ

Almighty. What a mess."

Tam said nothing. She was not exactly intimidated; there were few people on earth who could manage that, but the Deputy Director of the National Clandestine Service, answerable only to the agency's director and the president himself, was her boss, and right now, she needed to be in his good graces.

"I've burned up a lot of chits to get you out of this mess," he went on. "First that business with Stone, and now…For God's sake, you invaded Mexico. Please, tell me this is worth what I've paid for it."

That was the cue Tam had been waiting for. "You know I wouldn't be here if it wasn't."

The director heaved a sigh. "You were right about the Dominion before. That cuts you a lot of slack. But you're going to have to sell it."

"There's a local businessman named Roger Lavelle. He's Dominion. Version 2.0."

"What does that mean?"

"More interested in ruling the world than burning it down," Tam explained. "He's a predator, not an ideologue."

"Okay. Go on."

"Lavelle is working to destabilize the Mexican government so he can install his puppet, a guy named Esperanza."

An irritated frown crossed the director's bland visage. "Destabilizing Mexico isn't exactly a tall order. That's like deciding to make the ocean wet. And I'm not sure that ranks up there with the Norfolk attacks as an act of terrorism."

"There's more to it, but we're still digging. That's why I need to get back out there."

"How can you be sure?"

"Because Lavelle tried to kill us when we got too close to Esperanza," muttered Greg.

Tam nodded. "And he's working with the Russians. With Oleg Samsonov."

That got the director's attention. "Are you sure? Samsonov?"

"I was as close to him in Vienna as I am to you now." It

was an exaggeration, but only a tiny one. "Samsonov and the Dominion are working together, so whatever this is, it's a lot bigger than internal Mexican politics."

The director tapped his fingers on the back of the chair, then pulled it away from the table and sat down. "We've been monitoring troop movements in the Crimea. The Russians are fortifying their positions and it looks like they're prepping to push their invasion even deeper into Ukraine."

"Saber rattling?"

"It would be stupid for them to take it any further, but they're desperate. Their economy is sinking like the Titanic. They've got a surplus of oil that they can't afford to sell because prices are at rock bottom. A war to take back their empire is probably looking pretty good right now, but there's just one thing standing in their way."

"NATO."

The director nodded. "And specifically us. We wouldn't need to even put boots on the ground. The Russian oligarchs have invested heavily in American banks because the dollar is a lot stronger than the ruble. It's dirty money—mob money—and we know where it is. They know that if they try anything, we'll freeze and seize."

"Why haven't we already done that?"

"It's the new balance of terror. If we took their money, they'd have nothing left to lose, and things could get really ugly. And there's the fact that sometimes it's better to deal with the devil you know. If the oligarchy goes down, the men who replace them would probably be even worse."

Tam considered this. Was Destiny somehow designed to distract attention from what was happening in Eastern Europe? If so, it would have to be something more than just fomenting political instability in Mexico. She decided to let the director reach his own conclusions about that. "Samsonov met with Lavelle's men in Vienna. They have the ball now. If we can shut Lavelle down, we can stop whatever it is the Russians want to accomplish. You need to let me get back out there."

The director stared at the table, evidently weighing her request. "The State Department has made it clear that they don't want us interfering in Mexico's troubles. Our government's policy is to offer whatever aid is requested but to let things play out. We can't afford to be seen as empire-building."

The comment reminded Tam of what Samsonov had said to her outside the Hofburg. *The sun is setting on the American Empire.* "This isn't just about Mexico," she said, choosing her words carefully, knowing that she couldn't back them up. "The Russians are targeting us. America. Whatever they are up to, it's meant to hurt us."

The director did not meet her gaze but after a few seconds, reached inside his suit jacket and took something from the inner pocket. It was a phone. Tam's phone. Waller's men had taken it from her, along with her Makarov. He placed it on the table and slid it toward her. "I'm going to trust that you know what you're doing. If you let me down…"

He did not finish the comment, but Tam was able to fill in the blanks. If she failed to produce real results, or if the magnitude of the threat did not equal the political capital the director had invested in her, they would both be on the chopping block.

CHAPTER 24

Cuarenta Casas, Mexico

No one moved, but Stone could sense both Sievers and Kasey calculating the odds and bracing themselves for action. There were three gunmen, with pistols drawn and held at the ready, against the four of them, but Stone and Avery were unarmed. Moreover, Sievers and Kasey would have to draw their weapons in order to fire, and in the fraction of a second required for them to do that, the Dominion gunmen would have time to react. Time to fire.

They could miss, though at such close range, it seemed unlikely. If it came to a shootout, the odds were against the four of them coming out unscathed. Someone would get hurt. Someone would probably get killed.

The Dominion operatives were a completely unknown variable. People with guns were unpredictable, especially those without formal training, and there was no way to know what background these men possessed. One of them was the man he had faced down at the Library of Congress, but the circumstances had been very different. Stone knew that if he did not take control of this situation, things would spin out of control very quickly.

He took a step forward, arms raised. "Just take it. No reason for anyone to get hurt."

The abrupt capitulation surprised the leader of the group. Stone could tell that it also caught his own companions off guard. He turned, nodding to them. Would they understand what he was trying to do? Sievers might, but he was also former military, used to violence as a first resort. He let his gaze flicker in the direction of the tunnels behind them, but with the light pointed at the gunmen, he could not tell if the gesture had been understood, much less seen by the others.

He reached out to Avery, palm open. "Let them have it. It's

not worth dying for."

Avery stared back at him in bewilderment.

"It's just a piece of paper," he said. "It won't change anything."

Disagreement was writ large in her eyes. "Do you realize what it is?" She spoke in a low voice, her words clearly meant for Stone's ears alone.

"Why don't you tell us?" suggested the leader of the gunmen.

Stone frowned. If the situation dragged out, the chances of something catastrophic occurring would increase exponentially.

"We can't let them have this," Avery whispered.

"No?" The Dominion gunman feigned disappointment. "Well, I'll just take a wild guess then. It's an agreement to annex northern Mexico for the United States. Am I close?"

Stone could see confirmation in Avery's unblinking eyes.

Sievers laughed. "Is that what you're all spun up over? Shoot. I might have been daydreaming about girls in my high school civics class, but even I know that it takes more than a piece of paper to make that happen. Especially when that paper and everyone who signed it has been dead for a hundred years."

The folksy bravado was a front, disguising Sievers' readiness, but his words were not wrong. Without ratification from Congress, the document was irrelevant. The very fact that it had been lost to history was proof enough that its authors and signatories had not pursued the agreement following Bierce's disappearance.

So why did the Dominion want it so badly?

"Avery," Stone said, keeping his voice calm. "It's just a piece of paper. It's not worth getting killed for."

"You really think they'll just let us walk out of here?" she retorted.

Stone frowned. She was right, of course, but he did not want their captors realizing that they knew it. He turned to their leader. "You will, right? We give you the treaty, and everyone can go their merry way?"

The man gave an acquiescent, and completely insincere, shrug. "Sure."

Stone turned back in Avery's direction, but his eyes went first to Sievers then to Kasey. He mouthed the words, *Wait for it*, and closed his eyes for a moment, hoping they would get the message. When he opened them, he saw Sievers nod, almost imperceptibly.

Avery continued to clutch the portfolio.

"Avery. It's just paper. Trust me."

She held on a moment longer, then relented and held it out to him. Stone took the case and moving with exaggerated caution, walked toward the trio of gunmen. He started to extend the portfolio, but then drew back at the last second. "Just to satisfy *my* curiosity," he said. "Did you figure it out for yourself, or follow us here?"

An irritated frown creased the other man's face. "Once we realized where you were going, it made sense."

It was an obvious lie, but Stone let it pass. "And the Spear? It showed you the way?"

This time, the response was honest. "Not exactly. But the general was kind enough to leave us a little tip, so to speak, to prove that we were on the right track."

"Oh? We must have missed that. What was it?"

"A coin. A gold double-eagle. Part of the money that President Wilson paid to buy Mexico for the U.S." He grinned and looked past Stone, in Avery's direction. "You see, it's more than just a piece of paper. It's a bill of sale. We paid for it. The treaty just proves it."

Stone inclined his head. "Well, that's definitely going to change the history books." He started to proffer the case again. "I have your word? You'll let us go?"

"Cross my heart," the man said, a little too quickly.

Stone smiled and held out the portfolio, but then pulled back again even as the other man started to reach for it. "So how does this help you exactly? If northern Mexico has actually been part of the United States for the last century, that would mean that everyone living here right now would actually be an American citizen. Forgive me for being blunt, but it seems to me like the last thing the Dominion would want is a lot of brown people claiming U.S. citizenship."

The man grunted in reply. "That's not your problem." He held his hand out, shaking it emphatically. "Give it to me."

"Sure." Stone thrust the portfolio out and opened his hand, letting it fall.

The other man made a reflexive grab for it, just as Stone knew he would, but missed. Stone was already moving. "Now, Sievers!"

The chamber was plunged into ominous blackness as Sievers, right on cue, switched off his light, but the effect was short-lived as the chamber erupted with the noise and fury of gunshots. The muzzle flashes were almost blindingly bright, yet were too brief to provide illumination. The reports were deafening, causing Stone's ears to ring with the first shot fired, and the air stank of sulfur, but he did not feel anything that might have been a bullet tearing into his flesh.

At the instant he dropped the case with the treaty, Stone had launched himself away from the Dominion men and their guns, and toward the vertical support beam in the center of the chamber. His course was chosen deliberately, he knew with absolute certainty where each footstep would land and the exact moment that he would collide with the post. The only thing he could not predict was what would happen afterward.

His shoulder jolted with the impact, but then the post buckled under his weight, and he went sprawling into the darkness, half-entangled with the splintered remains of the rough-hewn timber. He felt, or perhaps merely sensed, a downpour of earth as the unsupported ceiling began to collapse down on top of him.

CHAPTER 25

At the exact moment when Eric Trent thought success was in his grasp, everything went to hell. As the treaty case started to fall, he did exactly what his rational brain told him he should not do: he reacted. Then the lights went out, and the word exploded into violence.

The reports from out of the darkness startled him and he instinctively tried to shrink himself into a protective curl, even as his knees hit the floor, and one outstretched hand found the smooth leather portfolio.

The glancing contact grounded him, just a little. This was what he had come for. No matter what else happened, he had to get away with the treaty. He grasped hold of it and pulled it in close to his chest, shielding it from the destructive chaos that was erupting out of the inky blackness that surrounded him.

Which way to the exit? He had a flashlight in one pocket. Did he dare use it? He and the others had crept silently into the mineshaft and followed the dim glow at the far end of the tunnel like a beacon, their own lights turned off to keep from betraying their approach. If he turned it on now, he would give his position away, and judging by the muzzle flashes, his men weren't the only ones with guns.

Something struck him on the back of the head. Not a bullet, he decided. If it had been that, he would have lost consciousness or even died instantly. No, it was a stone, dislodged from the ceiling and part of an increasingly heavy cascade of earth raining down upon him. The mine was caving in.

He turned, hopefully orienting in the direction of the exit, and crawled forward awkwardly using just one hand. His pistol was gone, but he did not spare a thought for it. The leather case was what mattered, and he would not risk damaging it by dragging it across the mine floor.

The cascading dirt hammered against his back, driving him flat, but he kept squirming forward until his outthrust hand encountered something that didn't move. He probed the wall, left and right and felt the rough texture of a support post, and just beyond it, nothingness. His first estimate of the tunnel's location had been off by only a degree or two. He kept crawling, and then after he put some distance between himself and the chamber where the gun battle was still raging, he risked getting to his feet.

A faint spot of light was visible directly ahead, and he hastened toward it, tripping and rebounding off the walls of the narrow passage as he went. He forgot about the earthen slope leading up to the tiny opening through which they had entered, and stumbled forward onto it, but with the end in sight, nothing could slow him down. He scrambled up the slope and thrust his head and shoulders into the hole, squirming toward daylight. When he reached the end, it was as if he had been shot out of a cannon. He slid headfirst down the far slope, the rocks tearing at his clothing and shredding the exposed skin of his face and arms before he finally came to rest.

For a moment, all he could do was savor the fresh air and the openness of the sky. Then he remembered what it was that had taken him into the dark bowels of the earth. He rolled over, inspecting the treaty portfolio. To his dismay, the dark leather was now a dirty gray-brown, scraped and scuffed like a worn-out pair of shoes.

"No," he gasped. "Please God, let it be all right." With trembling fingers, he opened the case.

The treaty was undamaged. It had survived his desperate escape without as much as a frayed corner. Trent closed the case gently and held it close to his chest again.

A cloud of dust billowed from the hole in the hillside. Trent stood and cocked his ear toward the mineshaft, but heard only the creaking sound of the earth settling after a disturbance. He waited a minute, wondering if anyone else would emerge, but no one did.

The enormity of this finally hit him. The men that had accompanied him were trapped, buried in the cave-in, probably already dead.

No, no probably about it. They were dead, and no amount of wishful thinking was going to change that. It was up to him to make sure that their sacrifice was not in vain.

He took a deep breath, gathering his wits and his courage, and then started up the hill. It had been a costly victory, but a victory nonetheless. The key to the Dominion's great plan lay in his hands. There was no time to waste.

Destiny would soon be a reality.

CHAPTER 26

The darkness transformed the already oppressive confines of the mine chamber into a tomb. Despite Stone's warning, Kasey felt paralyzed by the sudden weight of so much impenetrable lightlessness.

Then the chamber exploded with gunfire.

The heat of incoming rounds creased the air above her and she threw herself flat on the floor. Her training overcame the inertia of conscious thought; her pistol found its way into her hand and before she knew what she was doing, she was firing at muzzle flashes just a few yards away.

She could not tell if she was hitting anything, but as her mind caught up with what her body was automatically doing, she realized that her answering fire might well be giving her position away to the Dominion gunmen. She let go of the trigger and rolled sideways, into the embrace of darkness where she bumped against something and felt it move.

Avery?

Shouting down the irrational fears that would, she knew, become a self-fulfilling prophecy if she did not master them, she reached out with her free hand and found what she thought was a leg. She groped her way up, finding a hand—definitely Avery—and then dragged the other woman away from the incessant gunfire, toward what she hoped was the back wall of the chamber, where she knew a tunnel led even deeper into the mine.

That was when the ceiling began raining down.

The gunfire abruptly ceased, and through the ringing in her ears, Kasey could hear the noise of rocks hitting the ground behind her.

"Stay with me!"

She had no idea if Avery heard her, but she maintained a

firm grip on the disembodied hand and kept moving forward, found the wall, then the tunnel mouth. As she moved into it, she struck something…no, another someone.

"Who?" The shout was barely audible, but she thought it sounded like Sievers.

"Me! I've got Avery."

The shape moved aside. "Go!"

Kasey plunged into the darkness, dragging Avery behind her. The rock scraped through the fabric of her jeans, shredding the skin of her knees, but the pain was just one dull sensation in a symphony of stimuli. Time and space lost all meaning. She might have been crawling for days, or perhaps just a few seconds.

And then, with no warning whatsoever, light returned to the world. Kasey's spirits lifted, but only a little. The ebb of darkness revealed the unchanged hopelessness of their situation.

Avery was breathing fast, almost hyperventilating, with tears cutting tracks through the mask of dirt that now clung to her face. Kasey realized that she was not in much better shape and bit her lip until the tremors racking her torso finally subsided. Further back, she saw Sievers, his back to them, crouched in what she immediately recognized as a shooting stance. His flashlight lay on the ground beside him, pointing toward the mouth of the tunnel, but the beam was being reflected back from a shimmering impenetrable curtain of dust. After a few seconds of scrutiny, Sievers holstered his pistol, picked up the light, and began moving up the passage.

He was also covered in dirt, but Kasey did not fail to notice the darker hue staining one arm. "You all right?" she croaked.

"I've been better." His voice sounded distant, funereal. "It's just a graze."

Kasey bit back a pessimistic reply. "Stone?"

Sievers' face creased in alarm, and then he looked back the way they had come. "Stone! Give a shout!"

There was no reply.

"Damn it!" Sievers raged. He shouted twice more, then turned back. "Screw it. First things first. We have to get out of here." He shone the light up the tunnel. "Should we see where that leads?"

Kasey's first impulse was to shriek in dismay. Going deeper into the mine sounded like a very bad idea. But she resisted the urge and answered with an equivocal shrug. "Knock yourself out."

Sievers frowned but said nothing as he stepped cautiously over the two women and ventured along the passage. With the flashlight pointed away and his body mostly filling the tunnel, the oppressive darkness soon returned, and Kasey reconsidered her position.

"Come on," she told Avery. "We should probably stay together."

Avery nodded dumbly, then looked up. "What about Stone? We can't just leave without… without knowing."

"The best thing we can do for him is find a way out."

Avery blinked as if unable to comprehend this logic. Kasey reached out and drew her to her feet, then headed down the tunnel after the diminishing glow of Sievers' flashlight.

They caught up with him just a few seconds later, stopped cold at a dead end. "We're not getting out this way," he declared.

Kasey's heart began pounding in her chest. "Told you," she said, trying to sound cocky instead of vindictive or just plain terrified. Trying and failing.

"Let's head back. There was another tunnel."

"And if that one's a dead end, too?"

"Then we start digging."

Kasey felt Avery's hand tighten in her own and knew the other woman was probably as panicked as she. Kasey knew she needed to do something to distract them both from the harsh reality of their situation. "Avery, did I hear you right? That treaty made Mexico part of the U.S.?"

"What? Um…Yeah. I mean, not all of Mexico. Mostly just the northern states."

Sievers seemed to grasp what Kasey was trying to do. "There's no way that would ever fly, right?" he said as he nudged past them. "You can't just write a piece of paper and buy another country."

"Well, probably not anymore, but that's how America got as big as it is. That and conquest. The treaty mentioned unresolved land claims from the Mexican-American War."

Kasey tried to recall her American history lessons from college. "That's how we got California."

"And most of the American southwest. But during the war, American troops actually pushed as far as Mexico City, and a lot of your congressmen wanted to claim all that territory. Manifest Destiny. They were outnumbered by other lawmakers who thought it was a dangerous overreach of power, and in the end, the Treaty of Guadalupe Hidalgo drew the border pretty much where it is today, except for a bit of Arizona and New Mexico that came with the Gadsden Purchase ten years later."

Sievers set a slow pace, allowing Avery's impromptu lecture to calm all their nerves. "So what changed? Why did President Wilson think he could reclaim those territories?"

"Two things. First, in the 1860s, the French invaded Mexico and installed Maximillian as emperor of Mexico. This was in direct opposition to the Monroe Doctrine, which held that the Americas should be kept free of European influence, but because of the Civil War, there wasn't much that could be done. By 1867, the Mexicans managed to overthrow Maximillian. The Cinco de Mayo holiday celebrates the Battle of Puebla, which was sort of the opening shot in their war to kick the French out.

"The second development was the Mexican Revolution of 1910. Not only was there the possibility that the unrest would spill across the border—which did happen in 1916—there was also a very real chance that European powers might again try to regain a foothold in the Western Hemisphere. Wilson saw a chance to permanently end that threat and stop any future violence by negotiating with both rebel leaders and the governors of the northern states. My guess is that, when Bierce vanished with the treaty, Wilson shelved the idea. World War I came along and pretty much put an end to European imperialism."

"Did the Mexicans want to join the U.S.?"

"At the time, most of the political power in Mexico was in

the hands of wealthy property owners. If you were a rural farmer, you lived at the whim of whoever owned the land you worked." Avery shrugged. "It's not much different today I suppose. America is still the land of opportunity, right? If it wasn't, you wouldn't have such a problem with illegal immigration."

Sievers gave a noncommittal grunt. They had reached the end of the tunnel and were once more confronted with the settling dust cloud from the cave-in.

Kasey felt some of her panic rising again, so she forced herself to stay with the conversation. "Back up a second. You said something about Manifest Destiny."

Avery's eyes went wide. "Of course. How could I be so stupid? I was so fixated on the Spear of Destiny… It all makes sense. The Dominion wants to create an American empire to dominate the hemisphere. Their version of Manifest Destiny."

"I thought the Dominion wanted to overthrow America," Sievers said. "Not make it bigger." He shone his light into the dust cloud. "If those guys made it out before the roof fell in, it might be something we need to worry about."

Kasey thought Sievers was right on both counts. Something about Avery's explanation did not quite mesh with the facts, particularly with the Russians being involved. Still, it was the start of a working theory. "The Dominion has known about the treaty for a while. They knew it was out here somewhere, and what it said. My guess is that their plan is to go ahead with Destiny…whether they have the treaty or not."

"Which is one more reason we need to get our butts out of here," Sievers said. He took a tentative step into the haze. "Better stay close. And you might want to avoid breathing this crap."

Kasey tugged her shirt collar up in a futile effort to cover her mouth and started forward, just a step behind Sievers. The gloom enfolded him, almost completely eclipsing the rays from his flashlight, and Kasey's claustrophobia returned with a vengeance, not mere discomfort, but a panic so complete that it overwhelmed her voluntary nervous system. Without conscious thought, she drew back, letting go of Avery's hand and bolting for the relative safety of the tunnel, but just two steps out into the pervasive cloud had left her completely disoriented. She crashed into the wall, gasped and breathed in a mouthful of dust. She began to claw at the wall, desperate to find the mouth of the tunnel, if only to be free of the choking dust, then felt a hand close around her wrist and pull her forward.

Kasey screamed.

CHAPTER 27

Mexico City, Mexico

An unnatural silence reigned in the assembly hall as Esperanza took his seat. How was it possible, he wondered, for so many people, five hundred deputies and God only knew how many aides and journalists, to occupy such a vast space and yet make no noise at all? Were they all, like him, afraid to even breathe?

He glanced down at the pages spread out on the tabletop before him. The words that he had written, labored over, poured his heart into, seemed alien to him. Dangerous. Once he spoke them, there would be no turning back. Everything would change, and while he sincerely believed the change was vital to the survival of his nation, and perhaps in a very literal sense, his own survival as well, now, standing at the precipice, he could not help but feel doubt.

He began speaking, reading the words, not daring to look up.

There were many among the gathered deputies of the congressional union that he counted as friends, many who openly supported what he intended to do, yet he knew that there were also many who would stand against him. Even among those who professed to be on his side, there were some who did so only for cynical motives. Some of the deputies were complicit in the crimes which he was here to enumerate. Directly or indirectly, they were guilty of corruption, of receiving support from the criminal elements which now held Mexico in a stranglehold.

That was the great lie behind political clichés like the "war on drugs" or being "tough on crime." The policies and enforcement measures ostensibly created to stem the spread of drug trafficking and human exploitation often served only to make those endeavors more profitable, reinforcing the very problem they were meant to curb and enriching both the criminals and their cronies in positions of power. Even now, he imagined, some of them were considering how they would be able to reap profit from Esperanza's desperate plan.

In an almost mechanical tone, he recited the dire litany of crimes which stretched like creeper vines through the infrastructure of the Mexican political system. Tens of thousands dead—some estimates placed the number as high as 120,000—thousands more missing, either dead and buried in secret, or worse, sold into slavery and prostitution abroad. Billions spent, wasted really. And perhaps worst of all, the complete loss of faith in the government to protect its citizens. The military and police—those that were not already bought and paid for—were impotent in the face of the cartels. The rural farmers, in desperation, had formed their own vigilante militias to fight the oppressors, and many such were already organizing into revolutionary armies, ready to take the fight to the men they saw as truly responsible. Others, numbering into the hundreds of thousands, had simply given up on the country of their birth, fleeing to the United States of America, where even the endless ridicule, persecution, and exploitation were preferable to the hopelessness of remaining in Mexico.

Lavelle had been right about one thing. The situation was beyond fixing. Yet, could he now bring himself to utter the terminal diagnosis? To admit that the fight to save Mexico from itself was lost beyond all hope?

He paused as he reached the closing paragraph, not for dramatic effect as some would probably believe, but rather because he had reached the precipice. The words on the paper seemed to burn his eyes.

President Mendoza has failed Mexico. His inability to halt the spread of violence and his toleration of corruption in the military and police constitutes an act of treason against our nation. I call upon this body to indict President Mendoza for his crimes, to place him on trial before the Senate, and to remove him from office.

He opened his mouth, but no sound came out. The words felt like lead in his chest. If he spoke them aloud, it would breathe life into a creature over which he would have no control.

This will mean the end of Mexico, he thought. *Can I destroy my country in order to save it?*

In that instant, he knew that the decision was not his to make.

He folded the paper over, slid it into a pocket, and raised his eyes to the president of the chamber of deputies. "There are some here who believe as I do, that we have reached a critical moment in our history. We cannot succeed if we do not acknowledge how we have failed. Nor can we save our world without being prepared to make the ultimate sacrifice."

The words tumbled from his mouth, from his heart, sounding incoherent in his ears, but he pressed on.

"The sacrifice that I speak of is something that I have only recently learned about. It is something both wonderful and terrible that will change our world. But it is not my place to tell you of it. I have not been elected to lead, to serve. I do not have the right to make this decision for our nation. President Mendoza has that honor, and it is to him alone that I will reveal what I have learned.

"I call upon you, *Señor Presidente*, to meet with me here, to listen to what I have to say and to lead Mexico into the future."

A numb sensation spread throughout his body as the words echoed through the chamber. The deputies stared at him in stunned disbelief. This was not at all what was supposed to happen. The cheers, or in some cases jeers, with which they had intended to reply to the expected call for Mendoza's impeachment, fizzled like wet gunpowder. Esperanza himself was unsure of what to do next, but there was nothing more to say, so he stood up, fumbled with his chair, and then strode from the hall.

A rustling noise grew in the air behind him, but it wasn't until he reached the exit that he realized the sound had been applause. Only then did he know that he had made the right decision.

Roger Lavelle was waiting for him just outside the door. The Texan's arms were folded across his chest, and his face was a grim mask of barely contained ire. "You went off script,

Guillermo," he said in a cold, accusatory tone.

Strangely, Esperanza felt no need to defend his decision. "You would not understand. You are not Mexican."

"And I thank God for that," Lavelle said, but then his scowl softened. "Fortunately, you haven't screwed things up too badly."

The comment took some of the wind from Esperanza's sails. "This will be something for Mexico to decide, Roger. It's not up to me or you, no matter what this treaty of yours says."

"Oh, I wouldn't be too sure about that, but don't you worry. If Mendoza takes you up on your offer, and I've every reason to believe he will, then we might be able to pull this off after all."

He clapped Esperanza on the shoulder and then turned on his heel and walked away. As Esperanza watched the Texan's retreating form, he felt the numbness return. What kind of game was Lavelle playing?

CHAPTER 28

Cuarenta Casas, Mexico

Stone pulled the shrieking figure close and hugged her tight. "Kasey! It's okay. It's me."

The screaming stopped, but he could feel her shaking against him and knew that his reassurance was a temporary fix at best. "I found a way out," he continued. "The others? Are they okay?"

Her reply was a faint tremor that might have been a nod.

"Avery! Sievers!"

A faint glow appeared in the haze of dust, growing brighter until Stone could make out two human forms. "Stone!" Sievers shouted. "Damn, if I'm not actually glad to see you."

"Likewise, on all counts."

"We ain't getting out the way we came in," Sievers said. "It's totally blocked. I did find one of those guys. Not sure if it was a bullet that got him or the rock that caved his head in, but either way, he's toast. Don't know about the others."

"That's all right. There's another exit." He motioned for them to follow and led the way into the other tunnel which branched off the main chamber. As they moved away from the site of the cave-in, Kasey calmed down a little, but Stone knew she was at her threshold.

The passage was considerably easier to navigate with the aid of artificial light. In total darkness, Stone had been forced to grope his way through the unfamiliar environment, one hand extended to keep from crashing into low hanging obstacles and unexpected turns, the other maintaining constant contact with the wall to his right, while he shuffled his feet forward, testing every step before planting his weight. He had scouted the tunnel alone despite not knowing the fate of the others, in the belief that he could help them best by finding an exit. The gunfire had ceased shortly after the cave in, and he had known at that moment that they were either alive or dead, and their status would not change regardless of whether he turned back to check on them. Fortunately, he had quickly found proof to support his prediction that this tunnel would lead to an exit.

"How far do we have to go?" Sievers asked.

"Not sure."

"But you did find a way out, right?" There was a desperate quaver in Kasey's voice. "You said you did."

"There's fresh air coming in from somewhere up ahead," Stone explained. "I thought I felt it when we found Bierce. It was faint, but it was there."

"And you're just telling us now?"

He shrugged. "We had more pressing concerns."

He decided not to mention that the air might be coming in through a crack too small for a human to fit through. That information would not exactly have a motivational effect. Nor would his admission that he had caused the cave-in intentionally in order to prevent a protracted gun battle with the Dominion men, a battle that they could not have survived unscathed.

One drawback to the way in which Stone perceived the world around him was that other people did not see what he saw, and often there simply wasn't time to explain. Sometimes, even after the fact, those explanations did not sit well with others who saw his reliance on the deterministic nature of the universe as a form of gambling, trusting in luck. Nothing was further from the truth, but most people would never get that.

He had worked all the angles and determined that the others were far enough away from the support post to survive anything short of a catastrophic collapse—something that was unlikely considering that the support beam had not already given way—and made a unilateral decision. The cave-in would also make their enemies, if any survived, believe that they were caught inside, killed or buried alive, which would further increase their chances of escape. The greatest uncertainty lay with the possibility that the ceiling might not give way at all, but there was no better option. The outcome had validated his decision; they were all still alive.

The mine tunnel wound back and forth through the

surrounding rock, sometimes intersecting natural fissures. To fill the silence, Avery speculated aloud about the significance of the treaty which she now referred to as the "Mexico Purchase." Stone was amused and encouraged by her efforts to unravel the Dominion's schemes using methods that approximated his own. The problem that she wrestled with, however, was a different matter.

"The Russians have known about this treaty for a long time," he said. "They might have learned about it from Patton himself. Maybe he talked about his plans to run for president. That might have tipped them off. There might be other people who know, or who knew in the past, but decided not to come forward with the information."

"Why not?" asked Sievers. "I mean it's just a matter of history, right? A treaty like that can't possibly be binding, so why make a fuss?"

"It's hard to say how the treaty would be received today. I doubt the U.S. would attempt to enforce it, but they might try to use it for political leverage. But I would imagine that in 1945, the Russians would have taken it very seriously. An uncontested expansion of American borders, with a trove of natural resources and manpower, led by a president who made no secret of his desire to go to war with the Soviet Union—they couldn't ignore that."

"So why drag it out now?" Avery asked. "What's changed? No more Soviet Union. Russia is probably even weaker now than it was under Stalin. Why would they risk putting this out in the open? And giving it to the Dominion, of all people?"

"Figuring that out is the second on my list of things to do," Stone declared.

A few minutes later, they reached the first item on that list. It was a fissure in the surrounding rock matrix, about eighteen inches wide that laterally intersected the passage. The original miners had thrown down a bridge of planks to cover the gap and kept tunneling forward in search of ore, but the crack continued in both directions. To the right, it vanished into nothingness, but on the left side, the gap widened and seemed to open out to the surface world, though it was difficult to say for sure since there was no sign of daylight beyond.

Sievers checked his watch. "Sun might already be down. Not sure what time dusk is down here."

"I don't care," Kasey said. "I just want out of here."

Stone didn't wait for more prompting. He stepped out into the fissure, wedging his foot against the bottom, and began scooting forward toward the promise of fresh air. He turned his body sideways so that his shoulders would not get stuck, and inched forward until he was completely sandwiched between the vertical slabs of rock.

He heard Sievers' voice, muffled by the angles of the stone face. "I wonder why they didn't enlarge this. Make a second entrance."

Stone did not venture a guess. Speculation was irrelevant. The geological circumstances that had led to this seeming coincidence had occurred millions of years before, and were the result of preceding events that went back to the beginning of the universe. It was what it was, as he was fond of saying, because it couldn't have happened any other way.

As he crept forward, he caught a whiff of a familiar scent. It took him a moment to recognize it as the smell of wood smoke, not a fresh fire still burning, but the stale smell of old ashes in a long forgotten fireplace. The smell grew stronger, as if his body scraping along the rock was releasing vapors sealed away centuries before. He slid forward a few inches more, and suddenly there was nothing below him.

He gripped the walls of the slab reflexively and drew back until he felt solid rock beneath him. The fissure opened out into nothingness, but evidently not on the surface. Another mine tunnel? A natural cave?

He moved forward more cautiously, wishing he had asked Sievers for his light, and felt the edge where the fissure ended. He stared into it, aware now of shapes, barely visible, lit from below by a twilight glow.

He was no longer below the earth's surface. Somehow, he was above it.

As he kept looking, he began to distinguish shapes, some of them too precise to be naturally occurring, and at last understood where he was. The soot-streaked walls had been his first clue, and the stark vertical edges below that defined the presence of man-made structures were his second.

Now oriented to his surroundings, Stone scooted back into the cleft to let the others know that they were almost home free. "We're right above the cliff dwellings," he told them. "That's why the miners didn't try to turn this into an entrance."

"How high?" Sievers asked.

"Maybe twenty feet. We'll have to free climb a little to get down." When no one objected, Stone nodded. "Okay. Follow me."

He scooted back to the opening and lowered himself down. Once outside, he was able to see more clearly the south-facing hollow in which the Paquime had built their abode. Beyond, the last vestiges of daylight still hung in the sky, but the cliff dwellings were draped in shadow. There were handholds aplenty on the rock face, and after just a few feet, the slope began to curve out, allowing him to slide the rest of the way down.

Kasey came next, so eager to be in open air that she practically scampered down the cliff. Avery was next, less sure-footed but still able to descend without incident, followed lastly by Sievers. Of them all, he had the most difficulty, losing his grip and dropping onto the slope where he tumbled to the bottom. He hastily got to his feet and pronounced that he was fine.

"You're not fine," Kasey said, her demeanor considerably improved. "You caught a bullet."

"That's why I bring a sewing kit everywhere I go," he replied. "Come on. Let's get out of here. I don't know about you, but I'm ready for a change of scenery."

He got no argument. They made their way through the ruins, emerging through one of the distinctive T-shaped doorways the Paquime had used, and onto a more recently built boardwalk that skirted the edge of the sheer cliff. The sun had already dipped below the distant hilltops to the west, so Sievers lit the way with his trusty MagLite.

They reached the RAV4 half an hour later. Avery ran the

last few steps and collapsed on the SUV's hood. "Thank God that's over."

"Amen," said Kasey. She turned to Sievers. "All right, hero. Let's get you fixed up."

She used two full bottles of water from their supply to rinse away the crust of dirt and blood and expose the wound. The bullet had gouged a furrow in Sievers' biceps, and the flesh around it was inflamed and tender, but aside from the danger of infection, it did not appear to be a serious injury.

While they were occupied with that, Stone circled the little SUV, conducting a cursory inspection to make sure that the Dominion men had not sabotaged the vehicle. It was unlikely that they had. The smart course of action would have been to leave the car unmolested since any signs of damage might lead to suspicions of foul play.

Avery watched him with a bemused expression. "Anything missing?" she asked as he completed his circuit.

"Just one thing."

"What's that?"

"A second car. Their car. Someone else made it out of that mine alive, and I'm betting they have the treaty. I'm afraid it's not over yet."

CHAPTER 29

Chihuahua, Mexico

The four figures that trudged across the tarmac toward the waiting Learjet looked like escapees from a mine disaster, which Tam supposed, was pretty much what they were. Kasey had told her as much in the brief phone call six hours earlier, but somehow that report had failed to convey the enormity of what they had undergone.

She glanced over her shoulder to Greg. "And I thought we were in bad shape."

Greg just shook his head then winced a little as the gesture aggravated one of his many bruises.

Tam stepped down to greet them. "Turn around," she told them. "I know we've got a schedule to keep, but you are not getting on my plane like that."

No one protested.

They reconvened at a Holiday Inn that was a ten-minute drive from the airport. Tam booked two rooms, his and hers, and although they were only there long enough for everyone to shower away the dirt—a process which took longer than even Tam anticipated—she considered it money well spent.

Once back on the plane and in the air, everyone got a chance to tell their story. Avery took the lead for the group that had gone to Cuarenta Casas, focusing primarily on their discovery of the Mexico Purchase treaty. Tam was stunned by this revelation.

"We bought Mexico?"

"I don't think it's a legally binding treaty," Avery was quick to say. "First, the signatories on the Mexican side did not have the authority to enter into such negotiations. Not at the time anyway. Second, all treaties have to be ratified by Congress, and that never happened."

"So it's worth the paper it's written on, and not much

more. What does the Dominion hope to accomplish with it?" Tam looked over at Stone, who as she had expected, was listening far more than he was talking. "You figured that one out, yet?"

"I think I may have." He straightened in his chair. "There are some other parts to this we need to consider. The Dominion, specifically this Roger Lavelle, has been pushing to get the President of Mexico removed from power, presumably hoping to get his ringer, Esperanza, elected as the interim president."

"I don't think Esperanza is aware of Lavelle's true intentions," Tam pointed out.

"Perhaps not his secret agenda, but Esperanza does know about the treaty. That's why he reacted so strongly when you asked him about Destiny. He knows about the treaty, and he's prepared to honor it if he becomes president. He's desperate to stop the violence from the drug cartels, and Lavelle has convinced him that the battle is lost. The murder of those students in Juarez was the final straw, just as Lavelle knew it would be."

"We're already offering the Mexican government whatever support they need," Greg pointed out. "This sounds way too extreme."

"Without the treaty, I would agree. That's why locating it was so critical to the plan. Think of it as finding proof that you were switched at birth, and your real parents are billionaires. You might still identify with the parents that raised you, but would you be able to turn down the promise of wealth? Particularly if you were in a desperate situation?"

"It wouldn't matter," Avery insisted. "Even if Esperanza starts waving that treaty around, the U.S. would not be obligated to honor it."

"Why wouldn't they?" asked Kasey. "It's not every day someone gives you a whole country."

"And all the crap that goes with it," countered Sievers.

"He's right," Avery said. "To build on Stone's analogy, put yourself in the billionaire's shoes. Someone shows up claiming to be a lost heir, but they're a wreck—addicted to drugs, a criminal record, a mountain of debt."

"The first thing you'd do if you were the rich guy," Sievers said, "is ask for proof, and in this case, the proof will say that the treaty was never ratified, so it don't mean diddly."

Stone raised his hand. "Lavelle knows all this. You're forgetting what the Dominion really wants. The Russians, too."

"Which is?" Tam asked.

Stone pursed his lips for a moment. "You're not going to like this."

"Honey, I already know that."

Stone told her.

CHAPTER 30

Mexico City, Mexico

Lavelle found Esperanza waiting for him in the dining room of the Four Seasons hotel. The Mexican businessman seemed jittery, which might have been explained away as too much coffee too early in the morning, but Lavelle knew the real source of the other man's anxiety. He took a seat opposite Esperanza, and without a word, placed a scuffed leather portfolio on the tabletop. Despite the abrasions it had suffered, there was no mistaking the distinctive seal embossed on the front.

"That is it?" Esperanza asked.

Until Trent's arrival in the early hours of the morning, Lavelle had secretly wondered if the treaty really existed at all. It had sounded so implausible at the beginning, when the Russian had first told him of its existence and of the code in the diary housed at the Vienna museum. Even though the plan—Destiny—hinged on his being able to procure the treaty, he had always allowed for the possibility that the actual document might have been lost to the ages, so he had made sure that even without the treaty, Esperanza would be desperate enough to propose redrawing the borders, ceding the north to the U.S. as a way to stop the violence. It would have been a much harder sell, but then the beauty of Destiny was that it did not rely upon what could actually be accomplished, only on the fears of what might happen.

Lavelle spun the case around so the seal was facing Esperanza, and then slid it across the table. "As promised."

Esperanza reached out with trembling hands and opened it. He gasped, then his lips began to move as he read silently. Finally, he looked up. "It is true, then? Northern Mexico has been a part of the United States for more than a century."

"An undeclared territory," Lavelle confirmed, flashing a

disingenuous smile. "And everyone born north of the twentieth parallel during that time is already an American citizen, even though they don't know it."

Esperanza's expression was not quite so sanguine. "I wanted to save my country. This will destroy it."

"Nonsense," Lavelle countered. "You've been in the wrong country your whole life. This will simply put things the way they should have been in the first place."

"I don't think it will be quite as simple as that, my friend."

"It will be when you're the president. Your word will be law."

"I have already made my position clear. I will not try to have President Mendoza removed from power. I will show him this, but what he does with it will be for him and the congressional union to decide."

Lavelle waved his hand as if untroubled by such a prospect. "Things will work out. I'm sure you'll be very convincing when you meet with him." He took out his phone and glanced at the time. "Speaking of which, I should let you be on your way. I've got a plane to catch."

"Back to El Paso?"

"The company won't run itself. And I suspect you're going to be pretty busy as well."

"A pity you can't stay," Esperanza said. "If this works, it will be because of your efforts, not mine. You deserve the credit."

Ain't that the God's honest truth, Lavelle thought. *But I'm going to be long gone when the shit hits the fan.* He pushed back from the table. "I just found the treaty," he said. "You're the one who has to make it work. Good luck, Guillermo. You're surely going to need it."

From a table across the room, Eric Trent watched Lavelle hand the treaty off to Esperanza. Even though this had always been the plan, he felt a pang of loss at seeing the priceless historical document simply given away. It was not for him to question the decisions of the Dominion's leaders, yet he could not help but think that there was a better way to make use of the treaty.

There was a great deal of wealth in the north of Mexico, natural resources that could be exploited, human resources, too… but no, the problem with annexing part of Mexico was the same as it had been in 1848 at the end of the Mexican-American war when the U.S. had relinquished most of the territory it had captured.

Mexico was full of Mexicans.

Letting them mow the lawns and pick the lettuce was fine, and all the better if you could pay them under the table, but if the treaty was enforced, they would have the vote, and that could never be allowed to happen.

Maybe there was no better way to play this wild card, but Trent had sacrificed too much in getting the treaty to feel good about simply letting it go. He had barely escaped with this life. The two men that had accompanied him into the mine would remain buried there forever. Nevertheless, Lavelle had promised him that when the plan finally bore fruit, it would all be worth it.

He watched Lavelle leave and quickly finished off his own breakfast. The clock was ticking now. Despite having only gotten a few hours' sleep, Lavelle had ordered him to keep an eye on Esperanza, just to make sure that the Mexican didn't make any more unexpected changes to the plan. Lavelle had been able to adapt to accommodate Esperanza's little kumbaya moment in front of the Chamber of Deputies, but now that the man had the treaty in hand, it was essential that he not deviate from the script.

He took a sip from his coffee cup and watched as Esperanza perused the document again. In just a few hours, the world would know about the treaty, and then the true purpose of Destiny would be revealed. When that happened, he would make his way back to Texas, to take his place at Lavelle's side, where together, they would forge a new nation, a true republic that enshrined the freedoms of the U.S. Constitution, but without the bleeding-heart permissiveness that encouraged laziness and perverted lifestyles, and was destroying America from within like a cancer.

It was too bad that, in order for America to be saved, it would first have to be put out of its misery.

Out of the corner of his eye, he saw someone approach Esperanza's table. He assumed it was a waiter, but when the businessman subsequently stood up to leave, Trent took a second look. He caught only a glimpse of the person leaving the dining room, walking alongside Esperanza, but that was enough for him to recognize her. For a frantic moment, he didn't know what to do, only that he had to do something,

He dug out his phone and placed a call. Lavelle picked up on the first ring. "What is it, Eric?"

"They're here. One of the people that I left in that mine. She's talking to Esperanza right now."

"What?" Lavelle's voice exploded in his ear. "You said they were all dead."

"I thought they were."

"Stop her. Do not let her get ahold of that treaty. I don't care what you have to do."

Trent licked his lips. The hotel was a public place. What could he do?

He hurried after Esperanza and the woman, closing the distance until he was just a few steps behind them as they exited out into a luxurious garden courtyard. There was no sign of anyone else on the tree-lined walk, and no one looking down from the surrounding patios. If he was going to make a move, there was no better place.

He weighed his options and decided the best course of action was to separate Esperanza from the woman. He would say that Lavelle needed to speak with the Mexican businessman on some urgent matter. The woman would probably recognize him, but what could she do? It would be her word against his.

A hand clapped down on Trent's shoulder, stopping him in his tracks. He tried to pull away, but the grip was like iron, and before he could turn to confront his assailant, another hand snaked around his head from the opposite side and covered his mouth. Panicking, he struggled against the hold, flailing to break free, but to no avail. His unseen attacker lifted him off the ground and dragged him off the path and behind a tree. He felt a faint stinging sensation on the side of his neck, replaced almost immediately by a cold spot that began to spread outward until his entire body felt numb and heavy, and then he felt nothing at all.

CHAPTER 31

Avery was aware of what had just happened behind her, but she resisted the urge to turn and look. Sievers had waylaid Trent without even a scuffling sound; the last thing she wanted to do was make Esperanza turn and look. She had gotten him this far by claiming to be a journalist from a Canadian news service wanting to interview him, a request to which he had happily agreed. She kept walking, making idle small talk until she heard a voice in her ear bud. "Bagged and tagged. You're good to go."

Avery nodded unconsciously and gestured to a nearby bench. When they were both seated, she pointed to the portfolio in Esperanza's hands. "I know what you have there."

He jerked it away defensively, as if fearful that she might try to seize it and run. "Who are you? You are not a reporter."

"No. I'm a historian. I was with the team that found that treaty yesterday. I've read it. I know what you think it means. But there's something you need to hear."

Stone sat patiently in a chair in the front room of the suite, facing the door. His arms were draped casually over the armrests, one leg crossed over the knee of the other, and he wore an expression of complete indifference on his face. The man who had just burst in—the suite's occupant, Roger Lavelle—was speaking angrily into his phone, completely oblivious to Stone's presence.

Lavelle lowered the phone a moment later, breathing rapidly and staring at nothing as his brain worked to process the news he had just received. By degrees, he seemed to take note of his uninvited guest, and when he finally spoke, there was no trace of alarm. "Who the hell are you?"

"The name's Stone," replied the man. "Sit down. We need to talk."

"You can talk to the police." Lavelle held up his phone as if to place an emergency call.

"I could," Stone agreed. "I could tell them all about Destiny." He chuckled. "Destiny. I do like the name, but even you must realize that it will never work."

"You don't know anything."

"I know that you're being used. Manipulated by the Russians. The only thing I'm not sure of is whether you've figured that out." Stone brought his hands together then spread them apart, palms up. "That's why I'm here. I'm trying to determine whether you are an unwitting pawn in Samsonov's game, or a willing accomplice committing an act of treason against the United States."

Lavelle uttered a terse laugh. "Treason. That's a joke."

Stone gestured to a chair. "Sit. I'll talk and you can tell me if I have it right."

Lavelle did not sit. Instead, he strode over to a side table where a bottle of single-malt rested on a silver tray, splashed some of the Scotch into a tumbler, drained it and filled it again.

"Go on," he said, turning to face his uninvited guest. "Tell me a fairy tale."

Stone smiled. Lavelle's decision to fortify himself with a dose of liquid courage would make this even easier. "We'll call it 'the man who didn't want to be president.' I'm talking about Esperanza, of course. I heard about what happened yesterday when he testified in front of the Mexican congress. That must have thrown you for a loop. You need him to take the presidency. It's the only way anyone south of the border will take that treaty seriously."

Lavelle took another sip, savoring the liquor in a futile attempt to hide his growing anxiety. "The treaty is what it is. It's up to the Mexican government to decide what to do with it."

"Of course, but you've been priming the pump with Esperanza. First, you hit him where it hurts. Twenty-two innocent students, people he was trying to help, butchered. You make him believe that it's the beginning of another cycle of violence, and then you show him the magic fix. A century-old treaty that will make the source of the problem vanish. Cede the northern states to the U.S. and restore peace and order, just like that." He snapped his fingers.

Lavelle conspicuously did not refute any of the accusations. "And why not? The Mexican government has had more than a decade to fix this problem. They've failed, and as long as they keep failing, it becomes our problem too."

"We both know that you aren't interested in fixing anything." He paused, daring the other man to take the bait. When Lavelle kept silent, Stone went on. "It has to be Esperanza. President Mendoza would never give up half of his country over a worthless piece of paper. That's why you wanted him removed from office."

Lavelle shrugged. "A lot of people want him out. He's tainted with corruption."

"Impeachment is a tricky business. You couldn't be sure that the senate would convict, but that didn't really matter. The important thing was to put Esperanza in the spotlight, show the country that he's willing and able to be their leader, ready to step in when Samsonov assassinates Mendoza."

Lavelle dropped his glass. It hit the carpeted floor with a faint thump. His mouth worked silently for a moment, as if sampling a variety of denials. He finally went with: "I don't know what you're talking about."

"Oh?" Stone let the lie pass. "Well, in any case, you need Esperanza to validate the treaty, if only to the public. There's no way it would stand up to scrutiny, but then it doesn't need to, does it? The real purpose of Destiny is to make people in America *believe* that Mexico is serious about becoming part of the United States."

Lavelle said nothing, but Stone could read the truth in the other man's scowl.

"You're counting on a frenzy of xenophobia. All those people who have been clamoring for a border fence, freaking out about the possibility of offering amnesty to illegal aliens…What will they do when they hear that millions of the very people they're so terrified of just became American citizens, a new voting majority that doesn't even *habla Ingles*?

"Just the possibility of that will be enough. The media will see to that. The fact that it will never really happen won't make a bit of difference. Can't have those pesky details getting in the way of a good story. It's all about the fear, isn't it? Make people afraid, and then promise them salvation. 'Washington can't save you, but the Dominion can.' There's a slogan for you.

"How does it play out from there? Revolution by ballot? No, that would take too long, and there would be no guarantee of success. Fear cuts both ways. While you're ginning up the bigots, you're also rousing the opposition—not just the arugula-eating, chai-latte sipping elites, but everyone who doesn't fit into your vision of what the world should look like. No, you'd never be able to make it work democratically on the national scale. But that's the point, isn't it? You want to destroy the Union."

Lavelle, with something like passion burning in his eyes, leaned forward. "One in four Americans want that. One in four Americans, who believe in the principles that this country was founded on, the freedom to throw off the chains of a tyrannical government that takes whatever it wants, while it spits on the values we hold sacred. This has been coming for a long time. I'm just giving the final push."

"A straw to break the camel's back," Stone said, nodding to acknowledge the tacit confession. He paused a beat. Up to this point, he had only been revealing things that Lavelle already knew, testing his deductions, and by all appearances, hitting pretty close to the mark. The next part, however, would be uncharted territory for both of them.

"Tell me this," Stone continued. "Did it ever occur to you to ask why the head of Russia's spy agency would hand you a jug of gasoline and a box of matches?"

Lavelle's head shook slightly in confusion. "Come again?"

"You're a businessman. The first rule of capitalism is self-interest. Do you think the Russians dropped this in your lap because they share your vision of freedom?"

The blank expression on Lavelle's face was evidence enough that he had not asked this question.

"After World War II, Russia, through the Soviet Union, dominated half the globe. Now they're a laughingstock. A nation of gangsters. Their economy is circling the drain. They've got the military power and resources, and most importantly, the will to take back everything they've lost since the end of the Cold War and then some, but one thing is standing in their way: America.

"It's not the threat of nukes anymore," Stone went on. "It's sanctions. The only way to turn things around is to go on the offensive, but whenever they try flexing their muscles—South Ossetia, the Ukraine—they get hit with crippling trade sanctions. The United Nations, the European Union, NATO members—they all follow America's lead.

"If Russia is going to reclaim its empire, their own version of Manifest Destiny, they first have to deal with their biggest enemy, and what better way than to let America destroy itself from within. Even if your proposed Civil War failed to completely collapse the federal government, the American economy would crater, and take everyone else down with it. That alone would boost Russia out of recession. They win no matter what happens.

"You see, that's what this was always about. Samsonov has been using you, just like you are using Esperanza."

Lavelle stood in stunned silence for a full minute, refusing to meet Stone's gaze, but then the corners of his mouth twitched up in a cryptic smile. "So what? What happens on the other side of the world doesn't mean a thing to me, or to most Americans. We've wasted a century playing world police, sending our sons off to die fighting for people who laugh at us behind our backs."

"You think your new America will be safe?"

"We'll be strong," Lavelle snarled. "Once we've cut the fat and brought back the values that made us great in the first place, no one will dare mess with us."

Stone nodded slowly. Lavelle's reaction had been entirely predictable. He had not really expected the man to acknowledge the madness of his scheme, but then none of this had been done for Lavelle's benefit. "Did you hear all that?"

Avery's voice sounded in Stone's ear. "We did. Señor Esperanza heard it all."

Lavelle looked around, uncomprehending. "Who are you talking to?"

Stone rose and, ignoring the question, walked to the front door. Over his shoulder, he said, "It's not going to happen, Lavelle. Destiny has just been canceled."

He opened the door and stepped aside allowing Tam Broderick and Greg Johns to enter. Tam faced Lavelle, hands on hips, smiling broadly. "Hello again."

For the first time since entering the room, Lavelle appeared to panic. "I have to go," he mumbled. "I have a flight to catch."

"Yes you do," Stone replied. "But not the one you think."

In the courtyard below, Avery switched off the transmission and studied Esperanza's reaction, which was nothing short of devastated.

"I—I don't understand. Why would he do this?"

"He's a terrorist," Avery said, trying to keep her explanations short, sweet, and vague. "He doesn't like the way the world is, so he wants to ruin it for everyone else."

Esperanza seemed to accept this explanation. "Do you think he is really going to try to assassinate President Mendoza?"

"My friend is pretty good at predicting what people will do. And Lavelle didn't deny it."

"We must warn the president. Alert the police."

Avery took a deep breath. Tam had given her very clear instructions in this regard. "The assassin is a very dangerous man. A foreign spy. And we're in a somewhat delicate position. If we tell the authorities, then we'll have to explain how we learned about this plot. It could very well make things worse."

"The president is on his way to the San Lazaro Palace right now, at my request. If someone kills him there, or even makes an attempt, they will believe that I am part of the scheme, especially because of my connection to Roger."

"We're looking for the assassin right now. We'll stop him, I promise. You're going to have to trust us on this."

"Trust seems to be a weakness of mine. I trusted Roger. How did I not see the man he really is?"

"People like that prey on our trust, exploit our good intentions. That might be the worst thing about what they do. They make us afraid to trust anyone." Avery allowed the sentiment to sink in for a moment, and then gestured to the portfolio, still clutched in the other man's hands. "What will you do with that?"

Esperanza looked down in alarm, as if he had forgotten all about the treaty. "Is it true what he said? Would this destroy America?"

"That seems to be what Lavelle wanted," Avery replied.

"What should be done with it?"

"I'm a historian, so to me this is a very interesting discovery. I can't imagine that anyone would expect it to be honored, but there are a lot of fearful people out there who might want to use it as an excuse to cause trouble."

He held it out to her. "I think it would be better if this never existed."

Avery felt a sudden and profound sadness at the idea of keeping this discovery a secret, but deep down, she knew he was right. She took the portfolio from him.

"What do I do now?" Esperanza sounded utterly miserable. "I am supposed to meet with the president in half an hour, but I cannot tell him any of this."

"Lavelle may have set you up, but now you have a chance to turn his scheme into something good. Meet with the president, just as you planned. Come up with a better answer. Turn this into a victory."

"What if nothing changes?"

Something Stone said came to her. She didn't know if it was really true or not, didn't know if it would bring Esperanza comfort, or deepen his despair. "A friend of mine believes that everything that happens happens because it couldn't have happened any other way. I believe everything happens for a reason. Maybe it's the same thing. I don't know. What I do know is that you have to play the hand you're dealt."

Esperanza gave a solemn nod. "Then I will play to win."

CHAPTER 32

Less than five miles separated the Four Seasons Hotel from the Palacio San Lazaro, the seat of Mexico's legislative body, but the luxury of the five-star hotel was a world removed from the chaos at the heart of the federal district. According to news reports, the protests, which had been ongoing since the incident in Juarez just a few days previously, were nearing critical mass, evidently in response to Esperanza's passionate speech the day before, yet nothing Greg Johns had seen since arriving in Mexico City shortly before sunrise would have led him to believe that the government was on the brink of collapse.

But he knew well that appearances could be deceiving. Mass protests and riots usually began at specific aggregation points—government buildings, stock exchanges, large city parks—while just a few city blocks away, people went about their daily lives blissfully unaware that the foundation of their world was crumbling.

Most of the turmoil had been focused in the Zocalo, the famed plaza that had once been the center of historic Tenochtitlan, the Aztec capital that had become Mexico City. Known formally as Plaza de la Constitución, it remained a destination for visitors and a focal point for both the city and the nation. The square was of particular interest to the protestors since it was also the location of the National Palace, from which President Mendoza led—or some would say, failed to lead—the country. Today, however, some of that attention had shifted to the San Lazaro palace, where the president would be meeting with Juarez businessman Guillermo Esperanza to discuss, rumor had it, a matter that would have profound implications for the future of the beleaguered nation.

If the Myrmidons failed to stop Oleg Samsonov from assassinating Mendoza, the firestorm would begin there.

Lavelle had been surprisingly forthcoming. Greg suspected this was because the Dominion leader believed that it was already too late for them to stop Samsonov, but Sievers' gleeful offer to give a demonstration of "enhanced interrogation techniques" might also have been a factor. Unfortunately, Lavelle knew only that Samsonov planned to hit Mendoza as soon as he arrived at the congressional building. The exact means by which he planned to kill the Mexican president were unknown, even to Lavelle.

The weight of the decision had fallen on Tam. Alerting the *Estado Mayor Presidencial*—Mexico's military equivalent to the Secret Service—was an option of last resort. There was no guarantee that the warning would be taken seriously. If it was, there would be no way to conceal the discovery of the treaty, the scope of the Dominion plot, or the involvement of the Russians, and that might very well trigger the chaos they hoped to prevent. If the EMP ignored the warnings and Samsonov succeeded, the situation would be even worse.

On the other hand, if the Myrmidons could take Samsonov down quietly, it would be a major coup.

Stone's appraisal of the situation provided the deciding factor. "Samsonov will want to take care of this personally," he told Tam. "Just like he did in Vienna. He won't trust this to anyone else."

"But how are we going to find him in time?" Greg asked.

"Leave that to me," Tam had told them, a strange and eager gleam in her eye. With Sievers remaining behind to guard both the prisoners, and if things went badly, help Avery and Stone escape the city, the others boarded waiting taxis and dispersed to carry out the desperate plan.

As Greg and Kasey sped toward the congressional building, their route taking them just ten blocks south of the Zocalo, they began to see the first signs of the unrest they had heard about. Graffiti messages, demanding the ouster of President Mendoza and accusing him of collusion with drug cartels, were spray-painted on walls in letters ten feet high. Scorch marks on walls and pavement marked the places where random fires had burned. Plywood covered store front windows that had presumably been shattered, no doubt the work of hooligans using the political turmoil as an excuse for wanton destruction.

When they were still more than half a mile from the San Lazaro palace, all forward progress abruptly ceased. The road ahead was a veritable parking lot.

"I hope Tam's having an easier go of it," Greg remarked.

"No kidding." Kasey leaned forward and spoke to the taxi driver. In halting Spanish, she asked if the gridlock was due to the protests. The man's response was a machine-gun-like burst of words, of which Greg understood just a handful. Kasey's next utterance was in English, harsh and monosyllabic.

"What's wrong?" Greg asked.

"He says the street has been blocked by the president's security men."

"Nice of him to let us know." Greg threw a handful of hundred peso notes over the seat, more than the figure on the meter and a lot more than the driver deserved, then threw open his door. Kasey got out on her side, and they both took off running down the sidewalk.

The first few steps reminded him of the aches and bruises incurred from the previous day's border crossing, but the pain subsided as he found his pace. Tam held them all to an exacting regimen of physical training for situations just such as this. Under ideal conditions, Greg could easily knock out a six-minute mile, and the lithe Kasey was even faster, but it soon became evident that conditions would not be ideal. Mexico City was nearly a mile and a half above sea level. The altitude not only left the runners winded, but amplified the effects of air pollution on the crowded streets of the world's fifth largest metropolitan area, turning the atmosphere into a choking miasma of automobile exhaust and ozone. After just a minute of running, Greg's chest was burning, and a metallic taste filled his mouth. To make matters worse, the sidewalk was crowded with sign-carrying protesters and nearly as congested as the boulevard.

Tam's voice squawked through the speakers in his ear bud a couple minutes later. "I've reached the search area. What's your

ETA?"

She had to shout to be heard over the strident background noise. Her voice was already hoarse from breathing the foul air, and although it brought him no comfort, Greg knew that Tam was facing an even greater ordeal than he and Kasey.

He keyed his mic. "We're on foot. A couple minutes out."

"You'll need to do better than that. I've got eyes on Mendoza's car. Coming in from the north. He'll be there in two minutes."

Greg glanced over at Kasey who gave a resigned shrug and somehow managed to increase her pace. Greg attempted to do the same, and immediately felt a burn in his muscles.

They dashed across an intersection and beneath an overpass, slipped between unmoving cars, and reached the blockaded security perimeter. Foot traffic was bunched up in front of hastily erected barricades, beyond which dozens of police officers in riot gear stood ready in the event that the physical barriers proved insufficient. To the right, a tall metal fence, painted red, blocked access to the forested grounds of the San Lazaro palace. The west entrance, where President Mendoza would be arriving at any moment, was still a couple hundred yards away.

"End of the road," Greg croaked into his microphone as he skidded to a halt.

Tam's next transmission was an almost deafening shout. "I see him! Rooftop. Two hundred yards west of the entrance. Looks like he's picked up a Dragunov."

Stone had also told them that Samsonov would favor this method of assassination. Explosives were unpredictable. A close-range pistol shot would be difficult to pull off given the tight security, not to mention the problem of escaping afterward. It was hardly a stretch to anticipate that Samsonov, who had once been a former Spetsnaz sharpshooter before taking a job at the FSB, would have the highest degree of confidence using the reliably familiar Russian-made SVD "Dragunov" sniper rifle. His choice of weapons would in no way tie the Russians to the assassination. Soviet-era weapons like the SVD were common and easy to acquire on the black market, and the blame for the crime would almost certainly be placed on the drug cartels. At two hundred yards—a distance that every U.S. Army soldier in basic training was expected to hit using an M16 with standard iron sights—it would be extraordinary only if he missed.

Greg turned in the indicated direction. The specified building lay on the other side of a Metro commuter train line that ran parallel to the boulevard and the congressional building. The tracks were protected by a barbed wire-topped fence that ran unbroken in both directions as far as Greg could see. A signpost marked the location of an underground stairway leading to a nearby station and presumably a way to reach the other side, but a throng of protestors lay between them and it.

No time for that, he thought. Nor was there time to double back and get on the overpass. Which left only one painful option.

"Kasey! This way!"

He bolted across the street, weaving through the traffic jam, and mounted the grassy verge beside the tracks. Shouts went up from the crowd as people realized what he intended to do, but no one moved to stop him. He reached the fence and immediately leaped onto it, clawing his way up the chain-link. The barbed wire snagged his clothes and tore bloody furrows in his exposed skin, but he was channeling pure adrenaline now. Nothing slowed him. He crested the fence and dropped down onto the graveled rail bed, leaving half his shirt behind in the process.

He skipped over the rails, assuming at least a couple of them were electrified, and clambered onto the opposite fence. Fortunately, there were no trains moving through the station.

At least something is breaking our way, Greg thought. Out of the corner of his eye, he saw Kasey, just a few steps behind him, crossing the tracks. A few seconds later, they were both on the ground and running again.

"I see you!" Tam called. "Samsonov is one block west, northeast corner of an apartment building."

Greg spotted the building, a five-story block of flats, painted gray with red trim, jutting above the treetops of a small urban park. He veered left, sprinting through the greenspace as fast as his burning legs and tortured lungs would allow. There were signs of an earlier unrest here as well—more graffiti and fire damage—along with a few straggling protesters who appeared to be using the park as a rally point. Greg ignored their stares and made a beeline for the entrance closest to where Tam had spotted the Russian. The angle was too steep for him to make out the roofs, to say nothing of a shooter positioned atop one of them, but that meant Samsonov could not see him or Kasey.

He dropped a step, planted his left foot, and jammed the heel of his right foot into a spot just below the door knob. The door could have been unlocked for all he knew, but stopping to check would have robbed him of momentum. The door flew open, splinters of the door frame spraying like shrapnel, revealing a tiled foyer.

"Mendoza's car has reached the entrance," Tam advised. "Greg, if you can't make it—"

"I'll make it," Greg rasped. He spotted a flight of stairs and started bounding up, three steps at a time, whipped himself around the banister at the midway landing, kept going.

Tam's urgent voice sounded again. "Greg…?"

The stairs ended at the fifth floor landing, but an iron ladder continued up to the ceiling, terminating at a trap door. From its base, he could see that it was secured with a padlocked slide latch. Samsonov had evidently found a different route to the rooftop, but Greg did not have the time to look for it.

He drew his gun and aimed up at the latch. The noise would alert Samsonov, along with everyone else in the building, but it couldn't be helped.

He fired.

The 10-millimeter round smashed into the flimsy bolt, snapping it in two.

The report left his ears ringing, but through it, he thought he could hear Tam's voice. Perhaps the shot had startled Samsonov, frightened him into abandoning his deadly mission. Or maybe it was a warning that he would be waiting.

He glanced back at Kasey, who had her own pistol drawn

and aimed up at the trapdoor. "Stay close." He thought he might be shouting, but he could barely hear his own voice. "I'm going through fast. If he kills me…"

"Got it! Go!"

He went, scrambling up the narrow rungs like he had rockets strapped to his feet. He threw the forearm of his shooting hand against the door and pushed hard, throwing it up and out, and then in the same fluid motion, launched himself through the square opening.

Samsonov was waiting, just as Greg knew he would be.

Greg fired, even before he had a target. So did the Russian.

Kasey heard the shots, felt something hot on her face and knew Greg had been hit. Nevertheless, he kept moving, propelling himself through the trap door, clearing the way for her, and she was not about to let his sacrifice be for nothing. As she neared the top rung, she coiled her body like a compressed spring, and then exploded through the trap door, pistol extended and ready to fire at the first hint of movement.

A flash of daylight captured the instant like a freeze-frame. Greg, to her left, rolling away from the aperture, but still firing. His free hand was pressed to his neck, the fingers stained bright red, unable to hold back the tide.

Greg, no!

Ten feet away, the stocky form of a man, back turned, fleeing across the rooftops, leaving his own trail of crimson droplets. Greg had not missed either. There was a pistol in the Russian's hand. The Dragunov rifle, its deadly purpose thwarted, had been left behind. Kasey adjusted her aim, finger tightening on the trigger, but in that instant, Samsonov leaped over the side of the building and vanished.

Stunned by the unexpected development, Kasey's first thought was to rush to help Greg, but he waved her off.

"Go after him!"

After him?

She kicked herself for missing the obvious. Samsonov would not have simply jumped off the building. He was getting away.

So what? They had stopped the assassination. That was all that really mattered.

"I'm fine," he insisted. "It's just a scratch. Go!"

Kasey did not think he looked fine, but he was still alive, and he did seem to have the bleeding under control. If their roles had been reversed, she would have wanted him to go after Samsonov. "Promise?"

His brow furrowed in annoyance. "Go!"

She went.

It had been only a few seconds since the Russian had gone over the side, not enough time, she discovered upon reaching the edge of the roof, for him to reach the ground. Samsonov was descending one floor at a time, lowering himself onto the protruding patios that looked out over the street. Kasey arrived just in time to see him swing out over the edge of the second story patio, where he hung for a moment before dropping twelve feet to the street below.

As soon as he landed, he curled up and fell to one side. It was a move taught to airborne soldiers, a way to redistribute some of the energy of hitting the ground. Samsonov however was slow to recover, struggling to his feet. There was a conspicuous dark stain on the ground to mark the spot where he had landed.

Kasey tried to draw a bead on him, but Samsonov, as if sensing her intent, shrank against the side of the building, removing himself from the line of fire.

"We'll do it your way then," she muttered.

She holstered her pistol and dropped flat, rolled to the edge, and lowered herself onto the uppermost balcony. As soon as her feet touched down, she was moving again, following the Russian's lead but doing so with considerably more grace. She swung her body out over the balcony rail and let go, executing a controlled fall onto the patio rail directly below, and then without pausing, dropped into a crouch and lowered herself again, skipping down the vertical face.

When she reached the second story, she swung her legs toward the building as she let go of the balcony rail, planting her feet against the wall and rebounding away to mitigate the effects of gravity. When she finally did hit the sidewalk, she managed to redirect the energy into forward momentum, sprinting out of the half-stumble and charging after the retreating form of the assassin.

Samsonov rounded the corner before she could unholster her pistol. He was injured, slowing, and Kasey knew she could catch him, but she also remembered that he was still dangerous. She drew up short, pistol extended, finger on the trigger, and edged cautiously into the open.

Instead of a gunshot, the next sound she heard was of an engine roaring to life. Fifty feet away, Samsonov sat astride a motorcycle, shrouded in a cloak of exhaust smoke. In the moment it took Kasey to adjust her aim and fire, he let out the clutch and rocketed away into the street.

Kasey resisted the almost overwhelming urge to empty her magazine at the retreating form. The chances of hitting Samsonov were iffy at best, the possibility of killing an innocent bystander made it an unacceptable risk. She keyed her mic. "Tam, he got away. Motorcycle."

"I see him," came the shouted reply. "Go help Greg. I'll take care of Samsonov."

And then, her coming heralded by a familiar mechanical scream, Tam Broderick descended from the heavens.

While Greg and Kasey had been negotiating the snarled traffic of the Federal District, Tam had raced to a different destination, two miles further east: Mexico City International Airport, where they had landed only a few hours earlier. Tam's ultimate goal was not the Learjet itself, but something tucked away in its luggage compartment, an aircraft of a different sort, the GEN H-4 personal helicopter, which Kasey had used to whisk Stone away from the black site in Romania.

She assembled it quickly, double-checking every connection as she went, and within five minutes of arriving at the jet's hangar, was in the air.

The H-4's low profile made it virtually undetectable by radar, but it was by no means invisible to the naked eye. Tam stayed low, just a few feet above the open field surrounding the airport's runways, gaining altitude only when she was clear of the flight path. Even so, the little helicopter shuddered as it passed through patches of turbulence caused by the thrust-wake of not-quite-distant-enough jets coming and going.

Once past this unseen storm, she had moved immediately to the vicinity of San Lazaro Palace to begin looking for Samsonov. Finding him had been relatively easy; there were only so many places where a sniper could have positioned himself to hit the entrance to the congressional building. Stopping him, at least from the air, was a different matter entirely. If she had attempted to approach the rooftop, the strident whine of the H-4's engine would almost certainly have given her away, and Samsonov, with his long-range sniper rifle, would have easily picked her off before she could have even gotten close. Instead, she hovered more than three hundred feet above the rooftop, guiding Greg and Kasey to his position.

They had succeeded in preventing him from carrying out his mission, but success had come at a dear price and she regretted not simply taking her chances in the first place.

She would not make that mistake again.

As Samsonov sped away on his motorcycle, Tam pulled the control bar forward and dove toward street level. She saw Kasey, frustrated by the Russian's getaway, heard the young woman's voice in her ear bud, barely audible over the buzzsaw drone of the H-4's four little ten horsepower two-stroke engines. She had no idea if Kasey heard her reply.

She leveled out about thirty feet above the pavement, just high enough to avoid snagging the power lines that criss-crossed the street. The personal helicopter had a top speed of over a hundred and twenty miles per hour, but like most internal combustion engines, it couldn't sustain that rate for long without overheating. If Samsonov red-lined his bike for too long, it would stall out. If she pushed the H-4 too far, she would drop out of the sky. Fortunately, the would-be assassin was already easing off the throttle, confident that he had left the pursuit behind and unable to hear Tam's approach over the growl of his own engine.

Tam lined up directly on his six o'clock and eased off the

gas. The street below had transformed into an open-air marketplace, with stalls stretching for several blocks. Samsonov bullied his way through the milling crowd, while Tam was forced to climb higher to avoid the tall shade trees that lined the avenue.

At the first major intersection, a southbound one-way thoroughfare, Samsonov veered left and joined the flow of traffic, then began working his way to the far side. Tam called out the direction change as she banked the mini-copter in pursuit. It was nothing more than a habit really; the chances of Kasey and Greg finding a way to follow were effectively nil.

Out in the open, above the traffic, the sight of the little helicopter did not go unnoticed. Passersby gawked and stared, some pointing skyward. Samsonov noticed their attention and glanced back, a quick head turn, barely long enough for his eye to even register anything, before returning his attention to the road ahead.

Then he looked again, and Tam felt his eyes lock onto her.

"Crap!" She shouted into her mic. "He saw me."

If Samsonov was surprised at the sight of the H-4 cruising above the Mexico City streets, he gave no indication. A lifetime of military training had evidently insulated him against the shock of witnessing the extraordinary. He looked up, just for a second, then brought his eyes to the front once more, but this time, he did not merely continue on as before. Instead, he twisted the throttle and shot forward, riding the lane markers to slip between cars. The motorcycle abruptly cut right, narrowly avoiding a collision with a city bus, and headed onto a westbound street at full throttle.

Tam increased her speed as well, but now instead of following him, she knew that she would have to run him down. The H-4's controls did not allow for one-handed operation. Since she could not fly and shoot at the same time, her only weapon was the aircraft itself. She was still wrestling with the question of how to wield it without killing herself when Samsonov took another hard right turn and headed north.

She banked the nimble aircraft and followed without sacrificing any speed. From her high vantage, she could see several blocks ahead. For a moment, she thought Samsonov had made a fatal error; the street did not go through, the way ahead was blocked by an imposing colonial structure—a church, judging by the magnificent bell tower jutting up into the sky. Then she spotted a second bell tower. Not a mere church, but the Metropolitan Cathedral, the largest and oldest cathedral in the Western Hemisphere.

In that instant, she knew that Samsonov had chosen his route deliberately. The Cathedral was one of several historic buildings, built on the site of what had once been the center of the Aztec capital of Tenochtitlan, ringing the open square of the Plaza de la Constitucion.

"He's heading into the Zocalo."

The plaza was crowded with people, protestors in all likelihood, since the National Palace—the official seat of the executive branch—dominated the eastern edge of the square. The President was away, of course, probably meeting with Guillermo Esperanza right that very moment, but that evidently had not prompted the throng to disperse.

If Samsonov reached the Zocalo, he would be able to lose himself in the mass of bodies, disappear completely, never to be seen again.

Tam pushed the throttle wide open, surging forward to catch up with the Russian, even as he began downshifting in anticipation of a hasty dismount. She was over him in an instant. Unlike a traditional helicopter, the H-4 did not have a cyclic control to adjust the tilt of the rotor blades for lift. The only way to make the helicopter rise or fall in a hover was by adjusting the throttle. Finesse was required to find that sweet spot between settling gently and plummeting like a stone. Tam did not have time for finesse.

She cut the throttle, just for an instant, and felt her stomach leap into her throat as the H-4 dropped fast. She switched it back to full, but before the rotor blades could lift it back up again, the protruding footrest slammed down onto the back wheel of Samsonov's motorcycle.

There was a screech as the tire compressed down to the rim, then the vehicle shot forward like a bean squirting from its husk. Samsonov flew backward as the bike's front wheel popped up in an unexpected wheelie, and just like that, man and motorcycle were separated.

While the section of the street leading into the Zocalo was not nearly as crowded as the plaza itself, Tam's sudden plunge sent even the most curious spectators fleeing in panic. When the Russian hit the ground, there was not a soul within fifty feet.

Tam eased off the throttle again, less hastily this time, while pushing the right side of the control bar, carving a tight turn to come about, facing the fallen assassin a few yards away and less than six feet above the ground. Samsonov was crouching on the paving stones, a Makarov in one hand, aimed right at her.

There was only one place to go, and it wasn't up. Tam hauled back on the control bar, curling her body forward to tilt the twin rotor discs down. She saw Samsonov scrambling back, the pistol forgotten, barely clearing the sweep of the top rotor, and then the entire world seemed to come apart at the seams.

The rotor blades met the pavement and shattered, flinging fragments of carbon fiber in every direction. A tooth-loosening tremor shuddered through the lightweight frame, even as it continued to shift forward, dropping Tam toward the road surface.

The engines stalled, ending the vibration and most of the tumult. Tam fumbled for the safety belt, and then abruptly dropped a foot and a half to land face down on the street. She rolled away from the wreckage, kicking to disentangle herself from the footrest, even though she was no longer certain which way was up.

She did not think she had sustained any new injuries in the collision with the ground, but the impact and subsequent shaking reminded her of every single old one she had accrued over the past few days. She got to her hands and knees, and then remembered the reason for everything she had just done.

Samsonov was still crabbing backward, as if afraid to turn his back on her.

Smart, she thought, and went for her own Makarov.

The Russian, realizing what she was about to do, abruptly flipped over and sprang to his feet, racing headlong toward the still retreating crowd.

Tam sighted her pistol but held her fire. Too many innocent bystanders, too many witnesses.

She got her own feet under her and started after him. A spear of pain stabbed through her ankle, and despite her best efforts to grit her teeth and drive on, the best she could manage was an ungainly lurch. Samsonov was not doing much better. His left pant leg was soaked through with blood, most of which seemed to be coming from the same area as the ragged hole in his trousers, six inches above the knee. Nevertheless, he somehow managed to move at something approaching a jog, reaching the edge of the massed onlookers before Tam had closed half the distance. Samsonov pushed past an old man wearing a denim shirt and a cowboy hat, collided with a young woman in sandals, then veered left, behind both of them and vanished from Tam's sight.

"No, you don't," she snarled, willing a burst of speed that brought tears to her eyes. She reached the old man a second later, searching the sidewalk for some sign of her prey and found it: fat red stains on the dirty concrete. She followed them like a trail of breadcrumbs and a moment later spotted him.

"Samsonov!"

He kept going, not once looking back. Tam was closing the distance slowly, one painful step at a time, but if the Russian was feeling the effects of blood loss, it was not showing. The pursuit stretched down the block, and as he neared the intersection, Samsonov abruptly took a step toward the street, as if intending to dart out into traffic at the first opportunity.

A black Range Rover slid up beside him, and then without warning, the door flew open and slammed into the Russian, sending him sprawling backward.

Astonished, Tam barely managed to stop short of tripping over the stunned assassin. The SUV pulled to a stop alongside her, and she looked up to see Stone's face framed in the open driver's side window. "Need a lift?" he asked.

EPILOGUE: RIVERBEND

Alexandria, Virginia

The gate, badly rusted wrought iron hanging from two massive piers of river rock held together with crumbling mortar, looked as if it had not been opened in half a century. A decorative arch that read "Riverbend," spanned the distance between the gateposts. The driveway beyond was barely discernible through the tangle of broadleaf vines that partially covered the gate and eclipsed the adjoining fence altogether.

"Nice place you've got here," remarked Billy Sievers from the back seat of a rented Buick Skylark. "Is that poison ivy?"

Avery, in the front passenger seat, took a second look at the foliage covering the gate and immediately recognized the distinctive three-leaf clusters.

"It's a lot more effective than a 'no trespassing' sign," Stone replied from behind the wheel. He pulled the car forward until the front bumper was almost touching the gate and shifted it into 'park.' "Be right back."

As he got out, he produced a pair of nitrile gloves. After donning them, he walked over to the right-hand gatepost and carefully drew aside some of the vines to reveal a bronze plaque, which had oxidized to a whitish green. From the safety of the car, Avery could only make out a few words on the marker, just enough to infer that the property had been designated as a historical preserve by the State of Virginia.

Stone pressed on the plaque, and it swung open on concealed hinges like a medicine cabinet door. Beneath was a digital keypad that looked to be in considerably better repair than anything else Avery had seen. Stone tapped in a code and then pushed the plaque back into place. As he returned to the car, he carefully stripped off the gloves, while behind him the gate—evidently well maintained despite all appearances—opened without so much as a squeak of protest.

Stone settled back into the driver's seat and eased the car

forward. The overgrowth on the drive was no illusion. No one had traveled this road in at least a year.

"This is your place?" Avery asked, still trying to wrap her head around what she was seeing.

"Yes and no," Stone replied. "It's the old family place, but no one has really lived here since my great-great-grandfather passed away eighty years ago."

"I thought the government seized all your assets when they arrested you," Sievers said. "How did they miss this?"

Stone gave a wry smile. "I made sure that it was not listed as one of my assets."

When he did not offer to elucidate, Avery pressed the issue. "Does Tam know about this place?"

The smile faltered a little and Stone nodded. "She knows."

Avery sensed there was a lot more to that story. She couldn't help but wonder if the secret of the strange bond that connected Tam and Stone lay within the walls of the old abandoned mansion.

Avery had witnessed the strength of that bond for herself just a few days earlier in Mexico City, when Stone, despite having been told to hold fast in Lavelle's hotel room, had insisted on providing backup support for the others after their departure. He had "borrowed" the Range Rover from an unsuspecting hotel guest, and with Avery monitoring the comm network and Sievers literally sitting on their two captives in the rear cargo area, they had set out for San Lazaro palace.

Avery had been horrified by the news of Greg's injury. Samsonov's bullet had nicked his jugular vein, but immediate pressure on the wound, followed by prompt emergency field medicine aboard the Learjet as they winged their way back to the States, and subsequent treatment at Bethesda Naval Hospital, ensured that he would make a full recovery.

Tam had declined the invitation to accompany them to Riverbend, though at the time Avery had assumed it was for reasons other than personal. Since their escape from Mexico City, she had been busy with administrative details, little things like accepting a secret commendation for having thwarted Destiny, to say nothing of poaching the head of Russia's spy agency.

Roger Lavelle and Eric Trent were presently on their way to a black site, possibly even Stone's old digs in the Carpathian Mountains, but Oleg Samsonov was going to disappear into a hole so dark that not even Tam would be privy to his whereabouts.

The Spear of Destiny had been recovered from Lavelle's hotel room, only a little worse for wear, and would be returned to the Hofburg as soon as the arrests of Paul Karcher and Emil Zanger were confirmed. No doubt the two men would have some interesting things to say about Heilig Herrschaft. Avery had no idea what had become of the Mexico Purchase treaty; it would probably be locked away in a vault in the National Archives along with all the other secrets that were deemed too hot to handle. Nor would the world ever learn the true fate of Ambrose Bierce, though on reflection, Avery felt the mystery suited him better.

Kasey was with Tam at CIA headquarters, just a short drive away in Arlington. As an official member of the Myrmidons task force, Avery probably should have stayed too, but she had been unable to resist Stone's invitation to accompany him to Riverbend, where he intended to make good on his promise to Sievers.

Stone's integrity in the matter of returning the stolen data, not because it was the right thing to do, but because he had given his word, was just one more cryptic piece of the puzzle that Avery was determined to solve. He had challenged her to look past her prejudices, but thus far she had failed to see what truly motivated the man. Perhaps a look at his ancestral home would shed some light on the mystery.

A crumbling three-story Colonial mansion appeared from the trees. Stone drew up to the front steps, and as they got out, Avery raised an eyebrow. "How is this place still standing?"

"Looks can be deceiving."

Avery sensed that Stone was referring to something more than just the state of the old house, but the truth of his words was immediately evident. Although the door appeared to be as old as the house itself, warped and brittle, the weatherworn brass knocker concealed yet another digital keypad. Stone entered an access code, and the door opened out to admit them.

The interior was not quite the dilapidated ruin Avery would have expected from her first impression of the outside, but neither did it match with the more fanciful possibilities she had begun to entertain. It was simply an old house, musty, dusty and clearly uninhabited. Heavy white sheets shrouded the furniture. Paintings rested against the base of the walls where they might once have hung.

Stone led them through the house to a study, appointed with a heavy wooden desk and shelves lined with books. The bindings were creased and worn, indicating that the volumes were not merely for decorative purposes, but had been well-read in their day. There was a window seat set against the far wall, though the portal it overlooked was boarded over, and opposite that, a large section of interior wall was dominated by an enormous painting—a landscape of a plateau rising out of primeval rainforest. Stone took hold of the painting's wooden frame and gave it a firm tug. It swung out to reveal a wooden door, which Stone also promptly opened.

A dark stairway lay beyond, spiraling down into the darkness. Stone slid a hand against the inside wall, and a series of hanging lights flickered on, illuminating their way. Another door—this one metal—blocked the base of the stairs.

"I think it's a good thing Kasey stayed behind," Stone said as he opened the door to reveal a vast cavern that had been transformed into something that was equal parts museum, library, and mad scientist's laboratory.

"Wow," Sievers remarked as he stepped through. "You've got your own Fortress of Solitude."

Stone did not reply but moved through the vast space to a desk, cluttered with books and other miscellaneous objects. There was a laptop computer on the desktop, but Stone ignored it and instead pulled open a side drawer and took out a key-chain sized thumb drive. Without any hesitation whatsoever, he passed it to Sievers. "A promise is a promise."

Sievers regarded the slim piece of plastic that rested on his open palm. "I'll need to verify this."

Stone gestured to the computer. "You can use that. It hasn't been turned on in a while, but it should still work."

Sievers took a step toward the desk, then stopped and faced Stone again. He held up the thumb drive. "What the hell is on here, anyway?"

"It's a program. A predictive algorithm."

"Predicting what?" Avery asked.

Stone cracked a smile. "Everything." And then, evidently sensing that his answer was no answer at all, continued. "It's funny how people get excited at the thought of the government eavesdropping on their phone calls, while they think nothing of laying themselves bare to strangers on the Internet or sharing every aspect of their lives with corporations just to save a few bucks on their groceries. Social media, shopper loyalty cards, search engine usage, even those ridiculous quizzes people are always taking—it's all part of a massive data mining effort."

"The government is behind all that stuff?" Avery asked, skeptically.

"No, and that's the really scary part. If the government did it, it would be illegal. But people sign their lives away without even stopping to read the terms of service. Once the data is collected, it becomes a market commodity, available to anyone."

"What does it matter?" countered Sievers. "So some computer somewhere knows that I like to buy Lone Star beer and barbecue potato chips, or that I searched for season three of Top Gear on Google. I don't see how it makes any difference to anyone."

Stone turned to Avery. "Do you remember what I told you in Vienna?"

Her eyebrows drew together in a frown. "About everything being pre-determined?"

"With perfect knowledge, we could predict anything. Even the outcome of something as random as a coin flip." He pointed at the thumb drive. "That's what the algorithm does. It takes all that information and assembles it into a predictive model of human behavior.

"We aren't nearly as unique as we believe. That's why things like personality quizzes and horoscopes can be so freakishly accurate. With just a very small sampling of data, that program can predict the actions of an individual or an entire nation."

Sievers looked down at the thumb drive again as if seeing it anew. "They say knowledge is power. I guess anyone who has this would be damn near almighty."

"I can see why you didn't want the NSA to have it," Avery said.

Stone chuckled. "I'm afraid you've got the wrong idea about me, Dr. Halsey. I wasn't trying to keep them from using it. I wanted it for myself."

Avery gaped at him.

"There is an underlying pattern to everything," he went on, his tone becoming almost reverent. "The universal source code, written into the laws of nature. It's there, and it's not as complicated as you might think. Cause and effect. Action and reaction. It's present in the material world, and in human behavior. I have to know what it is."

"Why?" asked Sievers.

The question seemed to confuse Stone. "Why? Why not? Understanding the source code would be like knowing the mind of God."

Sievers scratched his chin. "I don't know about you, but I kind of like not knowing the score of a game until I've watched it. Predictions are great for the betting man, but when it's a sure thing, what's the point?"

Stone's expression darkened for a moment, then he smiled again. "I knew you'd say that, Sievers."

Sievers burst into laughter. "So tell me this: what am I gonna do now?"

Stone shrugged and spread his hands. "Surprise me."

With a grin, Sievers opened his hand and let the thumb drive fall to the floor. He then took a step forward and pulverized it beneath his boot heel. "A promise is a promise. If what you say is true, then I don't think anyone needs this kind of power."

Stone did not reply.

"Are you saying that everything you've done—the crimes

you've committed, the things you've stolen—it's all about trying to figure out this source code?" Avery said. "It's really that important to you?"

Stone nodded. "It's the only thing that matters to me."

Avery stared at the thumb drive. "Then why give it up now?"

For the second time, Stone was taken aback by an unexpected question. "I made a promise."

"You promised to give Sievers the data, and in exchange, he would let you help us stop the Dominion, stop Destiny. But why would you ever agree to give up something so important in the first place?"

"Because," he answered, almost too softly for her to hear. "Tam needed me to."

When they emerged from the underground room, they found Tam Broderick in the window seat across from the door.

"I see your key still works," Stone said, as if he had known all along that she would be waiting there.

Tam made an affirmative noise. "Had to come make sure you boys played nice."

Sievers grinned. "Absolutely. A deal's a deal. He's all yours."

"Good to hear." She cocked her head sideways and looked at him. "What about you?"

"Back to work, I guess. Reckon I'll get a bonus since I'm the guy who finally cracked Stone." He laughed at the unintentional pun.

"You could come work for me."

Sievers was taken aback. "You're serious?"

"Stone trusts you, and I trust him. I'll admit, your rough edges kind of rubbed me the wrong way at first, but there's no way we could have stopped Destiny without you."

Sievers turned to Stone. "And I suppose you're going to working with her, too?"

Stone shrugged. "It's better than the alternative. International fugitive, on the run, always looking over my shoulder."

"It is that."

"It's an official job offer," Tam continued. "I have the letter in the car. You'll be sworn in as an operations officer, seniority adjusted for prior service. What do you say? Ready to join the Myrmidons?"

"A Myrmidon," Sievers repeated the word as if trying it on for size. "Hell, why not? I was always happier getting my paychecks from Uncle Sam." He shook his head, then grinned at Stone. "I guess you saw that coming?"

Stone shook his head. "Nope. I can never predict what Tam will do. That's why I love her."

~End~

ABOUT THE AUTHORS

David Wood is the author of the popular action-adventure series, *The Dane Maddock Adventures*, as well as several stand-alone works and two series for young adults. Under his David Debord pen name he is the author of the *Absent Gods* fantasy series. When not writing, he co-hosts the Authorcast podcast. David and his family live in Santa Fe, New Mexico. Visit him online at www.davidwoodweb.com.

Sean Ellis is the author of several thriller and adventure novels. He is a veteran of Operation Enduring Freedom, and has a Bachelor of Science degree in Natural Resources Policy from Oregon State University. Sean is also a member of the International Thriller Writers organization. He currently resides in Arizona, where he divides his time between writing, adventure sports, and trying to figure out how to save the world. Visit him at www.seanellisthrillers.com.

20084046R00164